LIVING LITERATU

Vacant Pos~~session~~

a story of proxy
decision making

Hazel E McHaffie

Radcliffe Publishing
Oxford • Seattle

Radcliffe Publishing Ltd
18 Marcham Road
Abingdon
Oxon OX14 1AA
United Kingdom

www.radcliffe-oxford.com
Electronic catalogue and worldwide online ordering facility.

British Library Cataloguing in Publication Data

A catalogue record for this book is available from the British Library.

ISBN 1 85775 651 7

Typeset by Ann Buchan (Typesetters), Shepperton, Middlesex
Printed and bound by T J International Ltd, Padstow, Cornwall

Medical ethics – a living literature

In the privacy of general practices and hospital clinics a million people a day in the UK share stories of personal moment with healthcare professionals. Fragmentary and often tangled, their accounts may feature bizarre experiences, unpleasant sensations, weird situations, complex relationships, difficult choices, conflicting interests and extreme emotions.

This refreshingly different series of novels conjures up some of these lived realities, especially their medical and ethical dimensions. The stories draw us deep into moral quandaries alongside people grappling with health issues and difficult choices; they are tales of passion, perplexity and crime that hold the reader spellbound amidst the thoughts, emotions, plans and actions of their characters.

Hazel McHaffie, already an award-winning author, has woven together authentic clinical details and ethical dilemmas with a lightness of touch that transports the reader effortlessly and convincingly into the world of scientific medicine. In *Vacant Possession*, the first of the three books which launches the series, she tackles the complex issue of making decisions on behalf of patients unable to speak for themselves. Through the experiences of Vivienne Faraday, an unconscious young woman who becomes the victim of an appalling crime, she challenges preconceived ideas and drives us to reflect on what is done in the name of modern medicine and what, in similar circumstances, we would choose for our relatives and, indeed, for ourselves.

'Ethics is a complicated matter' writes the philosopher and educationalist, Mary Warnock: 'it is partly a matter of judgement and decision, of reasoning and sentiment, of having the right feeling at the right time, and every time is different'. These novels cogently and evocatively embody that heady mixture of elements, bringing ethics to life. They are accessible and compelling and will be enjoyed by general readers as much as by philosophers and health professionals.

Brian Hurwitz
NHS GP
Professor of Medicine and the Arts, King's College, London
Series Editor
February 2005

Website resource

Medical ethics is a fast-moving, constantly evolving hotbed of challenges. You can stay up to date with current controversies, laws and guidelines by visiting a website created to offer useful background information about the series and about the ethical and medical challenges these novels address.

For those who will use this unique and exciting resource to bring medical ethics alive in their teaching, additional educational material and references are also available free on this website:

www.radcliffe-oxford.com/livingliterature

About the author and series editor

Hazel McHaffie's first novel was published in 1994 and 2005 sees the publication of three more. She began her professional life as a nurse and midwife and later gained a doctorate from Edinburgh University. During her career as a Research Fellow in medical ethics she was the author of almost a hundred academic papers and books. One of her books *Crucial Decisions at the Beginning of Life* was voted BMA Medical Book of the Year in 2002. In her new novels she has woven an extensive knowledge of ethics and moral conundrums into gripping tales of passion and tragedy.

Brian Hurwitz is Professor of Medicine and the Arts at King's College, University of London, and a NHS general practitioner in London. He is a member of the UK Association of Medical Humanities and serves on the Editorial Board of the *Journal of Medical Ethics*.

Acknowledgements

In writing this book I have interrogated, emailed, corresponded with and generally disturbed a number of people, and I have met with nothing but patience and encouragement. I owe them all an immense debt of gratitude; a few I must single out for special mention.

Professor Kenneth Boyd, Mr Tom Russell, Inspector Stewart Sanderlands and Sister Penny Profit all gave me the benefit of their expert knowledge in ethics, persistent vegetative state, police work and Catholicism respectively. Dr Ninian Hewitt and Professor Ann Sommerville put me in touch with key contacts. Professor Brian Hurwitz and Gillian Nineham provided both constructive editorial advice and sustained enthusiasm for the project. My family maintained an unwavering belief in what I was trying to do, encouraged me throughout and read preliminary drafts with affectionate prejudice.

I salute them all but acknowledge that any errors and weaknesses in this book are my own.

Hazel McHaffie
February 2005

ONE

'Pregnant? *Pregnant?* But she *can't* be!'

The raised voice carried into the quiet of the room, bringing Geoff's head up abruptly. He'd been dozing, lulled by the warmth of the late summer evening and the stillness of his surroundings. He glanced at Rhona. No change. No indication she'd heard anything.

There was a low murmur of another quieter voice from along the corridor. Then the strident response again.

'She *can't* be!'

The door was shut, suddenly, firmly.

Silence again save for the rhythmic swish of the heavy curtain in the breeze from the open window beside him. Funny how regular recurrent sound had such a soporific effect – if it didn't irritate you to distraction first.

The voice had sounded like an exaggerated form of Bill's, but harder, sharper, almost hysterical. Certainly not like the Bill he knew, long-suffering Bill, who took life's knocks with not a hint of self-pity or superfluous emotion. And knocks didn't come much harder than Bill's.

Geoff was hugely impressed by Bill. It amused him to see a strong resemblance to George Baker, the burly Inspector Wexford of TV drama. Same powerful physique, same commanding presence, same grandfatherly warmth metamorphosing into a sternly uncompromising attitude when life demanded it. Even a similar gravelly voice, but in Bill's case without the regional accent. Geoff had idly wondered what he must have been like before the accident, before tragedy had robbed him of so much, but there was something indefinable about the present Bill that made him wary: the suggestion of a minefield with no clear danger signs. It was enough to quell any impulse to probe.

Bill's continuing dedication intrigued Geoff. How did this highly intelligent man, with his keen eye for the aesthetic, cope so calmly, relentlessly exposed to the sight of his only daughter, once a lively, talented girl of twenty-two, now a slavering wreck of humanity, dependent on other people for even the most basic functions of living? But he visited Viv every single day without exception. He'd retired early from his busy architect's practice; he'd even given up all commitments which took him outwith daily commuting distance of The Home. For hours he sat with her, talking to her as if her mental capacity was undimmed and she would be restored to him whole if he only persevered in believing it. And Geoff knew Viv's room was cluttered to the point of oppression with the offerings her father brought to her shrine – books, tapes, cards, posters, childhood toys – to stir that dormant memory. The drawers and wardrobe were crammed with her favourite colours. He'd heard the nurses cursing the clutter of expensive toiletries, vitamins, the latest herbal remedies, that tumbled out of her bedside locker.

So convincing was Bill's faith in her future that Geoff had almost come to believe it himself. He smiled wryly now, remembering.

He'd gone out into the garden only two weeks ago to sit on the bench amongst the roses, just for a break from the tedium of sitting indoors, the endless pointless sitting. Viv sat in the shade, a paisley throw tucked around her wasted legs, hiding the restraints holding her in the wheelchair. Wisps of dark hair escaped from under the brim of her hat, blowing across her still face, unheeded. She was alone only for a moment while her father had returned to collect a book and some juice. At a glance it looked as if she were watching the pigeons and their interminable posturing in the dust. Geoff hated pigeons. He hated their complacent cooing, hated their stupid rituals, hated their mess, their sheer ubiquity. Did she feel the same way? He'd called out a cheery greeting as he'd passed her chair, and felt a surge of genuine disappointment when the staring amber eyes remained unresponsive.

He'd given himself a mental shake. For goodness sake, get a grip, no point in taking on other people's tragedies. He'd more than enough of his own to be going on with.

But in spite of every good intention you did get sucked into other people's stories. He saw Bill and Viv most days he came to The Home. They all called it 'The Home'. At first he'd made a concerted effort always to say 'Chivenings'; it sounded upmarket, desirable. It seemed to capture something of the ethos of this exclusive residence for patients with intractable problems, offering hope to the hopeless. 'The Home' conjured up anonymous rows, inactivity, end-stage boredom. But after a few years it was just like any other name. The name just became that place. Like calling a child some outlandish name – Evangelina Matilda Charlotta Esmeralda. At first everyone recoiled in horror – you can't possibly! But after a while the kid just *was* Evangelina and you didn't bat an eyelid using the name yourself. That's how it was with 'The Home'. It just grew in amongst your defences and became a part of your norm.

Bill had chosen Chivenings for Viv for the same reason Geoff had chosen it for Rhona: 'the most progressive, most prestigious centre in the country', the advert said. After all these years the progressive ideas and prestige had lost something of their appeal, but where else was there to go?

Geoff envied Bill, envied him his unwavering hope. And his commitment. His own visits were of a different order. Oh yes, he came three times a week – unless, that is, he was away on business or on his one long annual holiday. He'd even blocked those two evenings and one afternoon out in his diary. And he worked – consciously these days – at stopping other things creeping up above them in his list of priorities. But deep down he knew once he relaxed his rigid rule it would get progressively easier to invade that time with other more fulfilling activities. It had become necessary lately to remind himself: he'd always valued loyalty. He mustn't lower his guard. Not now. Not after all this time.

Six years he'd been coming. Three times a week for six years. How many times was that he'd driven up that drive, walked through that door, sat in that same chair, said the same things, glanced repeatedly at the same clock, stared at the same pictures, watched the same face? Six years. Fifty-two weeks in a year. Three times a week. Nine hundred and thirty-six times. A few less for the weeks he'd missed on account of the holidays and occasional away-from-home work commitments. Getting on for nine hundred anyway. And on nearly every one of those nine hundred times he'd seen Bill at some point.

Of course Bill's tally was much higher than Geoff's. Total devotion there. And for nine years not just six. Nine years. Three hundred and sixty-five days in each year. Plus a couple of extra days for leap years. Three thousand two hundred and eighty-seven times. No breaks, no misses. No temptation to skip a daily slot there. Not for Bill.

Geoff couldn't avoid Bill's dedication. Viv's room was right next to Rhona's. The door was often open. He'd listened to the drone of Bill's voice reading to his daughter – he couldn't help hearing when it was silent in Rhona's room. He'd been fascinated by Bill's selection. None of your light-hearted frivolous stories, the usual reading for someone ill in hospital unable to really concentrate. Oh no. Not for Bill the easy route. Tolstoy's *War and Peace*. Jostein Gaarder's *Sophie's World*. Stephen Hawking's *A Brief History of Time*. It sounded to Geoff as if Bill was straining every nerve to convey the full sense of what he read; only through his voice would her mind fill with all this information. He was like a home tutor whose whole reputation hinged on the success of this one pupil in the final exam.

And in a way it did. Nothing in the world mattered to him as much as the outcome for this one girl on the receiving end of his ministrations. His obsession with her progress must have isolated him from the rest of life in many ways. Bill seemed to double as mother, father, sibling, teacher, nurse, everything, all rolled into one. Hence the three thousand and however many relentless trips without missing a beat.

And never before had there been a sign of disturbance in that paternal devotion. Until now.

Geoff hung suspended in time. It was none of his business he knew. The firmly closed door shouted at him to respect their privacy. But what was there to distract his mind? He'd concentrated on doing the caring things whenever he visited The Home but he'd got out of the habit of talking to Rhona beyond the first few civilities. He felt too self-conscious now to break the pattern. What was there to tell? What was the point of telling it?

He walked over to the TV in the corner and idly switched through the channels, keeping the sound low.

Sport – no thanks. Not when he'd had to forgo most of his own physical activities to fit in the visits. Cruel anyway with Rhona sitting there immobile.

Some absurd comedy with coarse voices, crude language, demeaning behaviour. He shuddered. Life was harsh enough without cheapening it further.

One of those ridiculous programmes that showed a team of DIY enthusiasts repairing the damage done by amateurs. Geoff watched it for a few minutes, willing the owners to see the changes for the first time and scream their horror at what had been done to ruffle their order of things. The inane victims, glorying in their moment of fame, beamed instead. Tears in the woman's eyes – how absurd! She darted from the flimsy bamboo screen, to the solitary inverted flower pot in the false alcove, and on to the walls lined with fishing nets hung with three starfish painted crimson, exclaiming in superlatives as phoney as the fixtures. Yuck! Geoff pressed the button on the remote control viciously.

The fourth channel gave him an old film of Brontë's *Jane Eyre*. His eyes flew involuntarily to Rhona. It had been one of her favourites. She'd told him once she'd read it six times. He'd laughed and teased her about having a high boredom threshold; she'd chided him for his philistine approach to literature. But the differences between them were part of the mutual attraction. In the old days Rhona had never taken less than eight long books away on their summer break. Geoff had left her to it and gone off exploring, tramping for hours to see an ancient ruin or a rare orchid growing in the wild. He'd spend weeks studying guides and maps of their destination, planning days crammed with activity. She'd prepare only to escape into her private literary world, revelling in two weeks free of all the demands of her busy working life in the publishing house.

The picture on the screen flickered occasionally but somehow the hesitant technology, the stilted speech, were more in keeping with the story than any modern slick presentation could have been, Geoff thought. Strange how actors back then looked so much older for their years. Who today would ever fall for an ageing Rochester like that? Good grief, he thought, I'm no screen god but even I look a sight more appealing than that!

His eyes moved to the mirror on Rhona's wardrobe. Yes, he was averagely good looking, a fraction under six feet tall, stocky build, grey eyes, dark hair greying at the temples and in a strip down the back of his head. Rugged charm, Rhona used to call it. His all-year-round tanned look helped, creating the illusion of a man used to the healthy outdoor life.

Seeing the slumped reflection he straightened his back and squared his shoulders. Yes, he looked better in profile. Except for the nose. He'd always hated his nose, so like his father's, long, thin, dominant. He wrinkled it in distaste and turned away.

The wedding scene drew Geoff into the story in spite of his cynicism. It was well done. The naïve innocence of Jane, the shattering announcement from the back of the church extinguishing her dreams, the grim march to see the depraved Mrs Rochester, locked away for safety. The mad woman to whom Edward was irrevocably shackled. A wife who was and was not. A bit like Rhona really. The thought sprang unbidden to Geoff's mind. He put it resolutely out of his head and turned back to the story. But the spell was broken. The present flooded back in.

What was happening down the corridor in the room with the firmly shut door? Geoff left the TV on but his eyes went only occasionally to the screen. Rhona's never did.

TWO

Bill stared from Dr Steven Wilkinson to Mrs Reed and back in disbelief.

Green eyes fell before the accusation in the blazing brown ones. Alison Reed fidgeted with a paper clip. Head of the nursing team she might be, but at this precise moment she looked more like a recalcitrant schoolgirl. She was a small woman anyway – no more than five foot one or two, Bill guessed – with an improbably auburn head of hair caught up in a rather old-fashioned French pleat designed to add to her air of elegance, but under the weight of his anger she seemed to shrink into obscurity.

By contrast Steven Wilkinson stood tall, shoulders straight, voice calm, gaze steady. His thick head of wiry hair needed a trim, and his rimless glasses would have benefited from a polish. But there was no mistaking his air of quiet authority now. He was every inch the Medical Director of The Home, his expertise, his status undisputed. The crisp white coat looked as if he'd donned it for the occasion, creases still stiff and angular.

'How *can* she be pregnant?' Bill asked again.

'We don't know.'

'Are you sure … she is?'

'We did a test,' Alison Reed said, trying to make it gentle.

'So … who did it?' The question escaped through clenched teeth.

'We don't know.' Pathetic. How could they not know?

'Well, was it a member of staff or a visitor or … ? What kind of a person?'

'I'm sorry, but we have no idea who it was. We've only just discovered Viv is pregnant.' Dr Wilkinson's grey eyes met his squarely.

'And just how did you "discover" it?' Bill sneered the word.

'Well, I'm sure you'll understand it's … well, it's not the sort of thing my staff are watching for. So … well, at first no-one noticed anything. But then one of the nurses became a bit suspicious – Viv's tummy was less flat than it used to be. She mentioned this to one of the senior staff – somebody who's quite often assigned to Vivienne – and they got talking and, well, they remarked that she hadn't had a period lately,' Mrs Reed said. Negligence. 'Well, just to rule out the obvious really, they did a pregnancy test. And, well, they thought there must be some mistake, or they'd got it wrong, or perhaps hormones got messed up after a time for people in a persistent vegetative state, or something. But, anyway, they repeated it. And, well, then they came to see me. And I did the test myself. And I'm afraid there's no mistake. It was positive.'

'*No mistake*? You have to be joking! There's been a bloody, almighty great mistake, Mrs Reed! Pardon my language. But … well, it's a nonsense to say there's no mistake!'

'I'm sorry. I didn't mean …'

The paper clip snapped in two, but still her restless fingers kneaded the fragments. The sight of her discomfort somehow inflamed Bill. His usual self-control deserted him.

'No, I bet you didn't!' he exploded, jumping suddenly to his feet and pacing the floor, glaring at them. 'But I'm sorry, this is one mistake you *can't* brush under the carpet! It's the tin lid! This is something I *can't* just overlook. Not like the times nobody got round to feeding Viv. Not like the times she didn't get her physio. Not like all the other things I saw, all the times *I* did what you people should have been doing. Thought I didn't notice, eh? I noticed all right. But Viv's my concern. She needs every scrap of my energy to get her better. Any energy directed anywhere else is less energy to give to her. I let it go because it wouldn't help her for me to antagonise you. But *this*? Oh, *this* is in a different league!'

'Mr Faraday, we're as horrified as you …' Steven Wilkinson interposed.

'What kind of a place is this? The best in the business, they told me. That's why I chose it for Viv. But now …' He struggled for words. 'My daughter has lain here for nine years, totally dependent on all of you for her protection, and someone – you don't even know who – has had access to her for long enough to … to *rape* her! And no-one knows anything about it?'

'I understand your anger …'

'Don't patronise me – *please*! I don't need your softly-softly counselling talk. Of course I'm angry! I'm livid. Of course you understand I am. So would you be if you were in my shoes. So you *should* be yourselves. Angry – and bloody afraid in your case.'

'We're all terribly upset by this. And we quite understand your feelings …' Dr Wilkinson was still irritatingly soothing. 'But our main concern is Viv.'

It stopped Bill in his tracks. Viv. What about *her*?

'Is she …?' He dared not voice it. 'How is she …?'

'As far as her personal physical health is concerned she's fine.'

'How far on …?'

'I'm afraid she's already eighteen weeks.'

'*Eighteen!*' That was getting on for half way! Bill suddenly sank down in the armchair he'd vacated earlier and dropped his head in his hands. His own daughter, his beloved Viv, was eighteen weeks pregnant. His grandchild was moving about in there. Recognisably a human creature. Taking sustenance from its unknowing mother. Viv, a mother. His fingers clenched and unclenched in his hair.

'We need to discuss with you what to do – now we know.' Steven's voice cut into his thoughts. Bill dragged his head up to stare at the doctor.

'Do?'

'Whether to do an abortion or let the pregnancy continue.'

Bill continued to stare, the horror like an incoming tide, gathering momentum. The doctor's words seemed to emerge through a fog, only impinging on his brain when they came closer.

'Because Viv can't tell us what she wants we need to decide on her behalf what's best. I'm sorry. It's our responsibility but we do need your input. I realise this has been an appalling shock. You need time to think. But unfortunately time isn't on our side here.'

'Whose decision is it?'

'I think we need to do this together. You – the family – anyone really who knows what Viv thought about these things – can help us. We need to know what she would choose if she were able to tell us. And we, as her medical team, will try to make the best decision in these circumstances. In consultation with you, of course.'

Bill shook his head slowly. He must shrug off this drugged feeling of unreality.

'I imagine you'll want to speak to other members of the family …?' Dr Wilkinson began tentatively.

Would he? Bill hadn't got anywhere near that in his thinking. He was still trying to get his head around the bare fact that Viv was pregnant. Other members of the family? Who? Who else really cared one way or the other? Frances? Kevin? Euan? Well, what did they know of Viv now? They'd pretty well buried her already. OK, they'd known her when she was a bright, articulate girl with strong opinions. But how much of what she thought then applied now? If she'd become pregnant then she'd have known what she wanted. Oh yes, she'd been very independent, sure of her beliefs and values back then.

His thoughts rolled back. Before the tragedy.

Viv at twenty-two was a striking girl. It wasn't that she was physically a head-turner. Pretty enough, yes, with her glossy dark hair, unusual amber eyes, but no model – only medium height, mouth technically too generous for her small face, hips wider than the catwalk would tolerate, fingers unusually short and square with nails bitten more often than filed. No, even Bill wouldn't describe her as beautiful. But it was her personality that reached out and grabbed you. She radiated interest in people. Her insatiable need to find out what they thought, how they ticked, was like a magnet. The intensity of her undivided attention made them feel their opinions were worth hearing. She left them feeling *they* had had an influence on *her* life and thinking. She bound them to her subtly, made them want to stay in the circle of her intimate friendship.

Her appeal was tangible. During term time her cluttered flat was a mecca for fellow students searching for the meaning of life or a sympathetic companion for a meal in a new Italian restaurant in town. During the holidays her parents stopped answering the phone it rang so frequently, almost always for her. They grew accustomed to finding unknown bodies ensconced in sleeping bags in any available corner of their house.

Initially at university she dabbled in philosophy alongside her main subject of modern languages. But she quickly found the thinking of the great minds of the past sat uneasily with her own inclination to charge at issues foursquare. She'd laughed telling Bill that Professor Aidan Marriott was mesmerised by her end-of-year exam paper and read it three times in order to give her views a fair hearing, before awarding her a scraping pass. The Professor was as relieved to see her drop the subject as she was to throw off the shackles of meticulous logic.

In all other areas of her course she was an enthusiastic and able student. She returned from her year at the Sorbonne with an impeccable accent and a handsome suitor. Pierre changed Viv. He took her heart by storm and she spent the long summer months, when she wasn't running herself ragged as a waitress in the local busy French restaurant, gazing adoringly into his eyes. For his part Pierre taught her all he knew about French wines, French cuisine, and French kissing. So attentive and adroit was he that nothing prepared her for the revelation that came three weeks before she was due back at university. While she had practised his idioms, and his culinary tips, on the guests at her allocated tables for nine hours a day, he was happily murmuring other phrases as he nibbled the ear of Maria from Barcelona, a would-be model looking for recognition in the hard world of commercial beauty. It was Maria who flew off with him back to Paris.

Bill had watched in silent awe as she'd stamped out her fury, vowing never to trust a man again. He'd breathed a long sigh of relief when she'd thrown herself with even more determination into final year studies. If she was destined to remain single for ever, she said grimly, she would make sure she excelled at her work and outshone her male counterparts. She'd show them! And Bill had assumed that's exactly what she was doing until that fateful afternoon ... until a bruised and battered Tony Partridge was wheeled into Intensive Care.

Tony became aware of Viv when she started working late in the library. Night after night she came. And always she worked with an obsession which absorbed her completely.

It was not until almost Easter-time that she even spoke to him. He was relatively new to the library staff and felt a surge of dread when she outlined her request. Would he be up to the challenge of tracking down an obscure paper in an unheard-of French magazine? It would be mortifying to have to apply to a colleague for help. Methodically he inched through the world of intricate foreign literature searches in pursuit of his quarry.

15

Her own enthusiasm and persistence encouraged him. When the article was finally snared she had turned to him with shining eyes.

'I spent six hours trying and didn't get anywhere,' she cried. 'You've done it in twenty-seven minutes. I could hug you!'

He was embarrassed by the sudden colour flooding his neck and face. She didn't mean anything personal.

'It's what I'm paid to do,' he stammered.

'Oh, but you've saved me *days* of frustration. At least let me shout you a coffee.'

Tony wasn't even sure where the impetus had come from. But somehow one-way gratitude slid into two-way interest. Coffee led on to lunch, then to an evening at a play they'd both wanted to see. Her lively mind challenged him: discussions ranged over everything from student opportunities, to equality of opportunity, to fair trade, oppression, war, holy war, fanaticism, their own religious convictions. By the time they reached a comparison between their personal moral codes he knew that he had found a soulmate. In spite of her declared intentions to eschew all men, Viv told him, he had crept under her defences. No-one was more surprised than Tony.

THREE

Then, suddenly and without warning, the accident drove an impassable barrier between them.

Tony regained consciousness after two days but remembered nothing of the event which had cost him those hours. The dent in the right side of his skull, two broken legs, a fractured pelvis, and a ruptured spleen, kept him immobile for much longer. But he badgered the staff day after day, night after night, to tell him about Viv. In the end they wheeled him to Intensive Care to see her.

It was terrifying. She lay immobile, unreachable, unrecognisable.

But in spite of the terror, he sat for long periods, just looking at her, occasionally self-consciously holding her hand.

'Talk,' the nurses said. 'Talk to her. About anything.'

He'd tried. It was the talking that had drawn them to each other after all. But it wasn't the same when she didn't argue, or challenge him.

And often her parents were there. Then he didn't even try. They had so much more to say – twenty-two years of shared experiences to draw on – and so much more right to say it. In their presence Tony felt crushingly inhibited. Even what he alone could say to her was not for parental ears. He wanted to tempt her with promises of so much more, future things he would not yet have dared to offer in the face of her frank gaze. He said none of these things.

When she was moved to a hospital closer to the Faradays' home it was much harder for him to see her. His own incapacity made him reliant on others for transport. Visits became much less frequent. And almost always her father was already there when he arrived, and saw no necessity to leave. Bill Faraday was scrupulously polite but there was no warmth, no encouragement.

The coolness made Tony fret about the accident. Was her father blaming him? If only he could remember what had happened. Were they keeping the details from him because it was his fault Viv now lay in a coma? Oh, he'd asked – again and again he'd asked. They would only say his car was involved with an articulated lorry and a Ford Transit van. No-one had witnessed the accident. The van driver had died trapped in his blazing vehicle. The lorry driver had broken his neck. Viv had been crushed beneath the wreckage – for too long. He'd been the lucky one. The police hinted that the van had been going too fast on a corner but no-one could say for sure.

It preyed on Tony's mind – day and night he agonised. He tried apologising when he saw Viv, but the tears choked him. He saw her father avert his eyes, but he'd seen the scorn. And in his tortured mind the conviction grew: he became the prime suspect. His fears congealed as his physical wounds healed.

He convinced himself that he was the last person Viv would want to see when she woke up. He'd let her regain consciousness first, give her time, then he'd give her a chance to vent her anger against him. It would help to resolve the conflict. And she would – she'd berate him. That was one of the things he loved about her, her fearless honesty.

He stayed away, phoning the hospital periodically to find out if she'd woken up yet. Twice a week at first. Then once a week … once a fortnight … monthly. When they eventually told him she was probably never going to come round, she'd never be able to tell him what had happened, the depression that had been swirling round his brain for months finally swallowed him whole.

It was six dark months before he could face the world again. He woke from nightmares drenched in sweat, crying out in terror. And he was now totally convinced that he could not see Viv while her father lived. He had no means of learning that Bill was at a loss to know how to handle an incoherent stranger, damaged in the same accident as his only daughter, but unable to rescue her from limbo.

When the doctors first told Bill hesitantly about the diagnosis, he cut them short. He'd get another opinion, he said. The two senior neurologists were sympathetic. Yes, by all means. They understood. When the third man reiterated it – persistent vegetative state – Bill felt the tentacles closing vice-like on his stomach. Was Dr Peters one hundred per cent certain? The consultant, holding his gaze, said very few things in medicine were absolutely one hundred per cent sure, but he'd say this was 99.999%. It was enough for Bill. Viv had always been the exception. If anyone could defy them she was the one. With his help she'd do it. He applied himself with single-minded devotion to the task.

It had been hard accepting the move to Chivenings. Bill hated the thought of her in a place with connotations of incurable conditions and bleak outlooks. But there seemed little option if this was the centre of excellence, the one place that pushed the limits further than anyone else could or would. Outwardly The Home bore the hallmarks of success: design awards hanging in the foyer; gilt-lettered plaques commemorating wealthy benefactors; touches of luxury for visitors in the soft carpeting, bone china and excellent 'Cath's Canteen'. The pace was much less hectic than it had been at the hospital, too, giving the staff space to tailor Viv's care to suit his comings and goings. There was rarely anything to stop him giving Viv his undivided attention now that Tony Partridge had stopped coming. He was free to visit as and when he chose, do what he liked.

The routine helped. And a form of peace settled in Bill's heart as the years passed. A fragile peace that was abruptly splintered now.

Standing looking down at his daughter Bill found he was shaking. He forced himself to look at her anew. Her eyes were closed, but today he noticed the deep mauve shadows beneath the fringe of dark lashes. The sunlight made her dark hair gleam. She wore the blouse he'd bought her for her birthday, chosen because it was her favourite shade of blue. It was stretched more tightly than usual across her chest. A wave of nausea jolted him. She was already showing the outward signs of pregnancy. Underneath the cover loosely laid over her knees her abdomen would confirm what he'd just heard. It seemed indelicate to look. Without her permission. If only ... if only she could give it.

'Oh Viv,' he whispered, 'help me.'

He dropped down beside her and took her two hands in his, moving until his face was aligned with hers.

'I'm so, so sorry, darling. How could this happen to you? I'd have stayed awake day and night, never left your side, if I'd thought for one moment ...'

It was unthinkable. No-one could have anticipated anything like this.

'But now ... what now? What would you say, Viv? All these years I've willed you to speak to me, I've never needed you to more than today – now. Tell me. Show me. Please. Please. *Please*.'

Viv's slack mouth remained unmoving. Did she know about the pregnancy? Was she struggling inside somewhere to voice her feelings? Who could ever know? They said people in comas could hear, when they regained consciousness they could tell of their experiences. Who knew about people in Viv's state of nothingness? In spite of what the doctors said about her, he had to assume she was aware at some level. That's why he'd talked to her, read to her, for all these years. Oh, it had been a struggle sometimes, stilling the doubts. Sometimes he'd even tested his own faith, deliberately telling her things he'd never mentioned to another soul, secret thoughts, things he would never have shared even with her before the accident.

'This is your baby, Viv. Do you want it? Will you want it when you wake up? I'll look after it, love it for you, until then ... if that's what you want. But do you? Do you want it? Or will it just be a horrible reminder of what he did to you?'

Nothing.

The silence, the fear, settled around them.

The chaos in Bill's mind made him unaware of the ache in his knees until much later when he rose to leave. He'd delayed having his name put on the list for replacement joints knowing it would stop him visiting Viv. It crossed his mind that now perhaps he should get them done in case he needed the agility to chase a small child. Misgivings zigzagged across his brain as he gathered together his coat and umbrella, books and papers.

How could he possibly decide? A faint flicker of hope tantalised him. Perhaps if Viv gave birth to a new creature – a fresh, innocent, healthy new person – something would stir in her, reach out to this part of her. Was the maternal instinct the one urge strong enough to override the shackles that held her? And if that process took time, well, in the meantime he would have this vibrant part of Viv to lavish with love. She – this mini Viv, this daughter of his daughter – would be to him a symbol of new hope. Watching her thrive, feeling her arms about his neck, knowing that he was her protection, her fountain of unconditional love, it would give him new impetus. And if the unthinkable happened and the doctors were right, Viv never did come back to him, then something of her would live on, his role would be perpetuated.

And he wouldn't be deluding himself. You heard of people who wanted replacements for those they had loved and lost. They needn't fling that at him. He knew nobody, nothing, could replace his beloved daughter. This wouldn't be *Viv*, but …

He must sort out what he thought, what he expected, what he felt. And he'd have to try not only to think what Viv would want, but to put himself inside the skin of the baby. What would it choose? Would it be appalled by its parentage? Would it hate the idea of a 'non-person' for a mother, a rapist for a father? What genes would it carry? Would it be better for it never to be born? But if it were never to be born … It was one thing to agree with abortion in principle – or at least not to oppose it – quite a different thing to request it. Could he, dare he, ask for a potential child to be killed … and that, not just any child, but *Viv's* child? Had he the right? Viv would be so mad with him when she found out.

It was unexpectedly dark when he stepped outside. The security light above the door was off for some reason tonight. Symbolic of the darkness of this day, he thought fleetingly. It had rained steadily for hours but he scarcely noticed the muddy water splashing his trousers as he strode through the puddles to reach his car, the only vehicle still parked outside The Home.

For once he didn't look up at Viv's window before he drove away.

FOUR

Dr Steven Wilkinson watched Bill's car vanish into the night. What a nightmare! Telling the family was only the beginning.

It had been a shock seeing the benign, rather avuncular Bill Faraday transformed into a very angry man. He had revealed a reservoir of grievances festering inside him and he was obviously not going to accept this latest enormity quietly. If news of this got out what would it do to The Home? At the best of times it was a constant battle to acquire funding for this sort of work. Celebrities, big companies, they preferred to put their money into the high-profile glamorous things – research, front-line medicine. There was nothing remotely glamorous about the work he did. No star would want their photographs taken with the Rhonas and the Vivs of this world. No, he depended on the efforts of the families, the friends. It was amazing what they managed to raise but The Home was never exactly flush with money.

Publicity about the rape would be disastrous. Who would want to send their loved ones to a Home where such a thing happened? The ensuing anxiety might even make families move existing patients out of harm's way. And who could blame them?

How could he keep this under wraps? Would the Faradays buy into a low-profile approach: protecting Viv, respecting the family's identity, that kind of thing? Was it even possible? Once the boys in blue started snooping around asking questions it would be sure to leak out. Maybe not the details, but folk would sense that something unsavoury was going on.

OK, what about saying nothing, just beefing up security themselves? They could organise CCTV cover, security locks on the doors, checks of visitors. Steven groaned aloud and ran his hand distractedly through his sandy hair. It would all cost money. He could picture them now, the dreaded finance people, shaking their heads, looking disapproving about the year's budget. But hang it all, if in the long term it prevented a drop in occupancy figures it had to be worth short-term economies.

Besides even the treasurer wouldn't want to see *this* story blazoned over the papers. Imagine the comments, the letters, the speculation! It'd be their death knell. And there'd be sure to be some smart-alec journalist who'd drop suspicions about the staff. Who else had such ready access to these vulnerable women? Steven's mind ran down the list of employees. It was unthinkable that any of them would do anything so … so … beyond the pale. No, he really couldn't believe it. But if not them, then who, how? How could anyone have found an opportunity for this?

Picturing Viv again, his mind moved on to the growing pregnancy. He'd need to check. Which option held the greater risks to Viv, continuing the pregnancy or terminating it? Were there even data on such patients? The number of women who became pregnant in a persistent vegetative state must be infinitesimal. Had any of them actually delivered a baby? Did they need a Caesarean section? Would they need a general anaesthetic? Not for pain presumably, but there'd be signs of physiological stress – bound to be. A general anaesthetic would dampen down the worst excesses. Yes, he'd definitely need to contact the obstetricians before he saw Bill Faraday again, to find out from them about the risks and how best to proceed from a medical point of view. He smiled ruefully. The renal people, the chest folk, the vascular consultants, he was used to dealing with them all, but it'd be a first contacting the team who dealt in pregnancy and childbirth. He could see them now, flocking like vultures, fascinated, wanting a piece of the action.

Steven sighed, shaking his head, trying to shed the whirling unanswered questions. There was still humdrum work to be done. And all these patients to protect. The sudden shrill bleeping of his pager forced him back into the routines of medicine.

FIVE

For once Bill phoned Kevin at work. It was simple enough to contact him directly, Kevin being a senior partner in his firm of accountants, but Bill had strong opinions about keeping work separate from domestic affairs. Only in a crisis could he be persuaded to break his own rule. But this was a crisis. Certainly not a moment for Tina's criticism.

Even now Bill found it hard to tolerate his elder daughter-in-law. He could just hear her shrill sarcastic voice: 'How like Vivienne! I'm sure I ought to be used to being let down by the Faradays by now, but one always hopes things might improve. But of course, there can be no replacement for breeding. And Vivienne was always so totally lacking in refinement. But a pregnancy – *how* unpleasant! I always knew she'd come to grief – so careless in matters of etiquette and good form – but even I didn't imagine she could sink this low.'

Mercifully she'd never once visited Viv since the diagnosis of persistent vegetative state was pronounced. Nothing like that had ever happened in *her* family, she'd said, her perfect nose flaring ever so slightly as if she had scented the beginning of a bad odour. Bill didn't think he could have kept up his resolve never to retaliate if such insinuations had persisted. And he would certainly never have allowed them to be said within Viv's hearing.

Kevin's secretary, Carol, transferred the call immediately. Bill struggled to find the words to convey the urgency of his message without divulging the detail. There had been 'a development', involving Viv, could Kevin call at Bill's house as soon as he'd finished work. Euan too. Kevin began to mumble something about Tina needing him to do … Bill cut him dead.

'Kevin. This is an emergency. For once, can't you just do as I ask? I wouldn't ask for anything if I didn't have to.'

It was true.

'Of course. I'll be there.'

Bill waited until he'd calmed down again before ringing Felicity. No point in trying to track down Euan who might be teaching anywhere in his large comprehensive school. Besides Felicity was completely trustworthy. She could be relied on to pass on a message without passing judgement.

'I'll tell Euan as soon as he gets in, Bill. No, better still, I'll contact him at work for you, and ask him to come straight round to your house from school. He'll be only too glad to escape from the fourth years a bit earlier.'

'Thanks, Felicity. He'll fill you in tonight.'

The two young men stood staring at him in stunned disbelief.

Bill felt a sudden lump in his throat. Though completely unalike in looks – Kevin thickset, dark thinning hair neatly parted, his immaculate suit buttoned as tightly as his emotions; Euan skinny and slightly dishevelled, his fair curls rampant, his five o'clock shadow a marked contrast to Kevin's neatly trimmed moustache – there was a strong family resemblance in their faces at that moment. So like their mother.

It was Bill who broke the silence first.

'I know. It's too nightmarish to believe. I can hardly believe it myself.'

'How could anyone … possibly …?' Kevin was lost for words. Bill felt himself bristling. 'I mean, how could anyone have got into The Home and into her room – for long enough … to … without anyone seeing them?'

'That's exactly what I said. But Mrs Reed – you know, she's the manager – says, once they're stable, patients like Viv can be left for as long as two hours between turns. The staff only need to ensure they can't fall or choke or whatever. So it's technically possible. And they sometimes get left for longer than that, especially at night when there are very few staff on duty.'

'So do they think he got in during the night?'

'Nobody knows.' Bill shrugged.

'I just … how can … I mean … if somebody isn't safe in a Home specifically for such people, where *can* they be safe?'

'Good question. And it's something I intend to pursue, I can tell you,' Bill said grimly.

'Could it have been a member of staff? They'd know when she'd be alone, where to find her, everything like that.'

'Yep. It could have been. Mrs Reed and Dr Wilkinson have already gone down the list. They couldn't *think* of anybody suspicious – anybody who they think might be capable of doing something like that, but they're looking at everybody employed around that time, of course, but …'

'But equally it could have been a visitor or an intruder – somebody quite outside. How on earth could they find out who visited – when? – well, presumably they won't even know exactly when whoever it was raped Viv. If they just did it once or …'

'Stop it, Kevin! Stop it! Stop it! Stop it!' Bill shouted, his eyes screwed tight, his hands clapped over his ears.

'Sorry, Dad. Sorry. It's … it's just … it's such a shock. I can't get my head round it.'

There was a long strained silence. Bill struggled for composure before he spoke.

'I know. *I'm* sorry. Didn't mean to shout. It's just that …'

Bill sank down onto the nearest chair, naked pain distorting his expression. Euan moved swiftly to sit beside him, a hand gripping his shoulder briefly.

'We understand, Dad,' he said. 'Doesn't bear thinking of. But Kev's right. Who knows what might have been going on in that place? Not just to Viv, to any of them.'

'I know. But it kills me to think … anybody could … do anything … to Viv. To my little girl. Makes me want to … ' Bill ground his teeth.

His sons exchanged a look over his head.

'What about the police? Are they involved?' Euan asked quietly.

'Not yet.'

'For goodness sake! A crime's been committed!' Kevin glared at his father. 'Well, hasn't it?'

'I know. But I discussed it with Dr Wilkinson. They rang me as soon as they found out. They'll *have* to report it but … well, it's something we have to discuss – as a family. Do we want to have an open investigation? Do we want it to be broadcast? Do we want Viv to be named? Do we want folk finding out about the pregnancy or … whatever? If the police are brought in, do the media find out anyway? Do we want that? Would Viv want that?'

'And if people find out how vulnerable people like Viv are, how easy it is to get access to places like The Home, will it put the idea into some other nutter's head?' Euan was thinking out loud.

'Exactly. Copycat crimes. It's not an easy decision. OK, yes, a crime's been committed, but we need to make sure the situation isn't made even worse.'

'Depends a bit if Viv has an abortion or goes ahead and has the baby, doesn't it?' Euan asked.

'To some extent. And that's really why I asked you to come tonight. What do you think? There isn't time to waste. Dr Wilkinson wants us to give him some idea of what we think Viv would want.'

Bill noticed with surprise that Kevin was absent-mindedly twisting the edge of his moustache. It was a childish gesture – only back then it had been a lock of hair behind his ear – that had always betrayed anxiety even in the face of outward defiance or conviction.

'She'd be mad as hell that some guy got her into this mess! That would be Viv's reaction!' Kevin sounded so certain.

'Too right. I can hear her stamping and shouting and screaming blue murder. Demanding castration at the very least!' Euan agreed.

Bill gave them a wintry smile. They were right of course. Viv would have been extremely vocal in her condemnation of any man who could do something like this.

'But what would she have decided about the baby?'

There was silence. Viv, the old Viv, was suddenly vividly with them. Eyes blazing. Striding up and down the room in her ethnic-look floating skirt and beaded hair, as always, somehow larger than life.

Bill struggled again with the picture of her contemplating pregnancy – an unwanted pregnancy – by a man she'd never consciously met.

'Nearest thing I guess is if she'd been at a party and got completely stoned out of her mind and somebody'd taken advantage of her drunken state,' Euan said slowly.

'Yeah, or if she'd been raped at knifepoint by a complete stranger, or something,' Kevin chipped in.

'So what would she have decided?' Bill persisted.

'I don't know.' Kevin shrugged his shoulders.

'Me neither.'

'I can picture her screaming blue murder at the guy one minute and dissolving into tears thinking about the kid the next,' Kevin said.

'She was always on the side of the underdog, wasn't she?' Euan added.

'Absolutely.'

'But the thing is – would she think of *herself* as the underdog? Or the kid? How would she see the pregnancy?' Euan was thinking aloud. 'It would depend on that what she'd do, I think. Would she think of it as an extension of this creep who was capable of raping a defenceless person? Or is it *her* kid?'

'I think you're right. She'd swither – one minute mad as hell, wanting to tear it out with her bare hands; next minute fiercely protective,' Kevin said, nodding slowly.

There was another long silence. Then Euan turned to look directly at Bill.

'Did she ever talk about abortion? What she thought?'

'To me, you mean? That's what I've been trying to remember. And she did – several times actually. But her opinions were different at different times. Depended on her mood and her latest fad.'

'That figures. That was Viv.' Both young men nodded. 'What did she say then?'

'I've been wracking my brains. It doesn't help much but for what it's worth … When she was just a small kid I remember her telling me about her friend's mum having a "borshun" as she called it. She wanted to know what it meant. I softened it all actually – so she didn't give the other kid a hard time. She wanted to know if your mother and I'd do the same thing. I said no because your mother was a Catholic and Catholics didn't, but she didn't need to worry because it wouldn't happen. She got sidetracked into how we knew that. But in the end just as she was leaving the room I remember she said, "I'm glad Mum's a Caflick. I don't want *my* baby sister killed." I remember thinking it was odd that she thought of it in those terms at that age. That's why it stuck in my mind, I think.'

'She was just a kid. What about later?'

'I can't remember anything else specifically until she was about seventeen/eighteen. Then I remember she tore a picture of a fetus sucking its thumb out of a magazine and pinned it on her wall. Your mother found it freaky. She asked her why. To help her think what abortion really meant,

Viv told her, to remind her about what it actually involved. Your mother of course was just relieved to hear Viv was so opposed to it – even though she knew Viv didn't hold with the Catholic blanket ruling.'

'No?'

'You know Viv! She could be pretty brutal in her judgements sometimes,' Bill said wryly.

'Often, I'd say.' A slow grin spread over Euan's face as he said this, affection not condemnation in his voice.

Bill smiled briefly too. Viv's exact words rang in his ears: 'How can a bunch of scraggy dried-up old bachelors who've never had a kid know anything about it? There's no way *I'd* listen to that old religious claptrap – not even if I was a Catholic. It's the woman's body. Let her decide.'

She'd been a rebellious teenager before she'd left home for university. There'd been many a steaming session. Bill remembered one particular occasion vividly.

SIX

Twelve midnight. One o'clock. Two.

Bill insisted Frances go to bed. He'd wait up – yes, he promised he would. Her agitation was affecting him. She wanted to contact friends, ring hospitals, call the police – *do something*! But Bill remained adamant – it was just Viv testing their limits. No point in making idiots of themselves as well as showing her up. They'd only have to call all these people back when she *did* turn up.

Every minute stretched endlessly as he waited. He lost track of the number of mugs of tea he'd made and left to grow cold. No phone call. Nothing.

His outward confidence in front of Frances was one thing. Left to himself, Bill's own growing anxiety refused to be suppressed. Where would he start to search? They had no idea where she was. Or with whom. She'd just gone out. Without a word.

Two fifteen. Two twenty-one. Two twenty-five …

More tea. Coffee even. It would help him to stay awake.

He must have dozed off eventually because the sound of the key in the door woke him with a start. Three forty-five – he remembered the hands on the clock to this day. *Three forty-five!* He was standing in the doorway when she turned from closing the door as quietly as she could. She started visibly, her hand flying to her mouth, her eyes wide.

He gestured her into the room and closed the door behind her. No point in waking the entire household.

With his face only inches from hers he hissed, 'Where the hell have you been?'

'Out,' she said with that defiant look.

'Don't you cheek me, my girl!' He wagged his finger menacingly in front of her nose.

'Or what?' she taunted, striking a confident pose with her hand on her hip.

Her insolence in the face of his justifiable anger was breathtaking. He knew a feeling of empathy with men who lashed out in the face of such provocation. He felt his face working with the effort of regaining control. But her brazen stare remained unflinching.

'Don't you realise your mother and I have been out of our minds with worry?'

'I didn't *ask* you to stay up. I didn't *ask* you to worry.'

'We worry because we *care*, you little demon!' he spat out between clenched teeth. 'Where the hell have you been, anyway?'

'It's no business of yours where I've been. I'm old enough to take care of myself.'

'As long as you're underage and under my roof, it *is* my business, so cut the clever-clog act! And in any case, if you were *really* grown up you'd behave with more consideration, not like some spoilt brat who doesn't stop to consider other people's feelings.'

'Huh! For goodness sake! Not that old chestnut again!' She could be unbelievably rude in one of her 'sassy' moods. But he struggled to hold onto the real point of his lecture.

'And even if you do feel you're responsible for yourself, there're things out there you can't control. You're young. You're female. You're vulnerable. But you're not wise enough to know the dangers. Out on the streets till all hours like this – anything could happen. It's asking for trouble. We're only trying to protect you. That's why we expect you to obey the rules.'

'Rules! Glory, hallelujah!' she said in the nasal voice of a negro spiritual, dancing back away from him, wriggling her hips, swaying as if in a religious fervour. 'Bring back the slave traders!'

'Stop being so … so … *provoking*! This is no joke! I'm serious.' Bill cut her dead.

'Yeah, yeah, yeah.'

She was infuriating. She made him say things he didn't mean.

'Well, don't come running to us when you get pregnant or get into trouble with the police or get hooked on drugs.'

'I won't, don't you fret. I can look after myself. I don't need two old fogies out of the ark to tell me what to do.'

'You are so cocky! So sure of yourself! But you mark my words, my girl, the higher up you put yourself, the further you have to fall.'

'Cliché number three hundred and fifty-six!' she'd yawned. 'What's the matter? Afraid a fallen daughter will besmirch your reputation?'

'You are so rude. I'm ashamed to own you as my daughter,' he spat back.

'You don't own me.'

'But you still expect me to provide a roof over your head and food and clothing and washing and … and …'

She shrugged her shoulders. 'Suit yourself. I can always move in with Chris.'

'Chris? Who's Chris?' His voice was sharp, higher.

'Just a guy I know. Wants me to move in with him anyway.'

'Vivienne! Don't be ridiculous. You're still a teenager. Still at school. You've got your whole life ahead of you. For goodness sake don't throw it all away to make a point.'

'Why not? *He* wouldn't shriek at me for being out late.'

'Then he doesn't really care for you.'

'Oh, he cares all right. He cares a great deal.' She let her voice purr over the words, giving him a smouldering look.

'Are you …?' Bill's stomach lurched into his mouth.

'Am I what?' She waited, knowing full well what he meant, daring him to voice his fear. Stubborn glare met obstinate stare. 'Go on, Dad, say it. Sexually active? Go on.'

'Well, are you?'

'Wouldn't you like to know?!'

'Probably not!' he said grimly. 'Have you thought about the consequences?'

'Babies and things, you mean?'

'You *know* what I mean. Have you?'

'Oh, I know where to go for an abortion. And I know where the nearest clinic is for the other stuff,' she tossed off flippantly.

She laughed outright at his outrage. 'People *talk* about this stuff nowadays. Not like in *your* day. It's not birds and bees any more – it's HIV and venereal diseases. We can take care of ourselves.'

'But you're *not* taking care of yourselves if you're risking things like that. Prevention – saying no – it's much safer than hoping to find a cure.'

'Yawn, yawn, yawn. You sound like that health education advert on TV.'

'Pity you don't take notice then. It's a serious warning. Knowing about abortion – that's not the way to go. You shouldn't even be having sex at your age.'

'Says who? The health education people? Huh! They get paid to say these things. Mum's Pope? Big deal. He wouldn't want to have sex anyway, would he? Easy for him to talk. Don't suppose *I'll* want to when I'm old like him either.'

'*Are* you taking precautions?' He hardly dared ask the question.

'Precautions? Me? Why should I?'

'So you don't get pregnant – catch anything – in the first place.'

'Nope.'

'Nope, as in you're agreeing with the reason? Or nope, as in you're not taking precautions?'

A long pause while she looked at him with an inscrutable look in her eyes.

'Both.'

'For goodness sake!'

'Aw, Dad! For goodness sake yourself! I'm tired. I'm not taking precautions because I don't need to. So get your knickers untwisted and go to bed. 'Night.' And she was gone.

As so often happened when she'd overstepped the mark, she was extra charming next day, going out of her way to do thoughtful little things to please her parents and show her affection.

But Bill had had a real scare and he wasn't going to let her charm her way out of this one quite so easily. When she tried ingratiating herself by giving him a hug, he held her firmly and talked to her seriously about the hazards waiting out there in the real world. He knew she was too stubborn to apologise, so it was something that she listened in silence.

It was during the course of this discussion that she'd told him she wasn't against abortion in principle but she doubted whether she could go through with it for herself.

For his own reasons Bill kept the first part of this story to himself and only shared Viv's conclusion with her brothers. Disturbed by the memories, he got up abruptly and moved to the window where he stood with his back to his sons, looking out at the cluster of shrubs and trees where a small girl had once scampered so happily. It was still painful recalling being angry with Viv.

'That the last time?' Euan's tentative enquiry brought him back to the present.

He turned slowly to face them again.

'No, actually. There was one other time – that I can think of anyway. She was home from university. Must have been in her – what? – second year, I think, and she was in reflective mood. You know how she could be sometimes. Like quicksilver – wildly excitable one day, deep in thought the next. Anyway, she was telling me one night about some lectures she'd been to. They'd put on a series of seminars, all about ethical issues relating to being a student. She'd gone along at first because somebody in her year had recently committed suicide and it had really shaken her. D'you remember that?'

Both brothers shook their heads.

'Well, maybe you weren't around at the time. But anyway it affected her a lot. The guy who committed suicide wasn't a friend of hers but he was her age. It was preying on her mind. How could you know? What if one of her own crowd was very near the edge? Anyway, apparently one of the seminars was looking at depression and suicide. She talked about that mostly. But there was also one on abortion. And that's the last time I remember her saying what she thought herself.'

'Which was?'

'She felt it was up to each woman to work it out for herself in these particular circumstances.'

'Hmm. Not much help to us, that.'

''Fraid not.'

There was another long silence.

'Did she mention it to either of you?' Bill looked from one to the other.

'Not to me, no.' Euan was sure.

'Well, she did once to me, actually.' Kevin looked uncomfortable, and again he was fiddling with his moustache. 'Well … OK, you know anyway … she never really took to Tina for some reason, and she could be quite … well, unkind … about her sometimes. She knew we didn't want to have kids and she once asked me what we'd do if Tina got pregnant by mistake. I told her and she said, "Each to their own, bro, each to their own." I thought she was making another snide comment about Tina – you know, not wanting kids – but she said she wasn't. She believed every woman had the right to choose for herself.'

'So that was much about the same as what she said to Dad,' Euan summed up.

Bill shot Kevin a glance, wondering briefly just what had been said. He could picture Viv making every question, every comment, sound like a criticism of her sister-in-law. There had never been any warmth of affection on either side there, and Viv hadn't made much effort to hide her scorn. But then he couldn't himself imagine Tina risking her perfect statistics by childbearing, or sullying her carefully manicured hands with dirty nappies. Yes, he could see her electing for as speedy an abortion as possible – day two preferably. Before there could be the slightest whiff of biological repercussions.

But Viv, now she was a different kettle of fish. Feisty, practical. Yes, he could see her taking to the whole business of motherhood with her usual over-the-top enthusiasm. Under normal circumstances. But would she under these? Who knew?

His attention was momentarily diverted by Kevin's changed expression.

It was painful. Even now Kevin smarted under the memory of Viv's open scorn of his wife. And it hurt too, acknowledging his own childlessness so openly. He'd always liked children, but Tina's resolute rejection of motherhood was unwavering. It had been a hard pill to swallow but he'd kept his sorrow to himself. Not even Tina knew how he felt. His wishes hadn't been relevant to her. There would be no children – full stop. But no-one else had the right to interfere, and he'd resented his sister's forthright ridicule.

'It's nobody's business but ours,' he'd told her sharply, 'so butt out and keep your ideas to yourself.'

'Keep your shirt on, brother dear,' she'd retorted. 'Tina'd make a lousy mother anyway.'

In spite of the family's dislike of his wife, Kevin told himself theirs was a good enough relationship, better than many he knew. Nobody but themselves to consider. Nothing to stop them enjoying a luxurious lifestyle. And as long as he pandered to her whims, she rewarded him by being a definite asset in his rising through the ranks. And she could be loving when she chose to be. On her terms …

His father's voice broke into his thoughts.

'So I need you both to think about this and tell me what you think she'd say if she could.'

'I think she'd say abort it,' Kevin said. Was he really meaning Viv?

'Oh, I don't mean this instant. You've only just found out about … you know … what's happened. Sleep on it at least. We can't decide something as big as this without proper thought. Go away and think about it. And we'll talk again.'

SEVEN

As he drove home Kevin was surprised by the depth of feeling stirred in him by the news of Viv's rape and pregnancy. For years she'd been quite peripheral to his busy life; now suddenly she had shattered his peace of mind rudely, demanding that he too engage with her interests. She would not be ignored. Her interests became the family's interests, her problems their problems.

If Tina noticed his preoccupation that night she didn't remark on it. And she made no attempt to find out why he'd suddenly gone to see his father. The less she heard about his family the better it pleased her. Besides she was totally absorbed in applying an avocado face pack and vitamin-enriched nail strengthener. Irritation with her local health store for failing to stock a special brand of apricot and pecan concentrate was dominant in her emotions. Kevin listened superficially to her annoyance for fully eight minutes but once her eyes were closed beneath the weight of a cucumber cleanser, he slid out of the room, and sought the sanctuary of his study where he sat motionless in the gathering gloom.

He left for work early next morning long before she surfaced. He'd packed his overnight bag for London himself the evening before and slept in the spare room so as not to disturb her with his early rise. Nothing unusual in that. She was used to and expected such consideration. But for Kevin it had not been a restful night. He was still so disturbed by the situation that after an unproductive morning where columns of figures blurred into dancing children's feet, and visions of Viv seemed to swirl across his computer screen and deliberately muddle the totals on his balance sheets, he left the office for an extended lunch break and drove to The Home to visit his sister. He told no-one where he was going. If Tina rang, his personal assistant, Carol, could say with perfect truth that she didn't know where he was. He grimaced in sympathy, picturing the shrill diatribe Tina would unleash if Carol dared such a thing.

The girl at the reception desk in The Home was apologetic about asking Kevin to sign a book to say who he was visiting and how long he stayed.

'New rules,' she'd explained vaguely. But when she saw his name and whom he'd come to see, she'd lowered her voice and added, 'Oh. You'll understand then.'

Viv was alone in her room. That was a relief. She'd been packed around with pillows in a big chair and looked for all the world like a young woman in a reverie. He marvelled again at her clear complexion and glossy dark hair. They certainly took good care of her in here. He didn't touch her. He never did. He wasn't the tactile kind and he recoiled from the flaccid unresponsiveness of her body. The only time he'd tried to hug her – early on – he'd felt as if she was rejecting his gesture. It reminded him of … It didn't matter. It wasn't relevant. Viv didn't know he was even there. She certainly wouldn't know how much he was revolted by the outward manifestations of her condition. Sometimes it made him feel physically sick. But he needed to force himself to take it all in today. He had to think – really think – what was best.

He leaned forward in his chair staring at her motionless face. He always found it unnerving, that nothingness. What had she experienced when that animal had raped her? Had she just stared ahead like she did now? Unaware, unmoved by what he was doing? How could the beast have continued in the face of that total lack of reaction?

His eyes involuntarily travelled down the length of her body. It was incomprehensible. Why would anyone choose to do it to a girl who was as good as dead? The old Viv, yes, he could understand that. She'd had spunk; her very fieriness was attractive. If she'd fought and protested even – he could see that could have been exciting. But this total immobility? Incomprehensible. OK, she wasn't bad looking. But it was only a shell. She'd always been nicely rounded – still was – so she'd probably feel good. In fact, if she hadn't been his sister he might have fancied her himself. He liked the ones with meat on their bones. He'd told Tina that once early in their marriage when she'd been wailing about an extra quarter of a centimetre somewhere. It had been a mistake; she was a disciple of – who was it? Wallis Simpson? Nancy Reagan? – well, whoever it was who said a woman can never be too thin or too rich. Yes, he could see a guy finding Viv's body desirable back then … but now? All floppy, like a rag doll, no resistance, no response? No. It made him feel sick just thinking of it. The man must be a total inadequate or mentally unhinged.

But whatever … he'd done it. Who knew how often? And now she was carrying his kid. Underneath that patchwork cover, that loose dark crimson dress, was a ferment of life. Her abdomen was slowly swelling. A child was growing inside that insentient body. She might not know anything about it but her body was nourishing it. Didn't bear thinking of – things just going on as normal in spite of this appalling thing that had happened to her. Things functioning so normally that she *could* conceive, could grow a child in that otherwise unoccupied shell.

'It's so unfair, Viv. You having a kid. And me not.' It came out as a groan.

It was grotesque imagining her sitting there nine months pregnant. It would be a travesty of decency to let it go on, then cut her open, take the baby out, sew her up again, go on as if nothing had happened. Take the kid away. Where? Who would care for it? Who would tell it about its 'nothing' mother, its perverted criminal father? Would it want to go on living, knowing its origins? Would it wish they had done the decent thing, scraped it out of her early on? Before there was any real evidence of its existence.

He shuddered. His eyes went to her face in a mute appeal.

'Surely you wouldn't want it, would you, Viv?' he whispered harshly. 'If you knew. If you could tell us. Can't you give us some sign? Something? Anything?'

Nothing.

He clenched his hands. It was so frustrating, this total lack of reaction. Surely somewhere in there she must know − something. It was like dealing with a stubborn child. She'd always been wilful. But this? This was worse − much, much worse. He wanted to shake her, get her to face up to what had happened, tell them what she wanted, not leave it up to them to discern her wishes. What wishes? She had none. She was nothing.

A woman wearing a badge he couldn't read tapped on the door and came in without waiting.

'Sorry, sir. May I ask? Who are you? Are you …?'

'Kevin Faraday. Her brother. Her older brother.'

'Oh. Sorry, sir. It's just that … Well, we have to be careful. I didn't know she had another brother.'

Why would she? He hadn't been for − what − eight/nine months? He felt annoyed with this stranger for making him feel guilty. Now. When he *had* come.

'Well, she has,' he snapped. 'Two brothers. I'm the older one − Kevin. Want to see my identity cards?' He dragged out his work disc, glaring at her.

'I'm sorry. Only doing my job.' She backed out of the room, leaving him feeling more guilty still.

'Now you see why I don't come!' he muttered in Viv's direction. The woman would be at the desk checking, phoning somebody. Was it true? Did the girl who was raped have another brother?

An appalling thought hit him. Did they suspect him? Or Euan? Or his father even? If the police started hunting, would they all be under suspicion? Her father especially. He was often on his own with her. There for hours on end. And he was obsessive about her. It didn't bear thinking about. Had it entered Bill's head? He hoped not. Much as he railed against Bill's total preoccupation with Viv, he didn't deserve that. The very suggestion would send him ballistic.

He dragged his mind back. Staring at his sister just seemed to add to the sense of unreality. It was just unbelievable that she should become a mother so totally unknowingly.

No. It just could not be.

He left the room precipitately with no farewell, no parting look. Only when he was a mile down the road did he remember he hadn't signed the book to say he was leaving. His foot jammed harder on the accelerator and he overtook an articulated lorry, an AA van and two fast saloons before he pulled back to a safe speed. There was no way he was turning back.

In the outer office, Carol opened her mouth to tell him about Tina's call, but seeing his thunderous face she closed it again, and slid down behind her computer. The office door slammed shut. She left the divert-call button down.

Kevin left for London earlier than expected. Tina had rung twice more before he left. Carol had tried to put her through but Kevin had simply not picked up the phone. He'd been dimly aware that his secretary must have left the phone lying on the edge of her desk, and was hammering the keyboard harder than usual to blot out the sound of Tina's shrieking voice. Poor kid. It was bad enough trying to pacify the people ringing on legitimate business, without getting embroiled in her boss' domestic squabbles. But he couldn't face Tina's calls himself. Not yet.

Felicity was halfway through a stack of ironing when Euan let himself into the house. It was a job she enjoyed – ironing the problems out of her life, she'd retorted when Euan had teased her about it. She was no career girl but she was quietly contented staying at home raising their three children and spinning clay pots on her electric wheel for pin money and fun.

One look at her husband's expression was enough. Without a word she went to put the kettle on.

Throwing his briefcase into the corner, Euan slumped into the nearest chair, not heeding the discarded anorak and the book lying on the seat, and dropped his head in his hands, his fingers clenching and unclenching in the tight fair curls, unconsciously mirroring his father's gestures. He drank the proffered tea in great gulps, and then sat cradling the warm mug in his two hands, staring unseeingly at the floor.

Felicity carried on ironing. The smooth pile grew.

His voice sounded stifled when he eventually spoke.

'You're not going to believe this.'

'Want to try me?'

He swallowed hard, opened his mouth to begin, closed it again.

'Is it your Dad?' she asked gently.

He shook his head. 'No. It's … Viv.'

'Has she gone?'

He shook his head again. They'd faced Viv's death so many times during those first weeks and months – before the diagnosis of persistent vegetative state. Every time the phone had rung. That would have been easier to say than this.

'She's been … raped.'

He watched Felicity draw back in slow motion, her flecked brown eyes widening as the news penetrated, the iron suspended above the dungarees on her ironing board like a giant crane about to drop its load. In slow motion she replaced the iron on its stand, tucking a stray strand of hair behind her ear with the other hand.

'Viv?'

'Yeah. Viv.'

'I don't understand … how could she …?'

She switched off the iron and leaned both elbows on the board as she stared at him. The strand of ash blonde hair flopped forward unheeded.

'They don't know. They only know she's …' – he closed his eyes – 'pregnant.'

Silence.

Felicity's hands flew to her mouth.

It was unbelievably painful recounting the story. But it helped. Talking about the options, discussing the implications, moved him towards his own conclusion.

It was she who suggested he go to see Viv.

'I just think you'd feel better if you tell her yourself how you feel. I know she can't hear you. She won't know. But you wouldn't feel so much like you were going behind her back.'

'Times like this I know why I married you!' he said.

'Gee, thanks!'

He grinned at her suddenly. She was no model but he'd rather have her matronly figure and warm scattiness than any number of icily perfect Tinas.

'Want me to come with you, or would you rather go on your own?' she offered.

'I think – if you don't mind – on my own. No reflection on you. I'd just feel self-conscious talking to her with anybody else there.'

'Yep. 'Course you would. That's OK.'

She rose to her feet and adopted a swaggering gait, a cowgirl drawl. 'Ah'll git awn wid yo'r bloomin' ol' shuurts, pardner.'

With a swing of her ample hips she was back at the ironing board.

He wrote his name with a flourish in the book at the reception desk. It was only four weeks since he'd seen Viv but he noticed the clerkess' quick scrutiny, her smile of recognition. So they'd learned something from this ghastly business.

Viv was lying in bed, propped up with the usual armchair shape of pillows.

Before he could lose his nerve he began to speak in a voice echoing Felicity's wild west drawl.

'Now see here, sis, you an' me 'uve gotta mide o' talkin' ta do.'

He swung the chair around to bestride it like a horse, both arms across the back of it. Her eyes were fixed on the door.

'Now, this lades' development o' yours. Could ya tell me, how yu feeull about it?'

Her eyes remained unblinking, unseeing, unknowing.

'Now see here, Viv, this won't do. Aah need t' know whad ya' feeull inside thad there head o' yours.'

The total lack of response was every bit as unnerving as he'd feared. He gritted his teeth. The mockery of his false accent had paved the way.

'OK Viv. Just listen up. I've got to tell you – because you can't tell me how it feels. If you're in there somewhere quit the act and for goodness sake let me know if I've got it all wrong. OK?' He glared at her. Nothing.

'This kid you're carrying – you didn't ask for it. Hell, you didn't do anything to get yourself into this mess at all. Nobody's blaming you. And I guess it'd solve a lot of problems if they just took it away and everybody forgot about it. But I keep remembering that poster you had. Remember? That one of the unborn baby – sucking its thumb. I looked up what eighteen weeks looks like – Felicity's got this book, you know. Shows you how they grow. Eighteen weeks – it looks like a baby, Viv. It's even got little fingernails! And it's moving around in there already. You'd be able to feel it moving – if you could feel things. It's real.' He stopped, swallowing hard.

'I remember when Felicity got to that stage with Nathan. She used to just stop still and hold her breath, waiting for it to move again.' He remembered so vividly the expression of wonder on his wife's face.

'You're missing out on all that, I know. And perhaps you wouldn't have let it get to this stage if – if things had been different. But now. Now it has, Viv, would you want them to snuff out that little life? Now? When it can kick and hold its hands and it's got these tiny little fingernails and little closed eyes and this big head and everything growing and developing? Would you? I don't think you would. I think you'd say, "Poor little blighter. What did he do wrong? Give him a break." Would you, Viv? Does that sound like you?'

He watched her face for a long moment.

'I can't tell you what I feel inside about the animal who did this to you, Viv. If I could get my hands on him – by gum, I'd make sure he never fathered another kid as long as he lived – with my bare hands! Nothing's too bad for him. But the kid. The kid's innocent. Wouldn't you say that?'

He rested his chin on his arms, staring at those unseeing eyes. It was a full five minutes before he spoke again.

'I just wanted you to know. That's how I see it. Felicity thought I ought to tell you. Don't want to go behind your back. Better you hear it from me. Before I tell Dad what I think.'

Felicity was right. It did feel better telling Viv.

'Oh yeah, and Felicity said I was to tell you, we'll help bring the little beggar up. I'll be able to tell him what a devil you were. Tell him he's had a lucky escape not being on the receiving end of your tongue! Yep, plenty of stories I can tell him about you, miss! And don't lie there thinking I won't just because …' His voice petered out. The cruelty of it all hit him foursquare.

Her staring eyes, her expressionless face, swam suddenly in his tears. He dashed them aside angrily and stood up abruptly. She seemed so small and somehow detached in the silence of the room, so vulnerable. He'd found it surprisingly painful when Bill had first brought in her own bedroom curtains, her patchwork quilt – to jog that latent memory. It was his father's attempt to imprint Viv's taste on an impersonal institutional shell, but to Euan it served only to underline her complete inability to put her stamp on anything – ever again. Not on the décor. Not on what she wore, what she ate, where she went. And it was still the same. Now she couldn't even tell them what she wanted for her own child. She was as much at the mercy of the family's decisions as she had been at the hands of the man who had raped her.

EIGHT

Bill read to Viv every day. He was now halfway through Umberto Eco's *The Name of the Rose*, and had promised the next instalment when he'd left her the previous evening. The routines were important to him. As always he began with a brief recap of the story so far.

'Remember, Viv, yesterday we were reading about finding the manuscript telling about the destruction of Margaret and Dolcino? How the men tore off the heretics' flesh with red hot pincers. How they made Dolcino watch while Margaret burned at the stake. Then they amputated his nose. Then his male member. Before they burned him too.'

Yesterday his voice had shaken reading that. He'd broken off, wanting to tell her that's what he'd felt like doing to the guy who'd violated her. His fingers had dented the pages of the book, so fierce was his grip. His composure had only returned when he got to the sentence passed on Brother Michael. It was all in Latin – never his best subject. He'd mocked himself stumbling over the words and in the humour found again the strength to read on.

The story was new to him, so he was unprepared for today's account of Adso's seduction. Mercifully the language was so archaic and biblical that he could get through it without drawing attention to his own discomposure. Would everything now bring thoughts of Viv's abuser crowding in on him? He knew it was crazy, persisting with the book. He could easily switch to something light and funny. She wouldn't know. But something made him persevere doggedly with every story he started, no matter how tedious, how unsuitable it turned out to be. Each one became a personal challenge. The harder the task the greater the satisfaction when it was done.

The quota of reading done he began brushing her hair. The static electricity made it crackle and stand around her head like a dark halo. He smoothed it gently with his hand.

'I see the boys came to see you, love,' he said. 'Did they tell you we all have to sign a book now? They're terribly upset by what's happened. I know they are. They're thinking about what's best too. Did they talk to you about their opinions? I know you'd listen to them – more patiently than I do, I suspect. I get so mad about it all. I'm mad inside because they don't come to see you more. I know, I know. You'd tell them not to bother, I know you would. "What good does it do?" you'd say. And I know they have their reasons. But it makes me short with them. I know it does. I'm glad they came now though. But even so a great big bit of me thinks they have no right to say what should happen now. They haven't stayed the course. But Dr Wilkinson insists. He thinks the whole family should discuss it. So I'm trying. Send me some of your patience, will you? I'll need it. Heaven knows what we'll do if we can't agree. But we'll find a way through this. Don't you worry about a thing. We love you. It'll be OK, Viv. We'll work something out. Don't you worry. You just concentrate on getting better. OK?'

But 'working something out' was proving even more difficult than Bill had anticipated. Fear compelled him to spend even longer at The Home but he found it increasingly painful to sit with Viv. There the unanswered questions seemed to shriek at him. He paced the gardens; he drew sketches of extensions to improve the architecture of the building; he sought distraction in extra trips to Cath's Canteen. The nursing staff grew uneasy in his presence.

When Libby Sinclair found herself in the room without a colleague she was hesitant about asking Bill to help re-position Viv. But action, especially routine tasks, held no threat and Bill agreed with his usual readiness.

'She's got beautiful skin,' Libby said, working cream into Viv's elbow. 'Not a mark. Did she always take care of it?'

'She did, but it was always good. Even as a teenager.'

'Lucky her. My daughter's going through the spotty stage. So self-conscious. And at that age they can't think beyond the teens. Anything over twenty's ancient!'

'I know.'

'And the hormones and everything right now are making Viv even more lovely.' It was the first time any of the staff had alluded to the pregnancy in his presence. Instinctively Bill tensed.

'Is that usual?'

'Oh yes. They say girls have a kind of bloom when they're pregnant. In fact some people reckon they can tell just by looking at a woman long before they're actually told that she is.'

'But no-one noticed when Viv …' Bill broke off abruptly.

'I guess none of us was even thinking along those lines.'

'No, indeed.' Bill heard the unintentional grimness in his voice. 'I'm sorry. I didn't mean to sound so critical. Not to you. You've been very kind.'

It was true. Only a limited number of nurses were allocated to Viv these days – a sort of damage-limitation exercise, Bill presumed. Libby was older than most of the attendants, full-time and often assigned to Viv when she was on duty. Bill respected her assured but gentle touch, and liked her quietly efficient manner.

'We're all desperately sorry about what's happened. But it's understandable if you're angry with us,' Libby said, not looking at him, still concentrating on Viv's pressure areas.

'I just wish we knew – I mean – if it was a member of staff, how can we know if …'

'Dr Wilkinson's not letting any of the male staff look after the female patients at the moment. And everybody's chaperoned. That's routine.'

'But still.'

'I know. You can't have confidence in us. Not after what's happened.' Libby's comments came out in short bursts as she massaged expertly. 'We sympathise. Really, we do. We're all devastated by this. It's hollow comfort, I know. Lots of us have youngsters of our own. It must be appalling – but we do feel for you. After the raw deal you've had already.'

'Thank you. It's kind of you to say so.'

'Oh, it's not kind. I mean it. We all feel terrible about this. But it's tough on the male nurses. It's getting to them most – this cloud hanging over them. They're all under suspicion until …'

Bill nodded slowly.

'I'm sorry. But I can't trust anybody. Not yet.'

'Everybody understands that. I wasn't trying to make you feel guilty. But they're a great bunch of lads. Hearts of gold. It's tough.'

'Must be. Poor return for all they do. I know.'

'But hey, don't you be wasting sleep over them. You've got enough worries of your own.' Libby flipped Viv over expertly, the words coming out in a grunt with the exertion.

'And I do know – it might be anybody. I'm feeling just the same about the visitors and the other relatives and any man who comes near the place. Getting pretty paranoid in fact about anything with a Y chromosome!' Bill tried to make it self-mocking. But it was true.

'I'm sure you don't want to broadcast what's happened – for Viv's sake – but what about *you*? Have you got people to talk to?'

'Just the family.'

'I was thinking of somebody who isn't caught up in the emotions around Viv. One step removed, as it were.'

'No.'

'Would it help? Just bouncing ideas off somebody unrelated sometimes helps.'

'I guess if I'm honest I'm just too angry to talk to the staff.'

'Oh, I can understand that. But a friend? Your minister perhaps, or somebody like that?'

'No. I'm not one to talk – not about things like this.'

'I know. But this is different. It's a huge thing to deal with on your own.'

Bill shrugged.

'Have you ever had anything like this happen in your experience before?' he asked hesitantly, smoothing the covers on his side of the bed.

'Never. And I can tell you I'm shocked to my socks. I can't imagine how hard it must be for you.'

'It's the pits.'

'And it's not just getting to grips with what's happened – you've got to decide what to do now.'

'Mmmhhm.'

'Well, don't hesitate. If you think any of us can help. Anybody would. We're all hating being so powerless to help.'

'Thanks. I'm OK.'

It was with this offer ringing in his ears that Bill stifled a rebuff when a young man approached him in the canteen. He was tall and rather lanky, with soft fair hair flopping over his forehead and an air of diffidence which Bill would normally have despised in a man.

'Excuse me, Mr Faraday. I'm one of the care assistants. Toby Bernard. I just wanted to say how sorry we all are about what's happened to your daughter.'

'Thank you.'

'I only met her on a couple of occasions – on full rounds. And I was only once allocated to her care. Mostly I work on one of the other corridors. But we all know about the young ones especially.'

'Do you?' So Viv's name was bandied around, was it, Bill thought grimly.

'It's doubly sad, when they're young. Ending up in a place like this.'

'That's an understatement.'

'I'm sorry. I didn't mean to offend. I didn't mean to imply … I mean, this is the best Home I've ever worked in. We're all proud to work here. It's got a brilliant reputation. She's in the best place – as these places go.'

Bill felt all his hackles rising.

'I used to think so.'

'Something like this affects us all. It reflects badly on everybody. I just hope you can believe that we're all really sorry about it.'

'I'm sure you are, but sorry won't put it right, Mr Bernard.'

'I know. But I thought … well, perhaps it needed to be said.'

'Perhaps.'

It was a relief when the man moved away in response to a call from a colleague, but Bill knew he hadn't been fair. It must have taken courage for the care assistant to approach a stranger in these circumstances, and to attempt to apologise on behalf of everyone. Yes, maybe he deserved an apology too.

NINE

Bill brought in a pot of coffee and a plate of biscuits. It was intended to help them relax; instead it felt all wrong. The sound of shortbread crunching was inhibiting. He was impatient to start the discussion, move towards a solution to these endless questions.

His irritation was palpable – he saw it in their shifty glances, their untouched coffee, Kevin's hand straying to his moustache.

'OK. Let's see where we've got. What d'you think, Kevin?'

'Same as yesterday. I think she'd go for an abortion.'

'Why?' It sounded curt, unfriendly, even to Bill.

'Because she'd hate the thought of some guy forcing her into this. If she had kids she'd want it to be in her time, her choosing. And this isn't the right time. She's got enough else to contend with without that.'

Bill saw the raw emotion surge through his son, the sudden moisture in his eyes. He heard the tremble as Kevin forced himself to go on.

'Besides she'll never know the kid or be able to take care of it. So no sense in her going through the pregnancy and birth. I think she'd say quit now. She wouldn't want a kid to start off in life ... like this. Not if it could be prevented.'

Bill gave no reaction.

'And you, Euan?'

'I know what Kev means, but *I* think her first thought would be for the kid itself. OK, it *is* a bad start but I think she'd want to compensate – make it up to the baby as much as she could. I think she'd say keep it. Like Holly's puppy.'

How she'd fought for that puppy! Seven years of age, crouching down beside their dog, begging them, with tears rolling down her cheeks, to save the runt of the litter. She'd nursed that scrawny creature for hours together, feeding him milk, drop by agonisingly slow drop from a pipette.

'And you, Dad, what do you think she'd want?'

Both pairs of eyes were on him. Bill dragged his mind back to the present.

'I don't know. I just don't know. You're both right to some extent. She was so easily swayed by the emotions of the moment. She could go either way.'

'How do we decide then?'

'Try to think logically? I mean, we know some facts. She didn't have a *religious* objection to abortion at least, so it's not ruled out.'

'Like Mum you mean?' Kevin said.

Bill clenched his teeth. It was a long time since either of the boys had spontaneously mentioned her. It was still raw.

'Yes.'

'Have you told Mum?'

'No.'

'Shouldn't you?'

'She gave up her right to have a voice.' Bill was pleased at the level tone.

'She's still her mother.'

'Biologically speaking only.' He knew it sounded harsh.

'But … we know what she'd say, anyway.' Kevin tried for a conciliatory tone.

'She'd agree with me,' Euan said with a nod of reinforcement. 'No abortion. That makes two to one.'

'No!' Bill said sharply, slapping his hand on the arm of his chair. 'This is *not* about scoring points! Anyway, that wouldn't be a point. Not for Viv. Your mother wouldn't be thinking of what *Viv* would want, but of what she *personally* believes.'

'But Viv probably talked to her − *before* − you know. Probably more than she talked to you, Dad. About those sorts of things anyway. You know. Woman to woman stuff.'

Bill knew it was true but his heart screamed, *No*. No-one was closer to Viv than he was.

'Actually' − Euan was speaking slowly now, tasting new thoughts − 'if we aren't sure what Viv herself would say, doesn't what we all think count … more … sort of … anyway?'

'No. Why should it? It's Viv's life. We have to concentrate on what's best for her.' Bill had anticipated this.

'But nothing's best for her − either way. Is it? I mean, it won't affect her − either way, will it?'

'Of course it will − eventually.' Bill's statement was deliberate, forcing closure.

It was a shock when Euan picked up the forbidden gauntlet, holding his gaze, his voice firm in its challenge.

'No, Dad. We all know − you too, deep down − you know it won't. Either way Viv's the one person it *won't* affect.'

'I know no such thing!' Bill snapped, too quickly, too defensively. 'No-one can say that. I know she *will* come out of this. And then what? What would she say about a child? Or about anyone taking away a potential child? While she was out of it.'

'Don't know. But even if she *did* ever come out of this she'd never be fit enough to bring up a kid, would she?' Euan persisted.

'We don't know. She might. And when she does come back, she'll certainly know about the child and, if it lives, relate to it at *some* level at least.'

It always hurt unbearably hearing the boys had given up hope. He knew

46

they had. Long ago. But he still hated to hear them say so. Now the hurt stirred into anger against them. When she most needed them, would they let her down again?

'But then isn't the decision more up to the people who'd take the biggest strain?' Euan asked. It fanned the flames.

Bill struggled to quell the emotional response gripping him. Temper wouldn't strengthen his own case.

'It's not actually, no! It's *her* child. Not the family's. At the end of the day it's not for us to decide.'

'Then why are we …?' Kevin began, spreading his hands in perplexity.

'Because the doctors want to know from us what *she* would have wanted. We're the ones who knew her – before. If anyone knows what she would choose it's us. They suggested we should all talk about it – together. Try to reach a consensus view if possible.'

'And we haven't. So surely the next step is what *we* think is best.' Euan made it sound so clear-cut.

'Your personal opinions – any of ours – aren't relevant.'

'That's ridiculous!' Kevin said. 'It'll affect the family far more than Viv if she has a kid.'

That was it. A step too far. Bill felt his voice – ominously quiet – quivering with the emotions raging across his caution.

'Will it? Just who do you suppose it will affect?'

Both sons were silent for a long moment, eyes dropping before his glare.

'Kevin? Euan? Lost your tongues suddenly, huh?' The volume grew.

Aha. As he thought! As he knew!

'You going to bring the kid up, Kevin? You and Tina? Eh?' Bill was in full flight now, making no effort to moderate his tones. 'You going to get up in the night to feed it and change it and rock it when it's teething? Have your routines turned upside down? Your precious shiny surfaces all finger-printy? That'd put paid to those two foreign holidays a year, wouldn't it? Eh? Viv's kid. That's why you say abort it. Isn't it?'

'No, I didn't say that. I only said that's what I think Viv would say.'

'It's true though – you wouldn't be seen for dust.'

Kevin flushed but compressed his lips.

'Euan? Fancy bringing up this one? Or will you run as hard in the other direction as you did when Viv went into The Home? Eh? First your own sister. Now your sister's kid.'

'I don't know, Dad.' Typical Euan, striving for a quiet tone, trying to deflect argument, keep the peace. 'It's not just up to me. If she does have this baby, we'd all have to discuss it. Where it would go? Who'd bring it up? Felicity and I talked about it and we agreed we'd take our share. But that's further down the track. The important thing now is … Well, it seems to me it *does* matter how *we* all feel. It *is* part of the equation. It's relevant. I don't think we *can* rule out the effect on the family. You can't just say Viv's the only one who counts here – what she would want.'

Again Bill squirmed in the face of the calm maturity that dared to question his paternal authority. He must regain his position.

'So then, if that's the important criterion, *I* should decide. It'd be *me* who'd be most affected. You know it would – if you're honest. Neither of you would do it. Face the facts. But *I* would – for her. If I thought it was what she'd want for herself –and the baby – I'd do it.'

'Dad. You have to be realistic. You're – what? – sixty-eight now. You can't start again with all that baby stuff. You'd be in your eighties when it was a teenager. You can't! You just *can't!*' Kevin protested.

'I *can't*. You *won't*. Answer: abort it. Is that it?' Bill flashed back. 'Get rid of it. Eliminate it from our lives – just like you eliminated Viv.'

'We didn't,' Euan interposed, his voice firm, matter-of-fact. 'We haven't. We just don't let her dominate our lives and ruin things for the people who *do* know what's what.'

'So I ruin things for you, do I? Because I still love her and care for her.'

'No. You don't *ruin* things. We've got our own lives now. But you've certainly changed them. We all hate to see you eaten up by this, Dad. It's ruined *your* life. And *our* family life with you is pretty much non-existent. I mean, it's heroic on one level, but the doctors all say she won't come out of this. And she could outlive you.'

'Ahh! So you're afraid you'd be left with it when I'm gone. That it?' Bill spat out.

'No, that's not what I meant. If she lives longer than you, you'll have sacrificed everything else on an outside chance.'

'Maybe I have. Maybe I chose to. You can all fend for yourselves. You don't need me. She does. She has no-one else.'

'Oh come on! She has an army of people caring for her,' Kevin said.

'Caring so well they let her get raped, you mean!' Bill flashed back.

'But that wasn't their fault. *You* care. And you couldn't stop that either.'

'*Don't ... you ... dare!* Don't you dare suggest I failed her!' Bill's eyes blazed.

'I'm not, Dad.' Kevin dismissed the idea with a flip of his hand. 'You know I'm not. Of course you haven't failed her. You can't be with her twenty-four hours a day, seven days a week. Maybe we've failed her. I don't know. I don't know what to think. But all I do know is that Felicity and the kids need Euan. Tina needs me. *They'll* know if we desert them to sit with Viv for hours on end. Viv won't. We have to balance things. Maybe I've got it wrong. But seems to me, Viv – the Viv we all knew and loved – she's gone. We have to live our lives, do the best we can for the whole family. And I believe that's what Viv would want us to do.'

'It's right, Dad,' Euan agreed. 'Viv was many things but she wasn't self-ish. She wouldn't want us to ruin our whole lives – for nothing. The way she is now, she doesn't really benefit from our being with her. It might make *us* feel better. We might feel we're doing our duty. But it doesn't really affect *her* one way or the other.'

'I don't do it out of a sense of duty. I do it because I love her.'

'I know you do,' Euan replied gently. 'And you've always loved her more than us. She was always your favourite.' Bill opened his mouth to protest but Euan waved the attempt away. 'It's OK. I understand. Dads are like that with their daughters. It happens in loads of families.' It was true. Euan did understand. Eloise was special to him – not to the exclusion of the boys, of course, but special, being their only girl. 'But I don't believe she'd want you to give up everything. Not when it's hopeless.'

'But we can't know that – not for sure. It might *not* be hopeless. Maybe she's locked in there somewhere. Just waiting for the right trigger to release her again. If there's any chance, any chance at all, and they can't absolutely rule it out, I want to make sure she gets that chance.'

'You have to do what seems right for you. Of course. I'm not trying to stop you – not any more. I know your mind's made up. But it really isn't fair blaming us for seeing things a different way. The doctors agree with us – it makes no difference to her if we're there or not. If it did we'd go like a shot. She's our sister, too. Not just your daughter,' Euan said.

'And I must say – knowing this – about the rape, I mean, it's made me realise just how much I *do* still love Viv.' Kevin's voice was suddenly softened.

'OK. Whatever,' Bill said less harshly. 'But what about now? You think she'd choose abortion. Euan thinks she'd carry on. I just don't know. It's stalemate.'

Euan looked thoughtfully at his father as he spoke. He stretched out his legs and propped one heel on the other toe of his shoe. Bill noticed incongruously how scuffed they were. Looked as if they never saw the inside of a tin of polish. Frances' voice was suddenly vivid: the state of their shoes tells you a lot about a person. What? What did it say?

'We've never even acknowledged *to each other* just how we feel about this whole business with Viv,' Euan was saying slowly. 'We're always skirting round things, trying not to upset each other. But now there's a baby on the way – or there may be – that changes everything. Now we're talking about things that go on and on and on. Way beyond Viv's lifetime. Our lifetime. We can't just single out Viv and say it's only her interests that count. Yes, she's very much part of our family. We love her and we're all affected by what's happened to her. But she's only *part* of that family – not the only bit of it that counts.'

'That's exactly right.' Kevin nodded. His shoes were burnished black. 'And it could be that what's best for the family as a whole isn't ideal for Viv herself. It could be. And it seems to me that because she's unaware of anything that happens …' Bill saw Kevin faltering in the face of his glacial glare. 'Well, I think it's right that we put the interests of the family ahead of hers – if there's a conflict of interests.'

'You've already put your own and Tina's interests first,' Bill said, packing his words in ice.

'But Dad, it's what Viv would have wanted us to do – in the circumstances,' Euan protested. 'She'd have wanted us to get on with our lives, be happy, not totally wrapped up in her to the exclusion of everything we need or want for ourselves.'

'And it's precisely because she was that kind of person that we should put her first now,' Bill persisted.

Silence fell. They were not going to persuade him. He refused to be moved. It was Euan who eventually broke through the impasse.

'Should we talk to the doctors – take advice? See if they can help us all come to an agreement?'

Bill's head reeled from the endless vortex of questions. He needed to get away from these rational arguments. He needed space to work logically through his own thoughts. Dismissing offers of help he carried the cups into the kitchen and sank down on a stool, staring blindly out into the mist swirling in from the east.

Kevin, left alone with his brother, felt suddenly bone weary. Standing with his back to the fireplace with its portrait of Viv on her twenty-first birthday, he eyed Euan rather sheepishly. This new honesty was unnerving. The spoken words hung uneasily between them.

'At first, you know, I thought of him as a sort of selfless hero. But now ... well, I can't. Not any more. It doesn't make sense,' he began, tentatively.

'But he's sacrificed his life for her.' Slumped on the settee, Euan picked up a cushion and hugged it to his chest.

'I know. But, you know, I've thought about it a lot and I've come to see it as something else. I think this "beyond the call of duty" stuff is a cover.'

Euan threw a sharp look at his brother.

'For what?'

'For guilt.'

'Guilt? Why would *he* feel guilty? Of all of us he's got the least to feel guilty about, I'd have thought.'

'Well, I think maybe he feels he failed her in some way, didn't do everything he should have. I don't know. But this over-the-top doing things now – seems to me, he's trying to compensate for something. Some failing or something.'

'Don't see what.'

'Well, you're a parent. Don't you sometimes feel a ... responsibility? Feel like you're not as good as you should be at it?'

'Often!' Euan gave him a sheepish grin.

'Well, imagine something like this happens to one of your kids. Wouldn't you maybe feel you hadn't protected them or something – you know, if only ...?'

'But Dad couldn't have stopped Viv from going in that car. I mean, she was away from home, independent.'

'I know. But even so …' Kevin shrugged. 'Or maybe he feels responsible for Mum leaving.'

He plunged his hands into his trouser pockets and absent-mindedly jingled the loose change. There was no Tina to tell him sharply to desist.

'*Was* that his fault? I've never understood why she went,' Euan said slowly.

'No idea. He'd never talk about it. But could be. I don't know.'

'Know what I think?' Euan changed tack, twisting the cushion through ninety degrees. 'I sometimes wonder if he hasn't got a sort of sense of survivor guilt. You know, feels unworthy to have survived all these years when Viv's only had twenty-two years of life. It happens.'

'Could be.'

Silence fell.

'Easy to stick labels on folk though, eh?' Euan observed. 'I mean, if it had been *Mum* doing what Dad's doing, we'd probably be saying it was a sense of inferiority. A lack of self-worth: I'm not important, I'm here only to serve, sort of thing.'

'True.' There was another long pause. Kevin moved to perch on the arm of the nearest chair. 'D'you think the doctors maybe put too much pressure on him – you know, early on – when we all had to keep talking to her to try to get her out of the coma?' he mused. 'I mean, you can see that, at first, when there was a chance she'd come out of it, her medical needs were more important than our personal ones. And I know Dad sat up all night – often. And Mum did, too.'

'But that was different.'

'That's what I mean. It *was* right then – when there was a chance it'd make a difference. But maybe nobody's given him permission to stop making that kind of effort now. Maybe he needs somebody – somebody official I mean – to tell him outright not to sacrifice his life for nothing; she's not coming back. I guess they've tried to spare his feelings and just sort of skirted round it. Don't want to take away the hope he's hanging on to.'

Euan shrugged.

There were no easy answers but they had together acknowledged the problem for the first time in nine years.

The questions swung backwards and forwards relentlessly in Bill's mind. Maybe he did need someone outside to talk to, as Libby had suggested.

Catching sight of Toby Bernard leaving the canteen, as he entered it, he remembered his own harsh response to the young man's overtures.

'I'm sorry I was rather rude – last time we met.' Bill didn't look directly at Toby.

51

'It's OK. I understand.'

'No excuse.'

'How're you coping?'

Inexplicably Bill was suddenly aware that the younger man had been eating raw onions. He instinctively stepped back a pace.

'Well – so so.'

'Must be grim. Shouldn't want to make that decision myself.'

'Nobody would.'

'Mr Faraday – I know it's none of my business, and I'm not even a qualified nurse, but d'you want to talk about it? I mean, say if you want me to butt out but ...'

Bill drew back again, brushing against a girl behind him collecting used cups and dishes. He sidestepped with a curt apology.

'Thanks. I know you mean well. But I'll work it out,' he said without looking at Bernard.

'Fair enough.'

'Nothing personal.'

'I know. See you around.'

Bill sat for a long time staring into his coffee cup, oblivious to the activity all around him. A lifetime of keeping his own counsel was hard to overturn, but this silent internal struggle was threatening his physical as well as his mental health. These new pains in his chest, the loss of appetite, the insomnia, they were all taking their toll – on top of the constant ache and stiffness caused by his arthritis. He'd better watch out or he'd be no use to Viv whatever happened.

'That was kind. Being nice to Toby.' Libby's voice at his elbow jerked him out of his absorption. She was carrying a tray and had stopped momentarily at his table.

Was nothing private in this place, Bill wondered. Did she also know how beastly he'd been to the man previously?

'It was nothing. He deserved it.'

'Well, it was appreciated, you saying something to buck him up. I probably shouldn't say this, but Toby's got ... well, personal problems.' Bill heard it with a pang of guilt. His own problems had blinded him to the realities of life all around him. 'He's an excellent carer. But we don't always get what we deserve.'

'No, indeed.' Viv hadn't.

Should he ask this kind woman to sit at his table, pour out his conflicts to her? She was the sort of person who invited you to share your problems – warm, motherly, sympathetic. Kind eyes. Maybe .....

She moved on with a smile and a waft of lamb stew.

TEN

The sight of the black figure bent in a posture of prayer beside Viv took Bill by surprise. He hesitated. Was this a friend of Viv's he hadn't met before? There weren't many of those left after nine years.

Or perhaps this was part of the service The Home offered. Maybe the different religious groups took it in turns to spend time with all these patients. He'd met the Protestant chaplain a couple of times. Seemed a decent fellow, sensitive. Said sensible things, none of the grating platitudes. Didn't do Viv any harm, he supposed. How Bill had wished he'd personally had an anchor in the darkest moments since the accident. Viv had shared his religious uncertainty. He smiled ruefully, remembering her more forthright and colourful comments on the subject. Some of it was just for effect, he knew. But at least she didn't know if folk were praying over her now. Like this person was. A mercy that! She couldn't sully those pure ears with her denunciations.

Should he wait? It seemed somehow tactless to intrude on such moments. It felt like hallowed ground, like going into a church to look around as a sightseer when the locals were using it for genuine worship.

He paced the corridor, occasionally glancing in at the bowed, still figure. Neither she nor Viv seemed to move by so much as a hairbreadth. He grew impatient. It was a good fifteen minutes before the woman raised her head. From where he stood, Bill couldn't see her face but her back was straight now, and she'd pulled a seat close up to the bedside. She seemed to be looking at Viv, saying something to her. Viv as ever stared steadily at the window, her flaccid fingers held in the nun's two-handed clasp.

The figure turned slowly as Bill entered the room. His deferential words of greeting died unsaid.

'You!'

'I came as soon as I heard.'

'Who told you?' The words sounded more accusatory than he intended.

'Kevin.'

'Huhh!' Too used to taking control in the boardroom, that boy!

'He was right to tell me.'

'Huh!'

'Bill, let's not fight over this. Not here. Not now.' Her eyes implored him. Turning back to the inert figure on the bed she stroked the hand in hers. 'My poor baby.' Bill saw the crystal drops splash on the black serge. He held back the burning words.

'What are we going to do?' The words were scarcely above a whisper. *We*? Did she really think she could steamroller in now – after all these years – and take over where she'd left off on that bleak September Monday? She seemed to be speaking to Viv, but the inclusive pronoun still grated. She had surely forfeited her claims long ago.

'Why're you here?' Bill's voice held no emotion.

'I had to come. To see her. To feel with her.'

'And are you staying?'

'That depends.'

'On what?'

'If I can be of any help.'

'How can *you* … help?' Bill glared at her.

'I don't know. But this thing … it's just … so … so … I don't know. As if the other wasn't bad enough. My poor baby.' She turned back to Viv, her hand stroking back the dark hair around the vacant face. 'My poor darling. Life has been so unfair to you.'

Silence fell.

'Kevin tells me they've asked the family …'

'To tell them what *Viv* would have said,' he finished her sentence firmly.

'And?'

'Nothing's decided. We're still discussing it.' He didn't want to tell her they didn't know.

'She was always so opinionated.' The gentleness of her voice softened the words.

'Meaning?'

'She was so confident about what she thought – now – this minute.'

'But she changed.'

'Oh, all the time. Exactly.'

'I suppose *you're* against abortion anyway. Whatever.'

'I am. But she wasn't. I understand the dilemma for you.'

'Do you? Do you really?'

'I think I do. Really.'

For one crazy moment he felt an urge to pour it all out, to share his torment with the one other person who had known the real Viv all her life as he had.

'There isn't much time' was all he said.

'I know.'

She reached out again to lay a white hand momentarily against Viv's cheek. The girl didn't even blink.

'I'd give my life to have spared her this.'

'But you wouldn't give your life to loving her – as she is – now.' He couldn't resist it.

'You don't understand …'

'Too right I don't! She's your own flesh and blood, damn it! How *could* you walk out on her? When she needed you more than she ever had. When we all did.'

'I did it for her.'

'No. You did it for *you*. You ran away. You couldn't face what had happened. You ran away so you didn't have to.'

'Do you think I could *ever* forget – this? For a single day? For a single minute? No, Bill. I …' Her voice petered out. 'Look, could we go somewhere? I'd like to explain. But not here – not in front of Viv.'

'Huh! So you're not sure, then? Afraid she might hear? Might understand?'

'No. But if there's even the remotest chance she might somewhere know anything, raised voices aren't what I'd want her to hear.'

His conscience smote him. After all these years, he had so far forgotten himself as to raise his voice in front of Viv. The act seemed to say he too believed she was beyond human reach. But, after all these years, *she* had remembered, had believed.

'There's a seat – outside. We can still see her window,' he said stiffly.

In silence she followed him out into the garden. He was acutely aware of the soft swish of her long skirt behind him. She took a seat at one end of the bench he indicated, he at the other. He pointed at the fourth window from the end.

'That's hers.'

'It's a nice Home, Bill. They take care of her well.'

'I used to think that.'

'Kevin tells me you come every day. Never miss.'

'She deserves that. There's no-one else.'

'The boys – it's not that they don't care.'

'Huh.'

'And I know you hate me for leaving, but it was the only thing left for me to do for her.'

'You could have stayed and fought for her.'

'You didn't read my letters?'

He shook his head. He'd been so angry with her, so let down, he'd burned them unopened.

'I didn't want to hear pathetic excuses.'

'They weren't excuses, Bill. I tried to explain.'

'What was there to explain? You deserted her. All of us.'

'It was over for us – you and me, Bill. You know it was. The boys, they had their own families. They didn't need me – not like she did.'

'And Viv? What did she have?' He rounded on her, his voice and look fierce.

'You. Every little fibre of you. You had no room left for any of us.'

'I was all she had left. No-one else had room for her. I had to make up for you all deserting her,' he bit back defensively.

'Viv didn't know if I was there or not. But there was one thing left that I could do for her.' She seemed to be talking more to herself than to him.

'Which was?'

'I could do penance for her. Take the punishment. Instead of her.'

'I don't follow.'

'If I gave myself to God I thought perhaps he'd release her. Give her back her life in exchange for mine.'

Bill looked at her with a mixture of amazement and revulsion.

'You honestly thought … this was … a punishment … from God? Your God?'

'I thought so … then. Now … I'm not so sure. Sometimes I feel I'm not sure of anything any more. Reverend Mother, Bishop Flaherty, Sister Mercy – they'd all be horrified to hear me admit it. But …' She shrugged.

He felt her loneliness in that brief moment before her face went back to its impassive mask.

'Good Go – I mean, good grief, Frances, I never did like what your religion stood for, but *this* – it's worse even than I thought! How could you care two hoots about a God who'd … who'd … who'd ruin a girl's life just to show his displeasure at some childish antic or other? Even we *mortal* parents understand the nonsense that kids get up to. We don't hold it against them. We know it's just part of growing up. How could you believe anything so … so …' Words failed him.

'Capricious?'

'More than that. Unfair. Unkind. Monstrous! Downright cruel!'

'I don't know. Maybe he was punishing me – not her. I don't know. I don't even know now *what* I believe. Not any more. Back then, I was clutching at straws. I needed to make sense of what had happened to my baby. I'd have done anything – *anything* … if only Viv could be spared.'

'You gave up everything – on the off chance?'

Again she shrugged dismissively.

'But *my* peace of mind – that's not important. I'm only telling you what my letters explained. But now – what about Viv?'

'I don't know. There's no easy answer. I wish with all my heart there was. What would she choose, Frances?' He was at rock bottom. Only desperation made him appeal to her. 'The boys thought you might know. She might have talked to you. More than me.'

'She did. Several times. Over the years.'

'And?'

'Mostly she was just challenging the Catholic position. She knew how to needle me – but you know that. She did it with all of us. She was like a terrier – once she knew your weak spot. With you it was your devotion to your little girl. With Kevin it was Tina. With Euan it was his socialist values. With me it was my faith. It was just Viv – the person she was.'

'So do you know – what she'd have wanted?'

'No. Much as I want to say she'd have opted to keep the baby, it wouldn't be true. I don't know. She could battle just as fiercely for the prosecution as for the defence. She'd argue black was white to score a point against any one of us.'

Bill slumped back against the bench.

'I know. Well, we all know it really. All four of us. But it doesn't help us here.'

'What do *you* think – in your heart of hearts?' Her enquiry was gentle.

'From a dispassionate point of view I think there's only one sensible course of action.' The silence was so long she had to prompt him.

'To … ?'

'To abort it.'

It took all his courage to say it. He couldn't meet her frank gaze.

'But … ?'

'But this is Viv's baby – my – our … grandchild.' He stopped suddenly, not wanting her to hear what that meant to him. He pushed his fingers hard into his hair, pressing the nails against his scalp until it hurt.

'And it's a way of holding on to her too,' she said softly, understanding.

'But that's not a good reason to have it. I know. I know it's not.'

'No. But it's natural to feel it.'

'I can't let her go, Frances. I can't.' Bill dropped his head in his hands, wrenched again by the despair. He saw her hand moving towards him instinctively, stopping suddenly, withdrawing into the security of the wide sleeves of her habit.

'She's lucky to have you. If she knows anything, it's that *you* haven't failed her.' It was balm to his soul.

'And one day – maybe …'

'Maybe. Who knows? Miracles do happen.'

'Do they? Do you still believe in miracles?' he asked.

'Well, sometimes things happen we can't explain logically, scientifically. You could call them miracles.'

'And – don't you see? – that's why I *have* to keep believing she's still in there somewhere, waiting to be released.' He slapped his knee for emphasis.

'I do see. And I'm grateful, Bill, more than you'll ever know. You've been mother, father, everything to her. If there's any possibility of recovery it'll be everything to do with you and your devotion to her.'

'Or will it be because you've paid the price instead of her?' He gave her a lopsided grin.

Her lips twitched momentarily. Or did he simply imagine it?

'But if she has this baby, Bill, what will happen to it? Who will look after it?'

'Me. There's no-one else.' It was a statement of fact. 'OK, I know. You don't have to say it. The boys've already told me. I'm over the hill. Incapable of starting all over again.'

'I wasn't going to say that. I was going to ask you, humbly – I know I've no right to do so, but Viv is *my* daughter too, and this would be *my grand-child* too – will you get someone in to help you? To get up in the night, take some of the physical strain. Leave you space to love the child without resentment, not kill yourself in the process. And to go on loving Viv.'

Bill stared at her for a long moment. She met his gaze unflinchingly.

'That's the first sensible contribution to this whole debate I've heard. Thank you.' She dropped her eyes, flushing under his unexpected appro-bation. 'All I've had up to now is "don't". *Don't* visit every day. *Don't* keep hoping. *Don't* take on this baby.'

'I know you're only doing all this because of your love for her. But you won't help her if you crack up yourself.'

He nodded. There was a long silence between them.

'Bill.' She was leaning towards him slightly.

'Mmhhmm?'

'I just want to say ... if you do decide ... for abortion ... I'll understand. I won't make things difficult.' It was hesitant, almost as if she would snatch the words back at any moment.

Ten minutes earlier he would have flared up at her. Quite right too. What right did she have to register a protest? She'd be far away, safe in her nunnery or whatever these places called themselves. Now he simply said, 'Thanks. It's good to know that.'

For another long moment they sat in silence, each lost in their own thoughts. It was Frances who broke it first.

'How are you these days, Bill? You look tired? This – all these years with Viv, and now, this latest thing – must have been a terrible strain on you.'

'I get by. Viv keeps me going. And you?'

'I still worry about you all,' she said, not looking at him.

Seeing Frances again had been a shock. What she'd had to say had been startling. Bill needed time to think. He'd asked her if she wanted to be involved in the family discussion with the doctors. She'd asked him if he wanted her there. He found to his surprise he did. She was the one person who might share his innermost thoughts and doubts.

The meeting was arranged for one o'clock the following day. Six eternal days since that first bombshell had shattered their fragile peace.

ELEVEN

Her high heels clacked noisily on the pavement as she walked briskly towards the bus stop. Several times she caught herself tiptoeing, and grinned involuntarily. Anyone watching her would be astonished. Tiptoeing went with children absorbed in a private game, or adults walking into a church or a hospital ward. It didn't fit with a middle-aged woman in a smart navy suit walking down a busy public street.

She caught sight of her reflection in a shop window. It felt odd. Especially, strangely enough, the sight of her legs, still shapely in fine tights. But everything about her felt disturbing today: the breeze lifting her thick hair, the silk of her shirt moving softly against her skin, the straight skirt restricting her stride. And the sound of her clacking heels echoing conspicuously around her. It was a curiously out-of-body experience altogether, like watching someone else doing things from a great distance. She wanted to fade into obscurity; she felt too exposed, too vulnerable.

In reality no-one showed the least bit of interest in an unremarkable well-groomed woman going about her business in a quite unremarkable way.

The Georgian house in Grosvenor Road was imposing without being ostentatious. She paused for a long moment to steady her erratic pulse before walking up the steps of number forty-nine. It was a relief to slip quietly on the soles of her feet. The brass plaque said simply: Wynne-Hope. She felt something rise in her throat, and swallowed hard.

It was fifteen years since she'd last seen Charles, almost double that since he'd been part of her life. They'd not been in contact for all these years. She knew nothing of what had happened to him; he knew nothing of her. But he'd responded with characteristic charm to her phone call and her request. Now here she was on his doorstep. What would he make of her sudden reappearance?

'Frances!' he cried, enveloping her hand in both his own. 'How lovely to see you. Come in. Come in.'

She was ushered into the wide hallway, and followed him to the end of the corridor and into a spacious sitting room. The sun streamed in through the bay window, throwing bright patches onto the cream leather upholstery.

'My word, the years have been good to you. You look fantastic!' he breathed.

She gave an awkward smile, feeling colour tinge her cheeks as his appreciative gaze lingered over her.

'And you, Charles? Has life been kind to you?'

'Good enough. Good enough.' He laughed with a sweep of his hand to embrace the luxury surrounding them.

He looked good. The same athletic trimness. The same smile. Same easy confidence. The once dark hair now white but still plenty of it, and still those errant strands that refused to lie flat … no, she mustn't …

'It's so good of you to see me at such short notice.' Frances heard her voice, stiffly formal.

'A pleasure, my dear. A pleasure. But let me get you a drink. Sherry? G and T? What's your tipple these days? Or would you prefer tea, coffee?' He was bending slightly towards her.

'Could I … would you mind … I'd rather have just a glass of water.' She stumbled over the words, pressing a trembling hand to her lips.

'Of course. Not a problem. Back in a sec.'

She took long deep breaths while she waited. She must stay in control, and keep up her guard. A photograph of Charles with Molly and the three boys caught her eye. The boys would all be established now, leading fulfilling lives. And Molly? Charles had said he'd be on his own when she called, but everywhere there was evidence of a woman's touch – glossy magazines stacked neatly on the coffee table, co-ordinated colours, an artistic flower arrangement in a corner alcove, a half-worked tapestry lying on the table. Yes, Molly must still be on the scene.

She took the glass in both hands to be sure she gave no sign of her nervousness.

'Charles, I know you're busy, so I'll get straight to the point.' She was into the safer zone of her rehearsed speech. It pleased her to hear the growing confidence in her voice. 'I have a relative, Kate, who's in real trouble at the moment. Her daughter, Ginny, developed leukaemia when she was four. She's ten now. She's had several courses of treatment and been in remission for the past nine months, but it's come back again. She's really bad at the moment. The doctors want to try a second bone marrow transplant. Ginny says she just wants to be left in peace. Poor kid, she's had so much to contend with in her short life. The thing is, the family can't agree on what's best.'

'It happens. It's fiendishly difficult. And everybody's emotions are shot to pieces,' Charles said gently.

'Exactly. Kate and Simon are out of their minds with worry. And the older kids – there are two older boys – are giving them a hard time. And Kate asked me what I thought, what I'd do, and I – well, I thought of you. All your experience with kids. All the difficult cases you must have dealt with and I thought …'

'Absolutely. You thought it might help to talk to somebody outside the family.'

'That's right. I knew you'd understand.'

'Of course. I'm only too happy to help. Fire away. Anything I can do …'

'Well, obviously Ginny's in no position to decide for herself.'

'Isn't she, Fran?' Charles leaned forwards a fraction. 'Why isn't she?'

Instinctively Frances tensed. It was so long since anyone had called her Fran. Only her brother and Charles had ever used that abbreviation. In the old days Bill had called her Franny.

'No. She's only ten. And she's ... she's so ill. I mean she's scarcely conscious most of the time.'

'OK. I understand that. But ... she knows what these treatments are like, doesn't she? And she's the one who'll have to go through it all.'

'But she's not ... she isn't ... *competent* to decide – not on something so important. She can't be. It's too big a decision.'

Slowly Charles sat back, looking hard at her.

'Competence. Hmmm. Well, I don't know Ginny, of course, you do. But you know, these little people – these ones who've been through so much – I suspect they're a lot more competent to decide than some of us older folk who've never been through any of these beastly treatments.'

'But she's not old enough to decide heaps of things. I mean, she's a minor. Legally even, she can't, can she?'

'True. But a kid can be competent to decide some things and not others, can't she?'

Frances had always liked the way he'd left things open to question, made her think she might be right, not forced his opinions on her – even when he was the undoubted expert.

'Competence is a funny thing. It's not a sort of blanket concept – you are or you aren't – at that age. I don't think so, anyway. In Ginny's case, for instance, some things will be totally within her comprehension, others won't. So I doubt very much if at that age she'd be competent to decide where to invest a large amount of money, or which party to vote for at the next general election. But maybe on second thoughts she'd be as good as the next man to do *that*! Bad example!' He shot her a brief grin before becoming completely serious again. 'But my guess is she's wiser than most when it comes to her medical management.'

'But we *can't* – we can't *surely* – let her decide something with such awful consequences. It's ... it's just not *fair*. It's too big a responsibility. Surely she'll only be thinking of how horrible it feels to be sick all the time, to feel all the miserable short-term things. I mean, the alternative's *dying*! Surely it has to be better to at least give it a sporting chance.' His steady gaze was unsettling. Her voice faltered. 'Doesn't it?'

'Well, I've never had chemo. I've never had radiotherapy. I've never had a transplant or been pumped full of toxic drugs. Nor have I ever died. But I've seen hundreds of kids doing all these things. And you know what, Fran?' He looked at her for a long moment. 'I'm not so sure.'

'Oh.' She wished he wouldn't watch her so intensely. It gave her a distinct feeling he was X-raying her thoughts.

'I know it's tough for parents to watch their precious kiddie slip away but for your – what is she? – sorry – Kate and her family, sounds like they've all been through a hell of a lot already. I don't know the facts but chances are they could put Ginny through weeks more agony and at the end of the day still lose her. Maybe they'd all be better accepting the inevitable, and stopping all the painful distressing things, and just filling her life with as much love as they can give her. Seems to me Ginny's got a big stake in this decision, don't you think?'

'Well, yes, but ...' She broke off. If she *couldn't* decide for herself ...

'I know. I know.' His soothing voice had a calming effect. She felt he really did know. 'What do Kate and Simon think?'

'Kate can't get past worrying what Ginny will feel like if they override her. She's just terribly upset and afraid of letting her down, failing her when she most needs her support. Simon – well, he just isn't sure. Ginny's the apple of his eye – he's just daft about her. Always has been. He's at the hospital all the time. And he just can't bear the thought of losing her so he wants to try anything – everything – to try to save her.'

'It's tough – unbearably tough – when it's your child. I can understand that. Not wanting to let them go.' His voice was very quiet.

To her horror Frances felt tears spill down her cheeks. She reached quickly for her hanky. The waft of delicate perfume from her wrist added to her sense of unreality.

'You're close to this family?' he asked gently.

'Very.'

'I'm sorry. Tough for you too.'

Frances took several gulps of water. The lemon slice slid against her lips diverting the flow, spilling drops on her suit. She dabbed at it ineffectually with her hand. Charles reached across to place his own folded handkerchief against the dampness, holding it there for a moment, withdrawing his hand without a word.

'What would you say? If you were her doctor?' she asked, mopping her lap, stalling for time, not wanting to look at him.

'I'd listen very carefully to all of them – one at a time and together. Try to get a sense of what was going on for them all, where they were coming from. And I'd look very carefully at the prospects – get a colleague to assess them independently.'

'And?'

'Well, it would depend. If I thought she really did have a sporting chance I might take a different line from if I thought there was pretty much no hope.'

'And you'd let Ginny have the casting vote?'

'Not necessarily. If I felt she really did have a chance, and her parents thought we should try, I might not.'

'Well! So what happened to her competence to decide? Sounds like she's only competent if she agrees with you!' Indignation made her look up. She saw the swift smile.

'I know it sounds like that. Paternalist! Despot! Autocrat! Know-it-all! Think you're God! I've heard them all! But it isn't like that really. Choosing death is serious business. Once you go down that route there's no going back if you change your mind. It takes a higher level of competence to decide for or against treatment with such serious consequences. So we have to be doubly, doubly sure the patient is competent to decide, knows exactly what they're doing, what the consequences are. And if we think it's – like you say – they can't see past the short-term symptoms, then we might have to override them – for their own sakes. There's an extra heavy duty on us paediatricians to be sure these children understand the consequences fully, and they're not just fed up of being sick, or depressed, or whatever.'

'And what about the parents? Would you always take their opinions as the final word? Or would you suspect their motives if they don't agree with you?'

'You're going to go away thinking I've got way above myself!' he said with a wry grimace.

'No, please. I didn't mean it like that. I'm so confused about all this. Really, I need to know. It helps talking to you.' She stopped, suddenly aware from Charles' narrowed eyes of the intensity of her appeal.

'OK. Well, no. I wouldn't always give them the casting vote either. I see it as a two-way thing. The parents expect me to use whatever skills and knowledge I have. After all I've been expensively and extensively trained, and I've had years of experience which they haven't had, so I do know things they can't possibly know. They expect me to apply all of that in their child's case. And they expect me also to act in their child's best interests. And that's right too. I do. But *I* have expectations of *them* too. I expect them to want what's best for their child. And I look to them to give me a sense of the family's values and beliefs and wishes – anything that might influence the decision we make. What they as a family think is best, what they need, what they'd prefer.' She was leaning forward now, watching him intently. 'So we enter into this collaboration. We each give information to help the other one understand. And we try to find a solution that fits with everybody's feeling that this is the best course for this child in these circumstances.'

'But you might not go along with their values. What then?'

'Well, it would depend on where the differences were.'

'Say they had a … I don't know … a religious scruple? … and they want something you don't think is best?'

'It happens. We have it with the Jehovah's Witnesses, for example. I know it's something that's really important to the parents, and if I can I try to avoid giving blood products. But if the child is at serious risk if I do, I might overrule them.'

'And what are you thinking inside about those parents?'

'It varies. Speaking personally as Charles Wynne-Hope, family man, I have a real problem seeing how you can possibly have your child's best interests at stake, and let them die unnecessarily. But I know the JWs attach more value to the afterlife than I do. And speaking professionally as Dr Wynne-Hope, consultant in charge, I respect that. So I do try to reach a compromise. Sometimes it's about me taking the responsibility, so they don't feel they've let their child or their religion down. But sometimes I have to go to court to get legal backing to save the kid.'

'But there are some things you wouldn't be so sympathetic about?'

'Absolutely.'

'So how do you decide – which value systems you respect and which you don't?'

'Well, I call it the "peaceful sleep factor"!' Charles smiled broadly at her. It had its old effect; her responding smile was involuntary. 'We doctors aren't robots – although sometimes we might wish we were! We have consciences too. And I for one want to be able to sleep in my bed at night, thank you very much. So I won't do anything that I can't defend to myself as well as – hopefully – to the GMC – sorry, General Medical Council!'

There was a long silence. Frances twisted the glass round and round in her hands.

'Say what you want to say, Fran.' He'd always been able to read her too well for comfort. It was disconcerting to find he still could.

'I'm sorry. This business with Ginny, it's made me ask myself a lot of questions. And I haven't got the answers.'

'Which is where I come in. I'm glad you felt you could come to me.' His voice was quiet. 'Ask away. I don't mind. I'm only teasing you – because I like to see you smile. We go back a long way. You can trust me.'

She wished he wouldn't keep introducing the personal allusions. It was vital that she didn't go down that track.

'Well. What if … Maybe you've got a different agenda. What then?'

'Explain?' he said, waving his hand as if unravelling the words.

'Say you're worried about the statistics for your hospital – or your reputation.'

'Wow! I didn't know you had quite such a low opinion of me!'

'Oh, I don't mean *you personally*,' she said quickly.

'I know you don't. I'm only teasing you again,' he said lightly, though his dark blue eyes were still too searching for comfort. 'You're right, we do have to worry about our figures. But I honestly don't think you'll find many paediatricians who'd put their hospital statistics above the best interests of one of their patients in these sorts of circumstances. *I* don't know any anyway.'

'But what if you were in private practice, say, and the patients weren't children? The success of the hospital or Home or whatever depends on good results, a reputation for excellence. Would you be tempted then?'

'You've been watching too many soap operas!' He laughed. 'Never been in that position – perhaps that's why I'm a humble jobbing paediatrician and not some millionaire in Harley Street, eh?' She half-returned his smile. 'But no, I like to think it wouldn't influence my decision. Hanging onto his illusion like grim death, you're thinking, huh?'

'No, I wasn't thinking that actually. I think you *would* put the kiddie first.'

'Phew! That's a relief. This is a bit like the third degree. Too close for comfort.'

'I'm sorry. I didn't mean ...'

'I know you didn't. Fire away. You were always good at getting to the heart of things.'

She concentrated on the glass still in her hands. Twisting it made the light refract, sending tiny rainbows along the pattern in the crystal. He didn't mean anything by it. It was just a figure of speech. But her voice sounded stifled in spite of her inner attempts at reassurance. She must get to the point, get away from here.

'What about if you had a girl – a patient, I mean – and let's say she was ... in a coma, say – and you found out she was pregnant. She can't tell you what she wants you to do. How would you decide?'

'Hypothetically speaking?'

'Yes.'

'Has she got a family, this girl?'

'Yes.'

'Do they have opinions?'

'Yes, but some of them think it should be terminated and some of them think she should be allowed to have the baby.'

'Was she in a steady relationship?'

'No.' Tony Partridge didn't count. Charles meant was there a father of the baby involved.

'Did she want to have a kiddie?'

'No.'

'And is she too young to have had a valid opinion herself – before the coma?'

'Well, nobody knows for sure what she thought.'

'Difficult one. I think I'd try to find out how everyone in the family feels, about what the girl would have chosen, what the family feel about looking after the baby. Lots of things. No simple black and white answer to that one.'

'And say she'd become pregnant against her will?' Her lips felt stiff saying it. 'Would that make a difference?'

'Rape, incest. That kind of thing?'

'Yes.'

'You don't make it easy, do you?' Charles grinned at her. 'Intuitively, I think, yes, it would make a difference.'

'So what would you advise then?'

'Sounds to me as if abortion would be in the girl's own best interests. Bit grim for a kid to wake up from a coma and find she's got a baby she didn't want, don't you think? And horrendous for the family to have a baby on their hands conceived by force. Unless of course the family know one of them did it and they're prepared to take it on – for other reasons.'

His direct gaze was unnerving. Frances rushed on. Every topic seemed to lead too close for comfort.

'Don't you find it hard making these decisions all the time?' she asked quickly.

'Not usually. Been doing it a hundred years – I guess that helps.'

'But the cases are all different. Don't you get … involved?'

'Prick us and we *do* bleed! Yes, I confess in the privacy of my own home, Madame Interrogator, some of these cases do get under my guard, even now. But I see the decision-making bit as the *art* of my profession. We can all learn the hard science, what drugs treat which diseases, how to do a particular surgical operation. But the real skill, I think, comes in the judgements we have to make. And a big chunk of medicine *is* about making judgements, weighing up alternatives. And as far as I'm concerned I can't make good choices if I don't care about the patients – if I'm not touched by the effect on the families.'

'That's why you've got such a good name.'

'Well, it helps to know *somebody somewhere* thinks I'm earning my crust!'

She smiled back at him more warmly this time. It was true. He'd always been a popular doctor with patients, families and colleagues alike. They knew he cared, really cared. It showed. It had been one of the things that made him so attractive.

She rushed on, too conscious of the inner conflict: needing to get away, wanting to linger.

'Are you ever tempted to skew the information you give to families? You know, steer them in what *you* think is the best direction? I mean, you have all the power; you could manipulate things if you wanted to, couldn't you?'

'To some extent. It's possible. In fact, some of my colleagues would argue that's good medicine because you don't want some ill-informed knee-jerk reaction, you want carefully argued and reasoned decisions. So as a doctor you should help them to a considered opinion.'

'And what if they don't like your advice? Does it bug you if they ask for a second opinion?'

'No. Why would it bug me?'

'Doesn't it feel like they don't trust you?'

'Heavens, no! Well, I guess if I'm honest, when I was younger and less secure in myself, I might have felt a bit threatened. But not now. In their shoes I wouldn't care about the doctor's pride. If this was my kid, I wouldn't care about anybody else's feelings! What do they matter?! I'd keep going until I was satisfied I had the best opinions available. Actually I quite often *suggest* a second opinion just to help them to accept the diagnosis or prognosis or whatever.'

'The "peaceful sleep factor" again?'

'Absolutely.'

'What if the family asks you what you'd do if you were in their shoes, would you say?'

'Now that's a tricky one. I can understand why they do it. And they often do, I must admit. I think I must be a grandfather figure or something!'

The shiver was involuntary. She knew he'd seen it, but she instantly dropped her gaze.

'Mostly I *do* say if I know from my own knowledge and experience what feels best. It's a bit of intuition sometimes as well as facts and rational arguments and everything. But sometimes what I think *they* should do and what *I* might do aren't always the same thing. If my values and beliefs and circumstances are completely different, it might not help them to know what I would do. Then I just say, "I'm not you and I can't pretend I know what this feels like for you." But I try to give them the knowledge and understanding to come to their own conclusion.'

The sound of a key in the door jerked Frances upright. She'd allowed herself to stay much longer than she'd intended. What was she thinking of? She leapt to her feet.

'I'm so sorry. I've kept you far too long. I must go.'

'Please don't go, Fran. It's only Henry, our youngest lad. He's back home for a few days – some business or other in the city.'

'No. I must go. But thank you. Thank you so much. It's helped. Thanks for fitting me in.'

As soon as she said it she knew it jarred. The slight frown between his eyebrows, the suddenly close scrutiny, just added to her discomfort. But she dare not begin to correct the impression, lest he make her say even more than she intended.

TWELVE

Bill arrived an hour early for the consultation with Steven Wilkinson, intending to spend time with Viv first. Preoccupied with the decision ahead he almost barged in on a silent tableau. The sight of the motionless figure swathed in black sitting close to his daughter made him clench his hands and grit his teeth. Abruptly he turned on his heel.

He'd go for a coffee; perhaps by then Frances would have gone. His feet were noiseless on the dark blue carpet. It was one of the things he liked about the place. The corridors of The Home were habitually hushed. It felt respectful, in tune with the surreal world people like Viv inhabited. There was plenty about the building that offended his architect's sensibilities, and he could never get used to the blanket of heat that hit you when you entered the place. To some extent he'd overcome the smell of medical care by ensuring Viv was always surrounded by her favourite perfumes. He'd slavishly replicated the ones left in her bedroom ever since she'd been admitted to hospital, at first in an effort to bring her back, more recently (if he was honest) to help him preserve the image and sense of the daughter he had known before. But whatever the shortcomings of the environment he always welcomed the peace of the place.

Now as he turned the corner that tranquillity was suddenly, sharply invaded. Such a cacophony of sounds assailed him that he instinctively backtracked towards the entrance to the building.

An ambulance stood at the door discharging a patient on a trolley. One of the paramedics deftly gathered up a trailing edge of blanket and tucked it in more firmly beneath the recumbent figure. A nurse moved alongside the patient's head, so much in step with their movements that it was as if she were attached to the trolley by an invisible thread. The quiet synchronised movement of the three professionals was in sharp contrast to the chaos behind them.

Biblical scenes flooded through Bill's mind. Swarming around on the drive were at least a dozen heavily draped black figures, accompanied by several swarthy men, and four small children with soulful dark eyes. The contrast between the raucous excitement of so many voices jabbering in a foreign tongue and the noiselessness within was so discordant that Bill simply stood and stared.

Out of nowhere Alison Reed, two doctors, and a nurse appeared. A terse instruction from Mrs Reed and the nurse whisked the patient and attendants out of sight. As if a switch had been thrown the din was suddenly no more than a muffled throb. The main doors had been abruptly closed, and

Bill could just see the backs of the medical men pressed against the glass as they barred the way. He watched mesmerised as the massed figures crowded closer to hear what the senior doctor was saying, darkening the hallway with their sheer solidarity. The mime of the exchange outside suggested a vigorous altercation, the gesticulations threatening without the sound to explain them. But little by little a form of order descended.

The doors were as suddenly opened. Mrs Reed's diminutive but upright figure, face expressionless, proceeded down the long corridor, the Arabic figures surging in a disorderly file behind her, the children skipping every so often to keep up with the longer strides around them. A small voice began piping a question; four adults shushed him instantly. They vanished out of sight. The Home returned outwardly to its usual calm.

Bill was idly tracing patterns on the table with a spoon when a voice at his elbow made him start.

'Care for some company?'

It was Geoff Archibald.

'By all means. Don't usually see you here this early in the day.'

'Rhona's got a urinary tract infection. I called in to check on her.'

'Doing OK?'

'Responding to the treatment anyway. They aren't worried about it. So I'm just grabbing this then it's back to the madhouse that pays my wages.'

The two men sat in silence. It was clear that Bill was distracted.

'You seem miles away. Everything all right?' Geoff ventured.

'Why d'you ask?' It was sharp, unexpected.

'Sorry,' Geoff said quickly, holding up a hand as if warding off something. 'Standard sort of question in here.'

'*I'm* sorry.'

'It's OK.' He paused, glancing briefly at Bill's unsmiling face. 'I noticed workmen outside this morning. Know what that's about?'

'Installing CCTV cameras.'

'Not before time. I wonder why they've suddenly decided to do that.' Geoff drained his coffee cup.

'Haven't you heard?' Bill shot him a sharp look.

'Heard what exactly?'

Geoff listened in absolute silence. He let out a low whistle when Bill stopped speaking, and swore eloquently.

'The police haven't talked to you?' Bill asked.

'No.'

'They must be focusing on the staff first, I guess.'

'Well, I've been out of town for a week. Maybe that's why I haven't heard anything.'

'I don't think I'm supposed to talk to any of the relatives about this, so keep it to yourself. But if I don't let some of this out I think I'll explode.'

'That is appalling,' Geoff said, leaning back in his chair, emphasising each word. 'I had no idea.'

Bill compressed his lips, fighting the emotions.

'Did you notice they'd taken all the male staff off our corridor?'

'Can't say I did. But I only just got back yesterday.'

'Until they're cleared, apparently, it's a women-only zone. Apart from Dr Wilkinson, that is.'

'Sure of him, are they?'

'Must be. But I really can't see him …'

'No. I agree. But presumably every male in the place is potentially a suspect. Me included. In fact any of us who're in and out a lot must be prime suspects.'

'To the police I guess, yes. But I know – somebody like you couldn't possibly … not when you know what it feels like, sitting with them day after day, year after year. You couldn't. You just *couldn't*.' Bill shook his head slowly from side to side as he dismissed the very idea.

'Like you say, *we* know that. But do they?'

'Presumably not. They've been asking us a load of questions anyway. Viv's brothers and me.'

'Thanks for telling me, Bill. But are the girls safe – now, I mean? If this criminal's still at large …'

'Indeed. Dr Wilkinson assures me the staff're being extra vigilant and they've employed additional security. But yes. The scumball might be anywhere.'

'So all the patients are at risk.'

'Well, yes. I suppose they are.'

'And the relatives don't know it.'

'Well …'

'You'd think that … But hey, what about *you*?' Geoff reached a hand across to the older man, not touching him but conveying his concern. 'And Viv. It's too late for her. I am so, so sorry. It beggars belief. What are you going to do?'

'I only wish I knew,' Bill groaned, sinking his chin back onto his hand. 'Whichever way we go it'll be open to criticism.'

'Don't waste your sympathy on the know-it-alls who'll criticise,' Geoff said briskly. 'It's what's right for *you* – your family – that counts here.'

'Trouble is we don't know that either. If only Viv could tell us.'

'Oh, how often have I thought that! Damnable, isn't it? – this relentless silence. I know. Churns you up, even though you know they can't help it. Must be even more frustrating for you now.'

Bill cast him a grateful look. Of course, Geoff knew.

'I thought I was getting used to it. Accepting it. But this – this has just opened it all up again.'

'Bound to.'

They sat in silence for a long moment. Bill drained his cup.

'We're sort of hoping the doctors can give us a bit of guidance. We've got a meeting with them this morning.'

'But at the end of the day it's personal, I guess.'

'Exactly. This isn't some textbook case. This is *Viv* we're talking about. And I know – I've seen it – the nurses and doctors and everybody, they're good with her but they don't see her as a real individual – not the person she was – before. Not like I do.'

'I know just what you mean. They don't know what kind of books she liked, that she preferred paté with bits in it, what made her laugh, the expressions she used.'

'It's ridiculous I know, but I get mad sometimes when I come in and find they've put a particular cardigan on with a skirt she especially liked. If she woke up that moment and saw them together she'd throw a fit!'

Geoff looked at him for a long moment.

'You're something else, you know that?'

'How d'you mean?'

'After all these years, still going on as if she might – wake up, care about something like that. I'm so impressed. How d'you *do* it?' The admiration in his look as well as his voice was genuine.

'She's my daughter,' Bill said simply. 'Actually I think I'm a real thorn in their flesh – being here so much. But tough! It's Viv who counts. And I'm damned if I'm going to let them do things she wouldn't like.'

'And that's what you need to hang on to now. Stuff the critics. They don't know her like you do.'

'You're right,' Bill nodded. Then after a pause he added sadly, 'Trouble is *we* don't know what she would want – not about this.'

'Not the kind of situation we tend to anticipate! I see it sometimes in my line of work – you know, living wills and all that. They only take you so far. Life has a nasty habit of poking fun at our advance preparation. Only in this case there's nothing "funny" about it.'

'Exactly.'

'Did she have anything at all – in writing?'

'No.'

'Only chance comments to go on?'

'Yes.'

'And nothing about being unconscious or being raped, I bet. And certainly not both!'

'Exactly.'

'Who ever would? What a bloody awful position to be in. If you wrote about something like this nobody'd believe it, would they?'

Bill caught sight of Libby who waved as she carried her coffee to a table. He returned the salute half-heartedly. He didn't want interruption at this precise moment.

'Staff have been decent, I must say. Not trying to pressure us or anything. And they're feeling this badly. Funny, I hadn't really thought about it – you know, you tend to notice all the little things that get missed and I know I've been critical over the years. But overall they're a dedicated bunch. And they're proud of the place and what they do. So it must be ghastly having something like this hanging over them. Couple of them have offered to talk it through with me. But to be honest, they can't really help. They didn't know Viv.'

'Exactly. I'd be the same if it was Rhona. It's so personal. And you don't need advice from every Tom, Dick and Harry. But by gum, I don't envy you this! I just do not know how you decide something as horrendous as this. I feel for you, I really do. Not that that's a scrap of use. Sorry.'

'Thanks. But that's the bottom line – there's nothing anyone *can* say to make it go away.'

'It's too soon to think of … but if you need a lawyer … well, I'd be only too willing to help. No charge.'

'Thanks, Geoff. That's good of you. I'll let you know. At this precise moment all I need is a flash of divine inspiration – or a message from Viv! I can't even get my head around the crime yet, I'm just so worried about Viv and what to do about … that.'

'You're right. Prioritise things – take it one step at a time. Once you've decided about the pregnancy that's time enough to think about the other. Just let me know. The offer stands. Whatever you decide.'

'Thanks again. Heavens, look at the time! Must dash. Can't be late for this meeting.'

As he strode along the corridor Bill cursed himself for missing seeing Viv first. But Frances hadn't had his opportunities; better for her to spend time with their daughter while she could. He'd make up for it later. When she'd gone.

Dr Steven Wilkinson and Mrs Reed were already in the small interview room when Bill arrived.

He hated this room. Whoever had chosen the frilly covers, the sickeningly pastel shades, had no idea how black the thoughts, how stark the prospects of families like his. Every time the staff had taken him here it had been to tell him more bad news about Viv. Every time he'd felt an urge to smash the shell-shaped ceramic lamp, rip off the fussy border along the dado rail. Even without the associations he'd have cringed here; his style in every building he'd designed had been simple, cool, elegant. Never fussy. The circumstances just made it more offensive.

He dropped into a chair with his back to the row of flower prints.

Frances entered three minutes after him. He felt awkward introducing her; referring to a nun as anyone's mother didn't sound right. But neither showed any outward sign of surprise and the moment passed when their two sons came into the room together. Everyone took their seats.

The family listened politely while the doctor went through the motions of apologising again, assuring them the staff were upset too, and that everyone was concerned to do what was best for Viv. Bill felt irritated by the smooth talking. Best for Viv indeed!

'And what do you think that is?'

Bill saw Dr Wilkinson's sudden frown. He'd probably had a careful strategy planned which would inch them towards the decision *he* thought was right. Probably no part of his plan to catapult them into potential conflict.

'Well, before any decision is reached on that, we all need to talk together.'

This time it was Kevin who interrupted. 'No disrespect, Doctor, but can you explain to me just how much attention you're going to pay to what we say? I mean, as I understand it from what my father told us, you need to know from us what Viv would have wanted. But *we* aren't allowed to decide. So if you think you know what's best for Viv, what difference does it make what we think?'

Bill watched Steven take a long, deep breath.

'As you'll all know I'm sure, we doctors can't just do things to patients willy-nilly. We need their consent. Now, we respect Viv hugely. I hope you feel we always try to treat her with the utmost dignity and respect. As we do all our patients. But unfortunately Viv can't give us consent to things. She isn't capable of doing so. Agreed?'

Stupid question. No-one deigned to answer.

'It's our philosophy here to see all our patients as individuals and as members of families. And it's my personal belief that you as a family have a special role to play in making this decision on behalf of Viv. Firstly, because you knew her when she was capable of expressing her own views on things. I realise, of course, that though you're in the best position to know what Viv's values and opinions and beliefs were, it can feel like a heavy responsibility to make such a big decision on her behalf. So I just want to reassure you that we do understand that none of us – not even you – can actually get inside her skin. The best we can all do is to give an approximation of her views and try to see where our own biases and prejudices might get in the way of what she would choose.'

Bill saw him glance at Frances and look away again quickly. Probably afraid of seeming prejudiced.

'And the second reason why you're in an especially strong position to make what we call a "substituted judgement" for Viv is because you have a particular and close interest in her welfare. She's part of your family. We have her best interests at heart, of course, as I've said, but because of the special bonds of love and affection in the family, we know *you're* especially concerned with what's best for her.' He paused to look at each in turn. One by one they all looked steadily back at him.

'Now, when we're dealing with children – below the age of understanding and consenting – the parents are legally responsible for deciding on their behalf. It's not just legally permissible but it seems morally right too. But in Viv's case, she's not a child. She's a woman. She's had many years of being fully autonomous – able to make her own reasonable and thought-through decisions, make up her own mind about things. So in the eyes of the law the same rules don't apply. Legally no-one else *can* make proxy decisions for her. We doctors can, of course, use our professional responsibility and privilege to decide what we judge to be best for her medically speaking in her day-to-day care. And if we run into situations where we aren't totally certain what's best, we consult colleagues elsewhere and experts, just to make doubly sure. And that's where you come in. *You* are experts – experts on Viv – the person you've known for years, the person she was before she came here. So we're needing you to help us to look at the various options and arguments and hopefully together we'll come to a decision that we can all feel is best on her behalf now.'

'Who else have you told then? Already?' Bill asked sharply, sitting suddenly bolt upright.

'Well, we had to report it to the police, as you know. We've had a couple of multidisciplinary meetings, and we've been talking to our lawyers and our chaplains who "we feel" might help us to make the best decision for Viv. All in the strictest confidence, of course. You'll understand that all our patients are especially vulnerable. We have to make sure their interests are properly protected. So for their protection we do seek outside advice and guidance to be sure we're playing fair by them.'

No-one pointed out the total lack of protection that had allowed Viv to be raped in the first place, but the thought hung in the air nonetheless.

'Although we've had discussions with other people,' Dr Wilkinson continued, 'I must emphasise, there's no decision made as yet. We're still trying to look at all angles and be sure we know what all the issues are that we must take into account.'

'So our opinion *might* influence you?' Kevin needed to hear it spelled out.

'Indeed. Your family opinion is important.'

'But say we said one thing – the thing that's best for the family as a whole – but *you* think that particular decision isn't the best one for Viv on her own. What then?'

'That's a very good question. I'm glad you raised it. There could be a conflict of interests – although I doubt it in this case – but the very fact that we're consulting different people will, I hope, help us be as fair as we possibly can be.'

'But Viv's top priority. Right?' Bill chipped in, a sharp edge to his voice, his finger drumming the arm of the chair in time with each word.

'Viv's top priority,' Steven repeated soothingly. 'As her doctor she's the one *I'm* most concerned about. I have a professional duty to her. And I'm sure I speak for all of you as well as all the staff here when I say that we *all* want to do what's best for her.'

'What if *we* disagree with *your* decision; is there anything we can do about that?' Kevin persisted. Bill had to admire the tenacity which drove him to establish the ground rules before they committed themselves.

'Well, we hope very much it won't come to that. The point of us meeting like this is to discuss everything together very carefully, and hopefully we'll all come to the same conclusion. But if it *should* come to that, you can ask for a second opinion, consult anyone else you choose to. And we would support you in doing that. Having said that, there is, of course, a real problem here. We haven't got much time. The pregnancy's already quite far advanced – further than we'd choose if we're going down the road of terminating the pregnancy. But that doesn't mean we're going to risk making the wrong choices by rushing the decision. We'll just have to concentrate our efforts and make the right decision sooner rather than later.'

'Do we have to sign things?' Euan asked, gesturing with an imaginary pen. 'Is it a legal sort of thing?'

'We do sometimes ask relatives to sign a form. Not because their consent is legally binding. It's not. But really just to show we've discussed everything with them, and they know what we're planning to do. I want to stress again we see this as a joint activity. We're on the same side. But professionally we have to document things to demonstrate that we've gone through the right procedures.'

Euan nodded. Fair enough.

'Have you had discussion with outside people yourself, Mr Faraday – any of you – about this?' asked Steven, his eyes tracking round the family.

'Not yet, nothing official anyway,' Bill replied, realising as he spoke that he had no idea who the rest of the family had consulted. 'It's tricky – because of the rape and everything. We want to protect Viv from – well, you know – publicity and everything.'

'Of course, I understand.'

'But if *you're* having these big discussions shouldn't one of us be there – sort of representing Viv?' Bill asked.

'If you wish to be, we can make arrangements for that,' Steven agreed. 'Perhaps you could make a note of that, Alison? Thanks.'

Mrs Reed nodded and jotted something in the notes she was taking.

'There's just one more thing,' Bill rushed on. 'Seems to me, we as a family – or perhaps even just one of us – might choose to take a risk and do something that *you* might think is unwise. You might even think it'd be a disaster for us as a family or for any one of us as an individual. But isn't it our right to take that risk?' He needed to be sure Dr Wilkinson understood that he, as this child's grandfather, might have a different agenda from theirs. His fierce gaze dared the doctor to deny him that right.

'Providing it's not a detrimental decision for Viv then yes. That's what autonomy's all about. Your concept of what's best, what constitutes a risk, may not be the same as mine. But if it feels right for you and you'll be the ones to cope with the consequences then, yes, I think we have to let you do it your way. I see my role as making sure that we give you the best medical advice and that you understand the consequences of a decision that might have serious ramifications for any of you. If you choose a difficult path knowing the risks, then that's up to you.'

There was a long pause. Steven Wilkinson's eyes went slowly from one to the other.

'OK. Anything more before we talk about the best decision for Viv?'

Bill, Kevin and Euan shook their heads. Frances still said nothing, and Bill felt her eyes on him.

'Perhaps we should begin with you telling us if Viv ever said what she thought about abortion.'

'We've discussed this and we all think the same – we all think that she felt each case should be decided on its own merits. It depends on the circumstances,' Bill summarised.

'So she wasn't opposed to it in principle?'

'No.'

'That's helpful. It means either option is open to us.'

'The thing is, though, she didn't ever talk about what she'd do if she was *raped* or anything,' Euan said.

'I can understand that. And of course, that means we don't know for sure what she'd actually say in these circumstances. Do any of you have a *hunch* about what she'd say?' Silence. 'Based on everything else you know about her.'

'We could see her going either way. It would depend how much she felt the baby was part of her and how protective she felt towards it,' Bill responded. 'We talked about that and we couldn't decide. It'd help if you could give us some idea of the risks for Viv. Either way.'

Bill noticed Steven's shoulders relax a little. He was on surer ground here, then.

'Well, there's not much evidence available as you'll understand – not for women in Viv's position. But our obstetric colleagues have advised us that there's probably a greater physiological risk in continuing with the pregnancy than in terminating it,' Steven said.

'Would she have to have a Caesarean section?' It was the first time Frances had spoken.

'Probably.'

'And there's an extra risk in that? Because she can't mobilise normally?' The fear was palpable in Frances' voice.

'Yes. Partly, but there's probably a fair amount of risk attached just to carrying the child for nine months too – for her. The obstetricians and physiotherapists say they could do a certain amount to minimise the risks but they couldn't eliminate them.'

'Would giving birth affect her quality of life in any other way?' Bill asked.

'I have to say, the real risk is to her biological existence, rather than her quality of life.' Steven's voice sounded almost apologetic. 'She simply doesn't know anything one way or the other, so she won't have an interest one way or the other whichever way we decide to go. But if continuing with the pregnancy killed her you could say it had not been in her best interests.'

'But if you mistreated her it would be fair to say her quality of life would be worse than if you treated her well,' Bill said, feeling a wave of irritation.

'Objectively we would say that, yes.'

'So *objectively* – would it make a difference?' Bill heard the sarcasm himself. But it was so … *pedantic*!

Steven thought for a long moment. When he did speak the words were slow and measured.

'It's difficult to say without seeming to be putting the emphasis in the wrong place. I think it'd be fair to say *we'd* feel pretty uneasy about watching her become increasingly pregnant. It just … *feels* wrong. So objectively we might say we think we should try to get back to where we were as soon as possible. Terminate the pregnancy in other words. But are we doing it for her or for us? We don't like it for her, but would we really be making that choice because *we* don't like feeling bad about this? I mean, Viv doesn't actually mind getting bigger. She isn't worrying about what people think, or what will happen next. She isn't feeling any discomfort. Or worrying about anything. *We* are, though – on her behalf.'

Bill looked at Steven with grudging admiration. He was trying to be honest, not churning out glib answers, not trying to gloss over things, not putting subtle pressure on them. Couldn't be easy for him. Not with all he personally had at stake.

'So what you're saying is that we can't use quality of life to decide. Yeah?' Euan asked.

'Not for her. That's right.'

'So what *can* we use to help us decide?' Euan appealed, leaning forward with his elbows on his knees.

'Well, I think it's fair to say that nothing is in Viv's own best interests because she neither knows nor cares, one way or the other – about any-thing. But it matters to *us* on her behalf – and all of you in particular. I mean, we all care desperately about this awful thing that's happened to her. *She* doesn't know. But *we* know and we're all appalled by it. It goes against everything we know instinctively is due to her – respect for her as a person, special protection due to her as an especially vulnerable person. So would it help for you to think what feels right to you *for her*?' Bill noted the emphasis and shot Steven a grateful look.

Bill became aware that Kevin, Euan and Frances were all looking at him. He took a deep breath – no point in pretending.

'We don't agree amongst ourselves on that,' he began, 'because we could all see Viv being mad about the rape and wanting to get rid of the result of it, but fiercely protective of this innocent baby.' He had to stop abruptly before emotion cracked his voice.

'OK, I can understand that. So you don't know what Viv would say. But I was thinking more along the lines of … well, let's come one step back from what Viv would say. What would *you* feel seems best? In these circumstances?'

The silence was long but nobody moved.

'I wonder – would you mind? Could we have five minutes on our own, please?' It was Frances who spoke for the family.

When the door had closed it was Frances who began the discussion. Bill noticed she was twining and untwining her fingers in her lap. The familiarity of the gesture unexpectedly hit a raw nerve.

'Given everything we've heard, I think it'd be helpful to think in terms of the cost of continuing.'

'What cost?' Bill asked, his voice carefully controlled.

'The cost to Viv's life and health. The cost to everyone watching the pregnancy continue – how bad it makes us feel for Viv. The cost to those who take on the care of the child – the effect of that on how they would care for Viv. The ongoing cost of having this constant reminder of what happened to Viv. The cost for her if she does ever wake up.'

'I think that's exactly the way to look at it,' Kevin said. 'The cost of continuing is too high. For everybody. I think the sooner we try to put this dreadful event behind us all the better. I'd say terminate the pregnancy.'

'But *you* wouldn't,' Bill said, rounding on Frances. 'Would you?'

'Speaking purely for myself, no, I couldn't. I can't personally support abortion. But I could for the family – and for Viv. I must confess I have real anxiety about keeping the child in the family.'

'Why? You wouldn't be here.' The words shot out, colder now, accusing.

'Don't let's make this into a personal battle,' Frances interrupted gently. 'I'm not thinking of myself. I'm thinking of all of you. None of you is in a position to bring up a child. None of you really wants to. And it does feel all wrong thinking of Viv pregnant.'

'It does feel different – put this way round, Dad, doesn't it?' Euan turned to address Bill directly. 'We couldn't agree on what Viv would want but it won't affect her. If you think about the whole thing from the family's point of view, then Mum's right. It would be better all round if we could try to put this behind us.'

'A baby would be a constant reminder, dragging you all back to this horror, wouldn't it?' Frances said, looking appealingly at Bill.

In spite of himself Bill was impressed. She was willing to suppress her religious conviction for Viv, for him. And he knew – probably more than the boys – how much loyalty to the tenets of Catholicism meant to her. What had made her change her mind?

'So you *all* think … that's the way to go, now?' he asked slowly. Three heads nodded.

'And you, Bill?' Frances asked quietly.

'You may be right.'

There was a long silence as they all assimilated the conclusion. It was Bill who finally broke it.

'Anything more you want to ask Dr Wilkinson first?'

'Would it be worth asking him – what *he'd* do in this situation?' Frances asked tentatively.

'I was wondering that myself,' Bill nodded, rising to go for the doctor.

'What would I do?' Steven repeated slowly. 'It's always difficult to say because I'm not you and I may have different values and beliefs from yours. But I do have a daughter. And if she were in this situation I think I'd go for terminating the pregnancy. But I must confess that's more about my personal feelings about the crime that's been committed than it is to do with medical facts. And I wouldn't use my choice to try to influence you.'

Fair enough, Bill thought, that's honest. And it was impressive that Steven didn't use any of these opportunities to exert pressure or plead on behalf of The Home.

'Thank you.' Frances and he spoke simultaneously.

It took two more days to decide. Bill gave no outward sign of his internal struggle but Frances' words hammered on his brain relentlessly: *None of you is in a position to bring up this child. None of you really wants to. A baby would be a constant reminder, dragging you back to this horror. You won't help Viv if you crack up yourself.*

Her own willingness to put her personal opinion to one side in the interests of everyone else moved him more than he was prepared to admit. Gradually the wisdom of her comments eroded his resistance and when he next gathered the family together he told them without emotion that he'd heard their strong recommendation and had decided that the majority family view must prevail. No-one interrupted him.

Steven immediately made the necessary arrangements. There must be no further delay, he told them. Viv would be transferred to the local hospital for the short procedure, a nurse from The Home accompanying her and staying with her to ensure her special needs were respected. They'd take every precaution to minimise the effects of physiological stress on her and return her to The Home as quickly as possible.

THIRTEEN

Steven Wilkinson let out his breath slowly. They'd soon have a clue to the rapist's identity. It would then be possible to eliminate the staff from the enquiry. It was incredibly stressful, everyone being under suspicion like this. Just having the CID men around the place – low profile though they said they'd be – had been awkward. Oh, they'd done as promised, muttered vague things about petty theft, just checking security, but he was under no illusions. Plenty of the visitors would be wondering; they'd soon smell a rat.

And several of the ancillary staff had objected – vociferously objected actually – to being interviewed by the police already. It only needed one of them to make his objections public to blow this whole thing wide open. Loyalty to The Home only went so far. And no-one could make them co-operate. OK, they knew it would make the police more suspicious if they didn't but they were quite within their rights to refuse.

The officer who'd interviewed Steven personally had been good. There had been no intimidation, no hint of suspicion. But he could well imagine some of the interviews being a lot less civilised! There were a couple of the chaps who'd give the police a good run for their money. Oh yes. Yes, the sooner it was over, the better. If they all agreed to the saliva swabs, they could soon hold their heads up fearlessly again.

And he had to admit, it would be a relief to have the evidence of the crime removed too. Thank goodness the family had decided for termination. Even the nun! It would have been impossible to have kept a pregnancy hidden from everyone, and how did you explain a long-term patient in a persistent vegetative state being heavily pregnant? The rumours would probably have been as lurid as the reality. Well, that wasn't going to happen now, thankfully. Things could go back to what they'd been five months ago.

As he strode through The Home the sound of drilling and hammering made him shake his head ruefully. Who was he kidding? No, there would now be no return to the old order, the old trust. The CCTV cameras, the security locks the workmen were fitting at this moment, the sight of plain-clothes police and security men wandering in the corridors – they'd all be an ongoing reminder that their safety had been violated.

And there remained the fearful, even if improbable, spectre of a repeat of the crime. If it had happened once could it happen a second time? Would they even know if he did it again – if he already had? How had he gained access to Viv Faraday? And what else had he done? Who else had been a victim? Rhona Archibald? Was this the explanation for these urinary tract infections?

Steven nodded at the heavily draped woman walking demurely along the corridor. The dark eyes dropped immediately as they always did, and she glided past him on her way to visit Room 11, the new admission. The names of these Arabian women were so difficult to remember and for the life of him he couldn't tell one from the other behind those veils or whatever they were called. So far he'd managed to avoid all their names except for the patient they'd just admitted in her own twilight world. And she wouldn't care. Would these ultra-modest women continue to come so freely if they only knew? Would their menfolk let them?

A sudden vivid idea came into his mind. Maybe they should put all the female patients on contraceptives! In spite of his worries he couldn't resist a grin at the cartoon pictures it conjured up. Imagine the face of the Arab patient's possessive husband at the suggestion! Fatima Omar had suffered a massive myocardial infarction and ended up in a persistent vegetative state. It happened. No-one was to blame. Even her husband bowed to the will of Allah. What didn't happen – in polite society anyway – was that such a woman was at risk of becoming pregnant. No amount of interpreting, of explaining Western values and customs, could sanitise that one.

Steven hoped devoutly that the cultural and language divides would prevent the Arabs from ever finding out about the rape. At least now there was every chance they would remain in ignorance, thanks to the courage of the Faradays.

But what of the staff and the aftermath for them? They all knew what had happened. The Home couldn't just eliminate the whole experience as easily as his obstetric colleagues would remove Viv's fetus – even if they were all innocent, as he presumed they were. He had to believe they were. It was unthinkable that anyone who chose this work could so abuse the trust placed in them as to commit so heinous a crime. Unthinkable. Some of them had taken the whole business very hard.

Thank goodness for the stalwarts like Libby Sinclair. She'd volunteered to take a personal responsibility for overseeing the care of the women in Viv's corridor. She was so discreet, so mature about the whole thing. And she was excellent with the relatives. If anyone could inspire their confidence and deflect anxiety it was Libby. It was a relief knowing she was keeping tabs on everything. The only surprise had been that Bill Faraday hadn't ever talked to her about his fears and doubts.

It was harder for the male staff, of course. No-one likes to be associated with the rapist of a vulnerable patient on any factor, even one as ubiquitous as gender. Steven saw it, felt it, wherever he went. Every man in the place was twitchy. The normally placid ones snapped at their partners and colleagues. The habitually brusque ones became volcanoes. Innocuous requests suddenly acquired sinister undertones.

In spite of the care the police took – the men from CID and the Family Protection Unit wore suits; DS Brian Latimer, the officer in charge of the investigation, smiled a lot and did his best to make them feel he was on their side – their very presence made the staff uneasy. What were they looking for? What did they read into what they saw? They were keeping things as low key as possible, holding the press at arm's length, but nobody likes having their private lives probed. Not even the innocent. OK, The Home had to be protected – their jobs along with it – but Dan, Iain, Sandy, George, Alan, all of them hated the way the policemen watched them, the casual way they asked penetrating questions, jumped on words.

And now Steven was about to face them all in the seminar room at one o'clock. Every man-jack of them. Doctors, nurses, assistants, kitchen staff, domestics, every rank, every man. On duty or off they'd been asked to attend all together.

It was an ill-assorted group, perched uncomfortably on the rows of seats, that faced him as he entered the room four minutes late. He'd always been proud of this room with its advanced technology and excellent acoustics. It symbolised success. Holding educational events here had been a useful way to promote their expertise as well as boost the funds. But the occasion he was about to stage today was much more likely to lead to a seepage of staff and bad publicity if anything.

He was grateful for DS Latimer's presence close behind him. Presence was the word too. The sergeant was not only six foot four with a physique to match, but he had an air about him that commanded respect, and a powerful voice that carried without assistance. Now, an imposing figure in a dark navy suit, he stood to one side of the conference desk surveying the men with a direct gaze that seemed to defy anyone to jeopardise his investigation.

The tension was palpable. Steven noticed several of the staff scanning their neighbours surreptitiously, doing a mental tally. A few missing faces certainly. Duncan, one of the senior nurses – well, everybody knew he was off because of a family bereavement. Ernie? The gardener? They said he was looking for another job. No. It *couldn't* be Ernie. Two sandwiches short of a picnic, old Ernie, but wouldn't have what it takes to plan a stunt like this one. Joe from the kitchen ...

Oh yes, he was very well aware of the seething unrest.

He rapped on the table for silence with his pen.

'Thank you all very much for coming. And thank you too for co-operating with the police. I know how unpleasant this whole business is. And what it feels like to be under suspicion – I am too. More than some of you as it happens, given my easy access to these patients.' He could see they weren't reassured by that one. 'I'm as anxious as anyone to get back to normal. And that's why I've asked you to come here all together today.

There's one course of action which might help us to do just that. Something which would allow us all to be eliminated from suspicion.' Now he had their interest. 'It's just a way of ruling each man out. Systematically. So we can get on with what we're here for.' He let that thought percolate. 'How would you all feel about having a DNA test? Just to rule you all out. No-one can pressurise you into it, of course. It'd be entirely voluntary.'

It had helped having Brian Latimer's advice on this. The police could do an enforced sweep if there were reasonable grounds for suspicion within a group like the staff. But in confidence he told Steven they hadn't anything strong enough to go on in this case, and they couldn't just trawl blindly in the hope that something might just come up. But it was self-evident that the staff were high on the list. Who else had such opportunity? Who else knew what they knew about the patients? Who else knew when the visitors left, when the coast was clear, when everyone else was busy, when the female patients were most vulnerable?

'But what motive could any of them possibly have?' Steven had protested. 'I *know* these blokes!'

'Somebody always does know these blokes.' Latimer smiled wryly. 'And they don't need a specific motive against a specific woman. Sex is a powerful drive in itself. And often in these cases it's more a need for power, not even sex, driving these men.'

'Fair enough. But I still can't see any of our staff *raping* anyone. Especially not someone like Vivienne Faraday.'

'OK. Well, of course I hope you're right. But in the meantime there's a sense that everyone is under suspicion until they're proved innocent.'

'So much for British justice – innocent until proven guilty, eh?'

'In this case, it's inevitable. Everyone feels uncomfortable because they know the staff are bound to be seen as prime suspects. And if it wasn't me, then is it him? Or is it him?' Latimer stabbed the air to indicate suspects in two corners.

'So you think it'd help to clear the air to just do a total sweep.'

'You could then get back to normal. Trust each other again. It'd then be all of you together against a common enemy – which feels much stronger.'

'Well, I must say it'll be a relief to get rid of this tension. You can *smell* it everywhere! I'll call a meeting. Put it to them. See how they react.'

One or two of them muttered about their rights, privacy, that sort of thing. But they knew – everyone could see it, DS Latimer didn't need to put it into words – if anyone objected or refused it'd make the others, and especially the police, mighty suspicious.

In the end they grudgingly agreed. The past three weeks of suspicion and doubt had been more than enough.

It was a more delicate matter asking the relatives.

Bill faced Steven Wilkinson and DS Latimer incandescent with rage.

'Hell's bells and buckets of blood! Are you *intentionally* adding insult to injury?'

'No-one thinks you did it, Dad.' Trust Euan to try the calming tone.

'Hogwash! Somebody somewhere must. Otherwise they wouldn't ask.'

He half-listened to the attempts to wrap the unpalatable suggestion up in layers of 'procedure' and 'routine' and 'protection'. But he remained unmoving.

'It's absolutely ludicrous. And I intend to have no part in anything so non-sensical. *Of course* it wasn't a member of the family! Full stop. End of story.'

Bill knew he was far too agitated to be able to sit with Viv. But support for his position came from an unexpected quarter.

He was pacing the garden outside her room when the care assistant, Toby Bernard, approached him tentatively.

'Mr Faraday, excuse me taking liberties. We met – once or twice. You probably won't remember me.'

'I do.' It sounded quelling even to Bill.

'It's just that ... I've just heard. I'm appalled on your behalf.'

'Is nothing sacred in this bloody place?' Bill spat out.

'I'm sorry. I don't mean to intrude ... but we're all involved in this. I just thought you'd like to know ... *somebody* supports you – taking a stand, I mean.'

'Thanks,' Bill tossed at him, continuing to march round and round. 'But it *doesn't* help knowing everybody's yacking about our private affairs.'

Toby fell into step alongside him. 'Oh, we're not. It's not like that. It's just ... well, I'm sorry, I was just passing and I couldn't help overhearing.' You wouldn't have to be that close to have heard the anger, Bill thought fleetingly.

'So some of your colleagues think it could be me too, huhh? Well, to hell with the lot of them.'

'No. Honestly. Nobody thinks you did it.'

'Huhh. That's why they need to test me is it, just for fun? Pull the other one.'

'For what it's worth *I* think it's insulting too. Asking you, I mean.'

'It's bloody intolerable. This on top of everything else.'

'I agree. It's bad enough for all the staff, being under suspicion. It must be ten times worse for you.'

'Hell's bells, she's my *daughter*, for heaven's sake!'

'Exactly. And you've been a father in a million. Who else would be as devoted as you've been all these years? That alone gives you the right to refuse.'

'I intend to! Bloody police. Who the bloody hell do they think they are?'

'It's my belief they haven't a clue where to start looking so they're just doing this to show they're doing something,' Toby said, soothingly.

'Wasting time too,' Bill ground out. 'They should be out there catching the animal who did this unspeakable thing.'

'I just wanted to say, there's a lot of support for you. Amongst the staff. Only you might not feel it – we're not supposed to be talking about this case or anything. I just thought you might misunderstand everybody's silence.'

Bill nodded stiffly.

'Times you feel everybody's looking at you sideways.'

'Only in sympathy. Because we care.'

'Pity the bloody police don't care then.'

'They can't make you,' Toby said quietly.

'Too right they can't.'

It helped marginally, knowing there was support for his position, knowing the evasion, the silence, was dictated. But Bill found it impossible to settle into anything resembling normality. His reading to Viv was perfunctory and most of the time he sat morosely staring into space.

Privately both Kevin and Euan advised their father to take the line of least resistance. This was no time to be taking a high moral position, they said. The sooner this whole thing was cleared up the better. Even Felicity tried to persuade him.

'Imagine if news of this did leak out,' she coaxed. 'And it might. With all these policemen involved. So many people already knowing about it. It'd only take one visitor to The Home overhearing something. The press would be sniffing around like bloodhounds, wouldn't they?'

'I know. Don't think I haven't worried about them too! Every day I go to see Viv I'm half-expecting to find them camped on the lawn.' Bill passed a weary hand across his eyes.

'It'd only take one little chance comment – just idle speculation, of course,' Felicity said, reducing the idea with the decreasing gap between her fingers and thumb. 'Something about the incidence of rapes that are carried out by men known to the victim, maybe. Just an apparently innocent, *little* fact. That's all it would take to start people speculating. And that would be enough to set minds ticking, tongues wagging. And then the gutter press – they'd drop more explicit hints. That's how nasty ideas seep out. You know what damage can be done just by innuendo.'

Bill heard. He gritted his teeth. Oh, he knew all right.

'So wouldn't it be best to have concrete proof? So the police can say, categorically, it wasn't any of the staff, it wasn't anyone in the family. Strangle the ideas at birth.'

'It's not that simple,' Bill repeated.

'The more you object, the more you make them think you're covering something up.' Kevin was notching up the pressure. 'I just don't understand what your objection is. You don't … you *can't* imagine Euan or I might be guilty – do you?'

'Of course not! It's the principle of the thing. How dare they even *think* it?'

'But the police don't know us, do they? They're dealing with families who *do* do this kind of thing. And most of them probably seem pretty ordinary on the face of it too.'

'But it's obvious *we* wouldn't. It's an insult. They can't *possibly* think any one of us'd do something ... something so ... unspeakable!'

Geoff, too, was cautious when Bill sought advice on his legal position, two days after the initial suggestion.

'I'm not sure that's really the question here, Bill. Of course I understand your revulsion. But I don't think anyone seriously suspects you. It's just that, well, where do the police start looking in a case like this? I think of it in a sort of list of groups. You know – the staff, the family, regular visitors, tradesmen, other visitors ... down through the ranks. The more groups you can eliminate completely the better, in a way. From their point of view.'

'But they *can* eliminate the family, without any work at all. None of us – absolutely no question – would ever do anything to hurt Viv. No way.'

'You know that. And I'm sure you're right. But the police can't be a hundred per cent certain, in all fairness, can they? They're trained to be suspicious of everybody. And hundreds of perfectly respectable families have black sheep in them. Or white sheep that once in a while stray onto the wrong side of the path. You know? Not that I'm suggesting that's the case in your family,' Geoff rushed on hastily. 'I don't think it for a minute. But the police can't just trust people simply on the basis that they seem like nice, decent, law-abiding folk.'

'Huhh!'

'Well. I must admit I'd rather welcome somebody testing *me* just so I know no-one's even wondering whether I did it.'

Bill shot him a sudden alert look. Geoff kept talking.

'And I guess the police are only doing their job. Much as I've had cause to curse them often enough in my years in court! But DS Latimer's probably got his superiors breathing down his neck, demanding proof of activity. "How can you be sure it's not the family, Latimer?" "No, you can't have extra resources to trawl six months worth of visitors to The Home, when the answer might be right under your nose." That kind of thing. Perfectly innocent reasons for Latimer suggesting this as a kind of second stage of the process. Check all the staff, check the family. Then spread the net wider.'

'I should have known a lawyer would side with the police,' Bill snorted and stomped off.

It became increasingly hard to resist DS Latimer's attempts at persuasion. Bill felt the mounting surveillance. It was unnerving. The policeman popped up at unexpected times, asking banal questions, questions which seemed to have no relevance to anything. Bill found himself furtively scanning the corridor, the car park, Cath's Canteen, dreading the sight of that close-cropped ginger head towering above everyone else. And always when he couldn't avoid a meeting, Latimer's eyes were vigilant, on the alert for Bill knew not what. He started to feel haunted.

The next stage was open challenge.

'You seem rattled about something, Mr Faraday.'

'Wouldn't you be rattled if your daughter had been raped and someone accused you of doing it?'

'No-one's accusing you. We're wanting to help you exonerate yourself.'

'I don't need exoneration. I didn't do it.'

'Are you trying to protect your sons? D'you suspect them?'

'Of course not.'

'They're both willing to give samples. They don't seem as if *they* have anything to hide.'

So Latimer thought he was hiding something. Bill said nothing.

Latimer leaned back in his chair, hooking his fingers into the belt at his waist, his eyes narrowing but unrelenting in their watchfulness.

'Mr Faraday, I'm considering applying for a warrant to test you anyway.'

'I have rights. You can't make me!' Bill ground out.

'I could actually,' Latimer said. 'I don't know why you're so opposed to being tested. But the more you refuse the more you make me ask questions. Why would you *not* want us to test you, if you know you're innocent and you believe your sons are too? You're just putting more and more doubts in my head.'

'Of course we're innocent. That's why there's no point in testing us.'

'Well, you haven't convinced me. So I'm thinking of getting a warrant from the Sheriff for DNA samples to be taken from all of you.'

'No-one can make me.' Was his bullish tone enough? Did his internal conflict show?

'They can actually, I'm afraid. The Sheriff has the power to override a family objection. And if I think you might be guilty, make no mistake, sir, I shall apply to the Sheriff for that warrant.'

Bill glared at him.

'Of course, I'd rather you agreed voluntarily,' Latimer said more gently. 'This has been a most unpleasant and upsetting experience for you all, I know. And it's not my intention to add to the distress. Only you're not leaving me much option.'

'You don't really believe I'm guilty, do you?' Bill threw at him.

'I'd like you to help me not to believe it, sir.'

There was a long silence. Bill leaned with his arms on his knees, playing with the nail on his forefinger. Without looking up, he said hesitantly, 'If you do the test … is the information … confidential?'

88

'Yeees. But presumably you're happy to have people know you're innocent?'

Bill nodded, still tearing at his nail. He felt the eyes boring into him.

'So you just tell us we're not under suspicion?'

'Yes. That's all it's for.'

'Nothing else?'

'Nothing else.'

'OK. No point in wasting the Sheriff's time. Do it. And then for goodness sake get on with the real business of finding this villain.'

Bill rose abruptly and left the room without looking at DS Latimer.

His shoulders slumped as he walked down the corridor. He felt suddenly drained of energy. This business of giving consent to things just showed how powerless people were when it came to the crunch. The law could override him as if he were no more capable of deciding than Viv. Somewhere deep inside did she too feel this sense of smallness, of insignificance, of being at the mercy of forces much more merciless, much less sensitive than their personal wills?

Goodness knows what DS Latimer was thinking. But those gimlet eyes would soon be trained on visitors, tradesmen, other men not connected with their family. His own seeming intransigence would soon be forgotten.

FOURTEEN

On the day Viv's pregnancy was terminated, Bill sat beside her for two hours beforehand.

Predicting churning emotions, he took evasive action. He started to read her a new book. He chose *Villette* by Charlotte Brontë, for no good reason except that he'd found Frances' copy lying on a shelf in Viv's old bedroom. Bill had no idea whether Viv had read it but on the fly-leaf in childish handwriting it said: *To Fran from Tom. Happy Birthday.* An early present from her brother. Years ago. It felt right keeping this day a family affair.

It was Bill who'd suggested – gently as it happened – that Frances should return to her convent. Better for her not to be associated with this act, he'd said. He'd noticed for the first time the lines in her pale face, the bleakness of her eyes, but resisted the sudden impulse to reach out to comfort. It felt awkward, inappropriate, to be hugging a nun. So he'd just touched her arm fleetingly, hoping his look conveyed something of his feelings.

Now, today, he found himself wishing she were here with him, sharing the anxiety.

It was a relief to see Libby Sinclair on duty. She'd been allocated to Viv for the whole day, she assured him. She'd be there in the ambulance, during the 'procedure', attending to her afterwards. They were handling things as sensitively as they could, Bill knew, keeping those involved to a minimum, but nothing could take away the enormity of what was actually being done. If Viv only knew … !

His superficial composure held until he watched them wheel her back into her room in The Home. It was over. To all outward appearances things were as they had been. He saw the look of compassion on Libby's face as she leant over the bed, smoothing back the damp hair.

The overwhelming surge of emotion hit him foursquare. Blindly he groped his way outside. Bitter tears fell unchecked as he paced the paths, lost to all but his own pain.

The light hand under his elbow took him by surprise. He jerked away instinctively.

'It's only me, Bill. I thought you might need a sympathetic ear to rage into,' Geoff said.

'Don't think your ears could take what I might let fly,' Bill responded gruffly, dashing a hand across his eyes.

'Try me. Not a lot I haven't heard.'

Bill shook his head.

'Thanks, but this is … I don't know … too horrendous for words.'

'Viv come through it OK?'

'So far. Shouldn't be any problems – healthwise, they say.'

'Thank God for that.'

'It's the only shred of comfort in this whole bloody awful mess. That she isn't suffering.'

'But you're feeling her pain as well as your own.'

'Never mind about me. It's what's happened to her that freaks me out. I just can't …' Emotion choked the words.

'I know. It makes *me* want to do something violent just thinking about it. I can't begin to imagine what it's doing to you.'

'They've got to find this swine. They've *got* to. But so help me, don't let him come anywhere near me!' Bill's fists and jaw clenched simultaneously.

'No judge in the country'd be lenient on this one.'

'That's something I wanted to ask you. If it does come to court …'

'*When* it does. You've got to hang onto that, Bill. They won't let this one go. Believe me. Latimer and his lot'll never drop this one.'

It was true. And Bill knew how persistent DS Latimer could be.

'These cases get right under their skin. They'll move heaven and earth to find this bastard. And now they'll have proof.'

Bill shuddered. That's all his grandchild was now – a source of DNA.

'But who knows what else'll happen before they do catch him,' he said, through stiff lips.

'Not likely to try this stunt again – not here. Not with everyone on the alert.'

'Aren't you worried about Rhona, then?' Bill shot Geoff a sideways look without breaking stride.

'Well, we'd be fools not to feel a bit anxious. But I honestly think she's probably safer here than anywhere else at this moment. What with the staff on the watch, the police in and out, all the extra security. I mean it'd take a lunatic to think he'd get away with it a second time, don't you think?'

'Case of lightning not striking twice, and all that, you mean?'

'Something like that.'

'Well, I shan't rest easy till this maniac's behind bars.'

'Where he'll get a helluva reception. Even the criminal fraternity take a dim view of blokes who abuse vulnerable girls.'

'Good. Can't be too hellish as far as I'm concerned. Frances – you know, Viv's mother – reckons I shan't get over this as long as I hate the beast who did it, but it's going to take me a lifetime to forgive anybody who could sink this low.'

'It's natural – just at first anyway. If you want a sounding board, just say the word. I shan't tell you to count your blessings!'

'Thanks. You're a mate,' Bill mumbled gruffly.

There was a long silence punctuated only by the sounds of their tramping feet. It was Geoff who eventually broke it.

'You were going to ask me something – before we were sidetracked?'

'In court … will they, you know, go into all the ins and outs of the family – ours, I mean?' Bill spoke straight at the ground, never once raising his eyes. 'Will they splurge it all in the papers, make it all grubby? You know what I mean.'

'I do indeed. Hopefully not. Get yourself a good lawyer, make sure he understands about Viv. Get him to keep the whole thing tight. It's up to you of course, I'm still willing, but you might have your own reasons for going to somebody else. I shan't be offended. It's your choice. Whoever you feel most comfortable with. Even so, I'd be happy to spell it out to the person you do go for. I could at least make sure they know from the inside what this whole thing feels like. Knowing about the persistent vegetative state and a bit about what it does to you.'

'I appreciate that. Thanks, Geoff. Sorry not to have said anything before. Haven't been able to think beyond today. But we will have to face the next bit now. And I can't think of anybody I'd rather have fighting our corner than you.'

Before Geoff could reply they saw Steven Wilkinson advancing through the garden. Geoff slipped discreetly away.

'Mr Faraday, how're you coping?' Steven asked solicitously.

Bill stopped pacing and stood tensely in front of the doctor.

'Just about.'

'I thought it might help to hear something about the medical side. I've just had the Infirmary on the phone.'

'No details,' Bill interrupted sharply, putting up a hand to ward off disclosure.

Steven nodded. 'Fair enough. But as far as they're concerned everything went smoothly. No medical complications. And Viv seems to be making a perfectly straightforward recovery. No reason to think she won't be back to normal very soon.'

'Thanks. And thank you, too, for – well, you know, having Libby there. Keeping it all as quiet as you could. I appreciate it,' Bill said gruffly.

'It's the least we could do. And Libby's the soul of discretion. You need have no qualms there.'

'Oh, I know that. And I must say I've been impressed. You've got some good people here. I know I've been a bit critical at times but since this happened – well, it puts a different light on things.'

'That's good of you. I'll pass the message on.'

'Even blokes who were under suspicion themselves had the courage to come and speak to me. Show their sympathy. That takes guts.'

'That's nice to hear. They're a good bunch on the whole. Hearts in the right place. Nice to know they did, all the same.'

It helped being able to pass on Bill's commendation to the staff at a time when everyone was in suspense waiting for the test results. Steven spent extra time going round The Home letting them know he understood their tension. But in spite of his inner conviction he found he was dreading the phone call.

When it finally came it was an anticlimax. Everyone was cleared. Stephen watched with a wry smile the men squaring their shoulders, lifting their heads again.

Bill saw his chance when he saw Toby Bernard standing talking to Steven in the main corridor.

'Excuse me, may I interrupt? This is one of the young men who was particularly kind – before.'

'Nice to hear that, Toby. Mr Faraday was telling me about people being good to him.'

Toby looked embarrassed. 'Only doing my job.'

'That's as may be. But there's the job, and the job done sensitively. I didn't take up your offer to talk but I appreciated it nonetheless,' Bill said.

'It was nothing,' Toby replied, watching his foot scuffing the carpet.

'I'm pleased to hear you're all in the clear. I know how much it was getting to everybody.'

'Thanks.' Toby walked quickly away.

'Strange young man. I can't quite get his measure. But that was kind of you, Mr Faraday.' Steven watched the retreating figure turn a corner out of sight. 'A bit of appreciation always helps.'

'He's proud of what you all do here. Said so earlier. Proud to be part of a place with such a reputation for excellence.'

'Did he say that? Mmmmm.'

'Yes. And I guess it made me feel I haven't appreciated it always as I should.'

'Oh, we aren't always excellent. Doesn't do us any harm to get the occasional critical comment. But I think this last little while has made us all sit up and take stock. Let's just hope that in time we can all start to move forward again.'

Bill shrugged and walked on to Viv's room. It felt like a vain hope as far as he was concerned right now.

No-one was surprised when the Faraday men were all proven demonstrably innocent of the crime of rape.

When the call from the lab came for DS Latimer, he was standing in Steven Wilkinson's office explaining to the doctor why it simply wasn't possible to mount a constant watch on The Home.

'Hang on a mo, Doreen,' he said, covering the mouthpiece with his hand. 'Sorry, Dr Wilkinson. By all means carry on. I know you've got clinical stuff to attend to. Don't let me detain you. I'll just take this call and then I'll be off. See myself out.'

He watched the doctor's retreating figure before removing his hand.

'OK, Doreen. I'm on my own. What news?'

As he listened he absent-mindedly picked up a paperweight with a fishing fly trapped inside the glass. He turned the glass ball idly, watching the changing perspectives of the intricate construction.

His attention was suddenly arrested. Uncharacteristically the paperweight was abandoned far from the papers it had originally secured. He reached for a pen from his inside pocket, snapped open his notepad. He automatically doodled around the two words he'd written on the top page.

'You sure? ... No possibility of the test being wrong?'

He underlined the words sharply, leaving score marks four pages underneath.

'OK, just leave it with me. Say nothing.'

He sank down into the swivel chair behind the desk. Phewww! What a turn-up for the books! Poor beggar. That explained a lot. Seemed like a good bloke too. Devoted to Viv. He'd given up at least ten years of his life to her. Positively obsessive about the girl. Did he know? Or did he just suspect? Would he have done all that if he'd known for sure? Who'd have thought it? And the mother a nun too! Presumably *she* knew. Well, what she did in her own life was her business. Maybe she'd become a nun just because she *did* know.

But Bill Faraday had made it plain. His consent was conditional on the results being confidential. If he had suspicions he didn't want them confirmed. No, no-one else would know, he'd make sure of that. It was simply a matter of confirmed innocence. Case closed.

FIFTEEN

It was five days later that Bill took the phone call. He didn't recognise the cultured voice.

'May I speak to Frances, please?'

'She's not here.'

'Could you tell her Charles rang?'

'She doesn't live here.'

'I'm sorry. Have I got the wrong number? Is that Mr Faraday?'

'Yes.'

'But there isn't a Frances living at this address?'

'No.'

'I'm so sorry. I do apologise for disturbing you.'

It had never occurred to Frances that Charles would attempt to find her, or that he would dare ring Bill's number. As far as she was aware he knew nothing of her private circumstances.

It was part of the attraction at the time – the air of mystery, the sense of free floating in space, unanchored by complicating ties – neither of them knowing much about their other lives, just savouring the tiny fraction of their week they shared with each other. The magical quality of something completely separate from the mundane routines, the duties and responsibilities.

She was four weeks short of her thirtieth birthday when she'd first met Charles. He'd told her later about the things that had captivated him – her air of other-worldliness, her infectious giggle, the way the thick swathe of dark hair fell forwards over her face when she moved, how she glanced around it tantalisingly rather than pinning it back. And he'd been intrigued by her ability to keep her own counsel.

She'd warmed to his gentle teasing and blossomed under his admiration. But even at her most abandoned she had made sure she remained an enigma to him. She'd had her own reasons for not letting him into her inner sanctum. On Thursday evenings she became a free independent spirit. She guarded jealously that one precious escape route. It wasn't a deliberate attempt to be provocatively mysterious; it was simply self-defence. The reality was that she was bored, resentful, and fast losing both self-esteem and confidence. Kevin and Euan kept her busy during the day but she was feeling increasingly devoid of intellectual stimulation. It was Bill who suggested the German evening classes.

'You've always had a yen to be fluent in a foreign language, haven't you?' he reasoned. 'This could be your chance. Going to classes, practising regularly, the discipline of going out each week, it'll help you stick at it. It'll be more fun if you actually speak it with other people. You'll soon be fluent if you have to use it. You can practise your accent on the kids during the day; I'll help you with the vocab if you like. Try it. You can't lose. I'll keep whatever evening it is free to be with the boys. Go on! It'll do you good, doing something for yourself for a change.'

It had been tough at first. Did having children squeeze liquid into your brain, turn the cogs rusty? But gradually endless repetition drove the basics firmly between the cracks where they lodged securely. She ventured more. It was confirming when she could have rudimentary conversations with her fellow students, about the weather, shopping, eating out. Although she couldn't ever imagine saying things like, 'I'd like a window seat, please,' or 'Twelve eggs, five pomegranates, two cups of white coffee with one lump of sugar, and a loaf of brown bread, if you please,' in real life.

When she was first paired with Charles Wynne-Hope she frowned in concentration as she asked in staccato bursts for a list of nine things. Three boxes of dark chocolates, four bags of brown sugar, a kilo of eating apples, two bags of freshly ground coffee, one packet of table salt, two sachets of salad dressing, a loaf of rye bread, a quarter of a kilo of strong cheese, and two cartons of full-fat cream, please. The creased brow vanished instantly when he sang, 'And a partridge in a pear tree!'

She warmed to him even more when he confessed, 'Haven't a clue what you need but as far as I'm concerned you can have the lot!' He was disarmingly frank about his own shortcomings with the language, and Frances discovered that joking about her deficiencies too took the sensitivity out of failure.

She became more adventurous when she was less afraid of showing herself up. It also felt good when he gave her an admiring look for using a new phrase or word. So good that she returned the compliment. It made sense to stay partnered with someone whom she could trust to be supportive.

By week twelve they had learned enough to be given a more interesting exercise. Using only German words they knew already they were to find ways of asking each other questions about themselves. Any lapses into English were scored against them. Frances felt frustrated. She had elected to be the first questioner and she was determined to spin it out so there was no time left for him to probe her life. But she found her limited vocabulary hindered her from discovering much about his either. She resolved to do more revision at home. He did his best to assist her, using extravagant gestures and expressions to augment his own inadequate repertoire, diverting her intensity into a smile.

His invitation to go for a coffee after the session seemed like a natural corollary, a chance to flesh out the rudiments she had acquired. The fact that it was delivered in German, and that he whispered under his breath, 'But I forbid you to utter a single syllable in this infernal language once we get out of here!' made it a harmless extension of their collaboration.

It felt strange at first, the freedom to say whatever they wanted to. Frances felt unaccountably shy. But Charles relieved the tension by doing a splendidly accurate caricature of their teacher, Frau Shröeder, a stout German lady from Heidelberg who had plenty of mannerisms which cried out for such treatment. It was harmless. Superficial. Frances wanted superficial. She didn't want to tell this man with his curiously intense dark blue eyes about what her life was really like. She wanted him to think her carefree, confident, at ease with him because secure in her other life. It would only change things if he knew how jaded, how hemmed in she felt by the sheer domesticity of her everyday life, how one evening out at a German class was the highlight of her social calendar.

She just wanted to feel the total absence of demands on her. She didn't want to have to think of stimulating things to say. How long was it since she'd had anything interesting to talk about? Charles wouldn't want to hear about her boring life. How she resented putting her teaching career on hold. How she got mad inside with Bill, free to pursue his career as an architect. How she hated the piles of his drawings that littered the dining-room table night after night. How she had stopped helping him with the colouring and shading, stopped phoning to remind him of appointments he'd been too busy to pencil into his diary, stopped going to the receptions which marked the successful completion of his projects.

She didn't want to dwell on it herself, never mind share it with a stranger. Especially an attractive, attentive stranger who made her laugh. So different from Bill. How long was it since *Bill* had laughed with her? How long since *he'd* sensed her insecurity, reached out to help her, encouraged her? How long since *he'd* spontaneously taken her out – even for a coffee? How long since *he'd* looked at her admiringly as Charles was doing right now? No, Bill hardly glanced in her direction these days. Just the effort of making conversation was too exhausting when you knew it would only invite a sharp retort. Life was more bearable if you just got on with the tasks of keeping the house in order, bringing up the boys, putting meals on the table.

But it was a mistake. Going for even a coffee was a step too far. She soon made her excuses and left. Good thing she had the car. She must remember that: always take the car so you can't accept a lift. And stay inside that room in the community school with its prescribed boundaries of syntax, conjugation and declension, idioms and accents. It was too dangerous to stray outside the rules of Thursday evenings. Just because a man made it obvious he was attracted to her didn't mean she could start to blur the lines between the fantasy and reality. It wasn't part of the escape to run into a different trap.

If he thought her steadfast refusal to be drawn into personal disclosures strange, Charles gave no indication that he did so. His warm smile continued to show her how pleased he was to see her again, he continued to choose her as his language partner, and he continued to make her laugh.

When Frau Shröeder suggested a weekend trip to Frankfurt to visit the Christmas markets there was an instant hum of excitement in the class. Frances turned to Charles with sparkling eyes.

'I've always wanted to do that,' she breathed.

'With my German I'd probably return with three French hens and two turtle doves instead of the gingerbread biscuits and the candles I really wanted,' he whispered back with a grin.

Bill raised no objections to her going; the boys would be fine with their grandparents for a couple of days. He told her again how good it was to see her happier, a person in her own right. He was glad he'd thought of the German classes.

Frankfurt just before Christmas was every bit as magical as Frances had imagined. The fact that Charles was there too was a bonus. Up until the week before she hadn't known if he was going. For some inexplicable reason she couldn't ask outright. But it was good to have someone to explore with, someone to share the excitement. They spoke in German most of the time, coining ridiculous words when their knowledge failed them, laughing together at their mistakes.

The crowds seething around the Christmas stalls were dense and determined. Charles pulled her hand through his arm and clamped her close to him as he said in her ear, 'For goodness sake don't lose me here! My German would probably put me in jail. I'm depending on you to give me credibility.'

Not waiting for an answer he surged forward with her towards the wooden ornaments he was bent on purchasing. In spite of his pleading, she refused to ask for the exquisitely crafted angel hanging out of the reach of damaging hands, behind the vendor in the Santa hat. No, she insisted, he must try. OK, but he'd practise on her first. He stood close to her, looking into her eyes as he rehearsed the request, twice having to look up the word for 'box' in his phrasebook.

'Brilliant!' she cried, clapping her hands, when the tree decoration was safely packaged and in his hands. 'Spoken like a native.'

'Given me a regular rush to the head!' he grinned. 'Let's go shopping!'

Essential negotiations successfully accomplished, they finally allowed themselves to seek their reward: Glühwein sipped from thick glasses as they huddled close together in the cold of December, their breath mingling with the steam and the heady aroma of the spices.

'We've certainly earned this!' Charles said, raising his glass in salute.

'It's like fairyland, isn't it?' Frances said softly, her eyes scanning the sparkling lights, the frosted roofs, the tinkling carousels.

'And you look as if all your Christmasses have come at once,' he teased.

'I'm a real kid about Christmas. I love it. And I've always wanted to do this,' she said, watching a noisy exchange at the nearby stall.

When he didn't speak, she turned back to him. The movement made her lurch suddenly. She instinctively put out a hand to steady herself, gripping his coat sleeve for a moment.

'Wow. This wine is going straight to my head!'

The expression in his eyes stopped her dead. She removed her hand quickly, dropping her gaze to her glass, feeling the warmth steal into her cheeks.

'I like to see you so happy' was all he said.

'Well, I think Frau Shröeder would be pleased with us,' she retorted quickly, her gesture sweeping their parcels. 'Not a French hen in sight!'

'And not a porter in sight either! How about we finish shopping and go back to the hotel to drop this lot before we venture further afield?'

It made sense.

They wandered slowly along the river, sat silently side by side in the spendour of the Gothic cathedral listening to the solemnity of Bach and Handel resonating through the arches, and tiptoed through other medieval, Renaissance and Baroque churches the city boasted.

They discovered a shared interest in history. Both were much more fascinated by the reconstructed fourteenth-century houses and Goethe's birthplace than by the colossal modern financial buildings.

They ate lunch on the move to save time but the hours soon passed and they had to run to fit in a last visit to the market stalls, where they lingered over a collection of quaint figures made out of twisted metal, polished copper, nuts and bolts. Charles chose a model called 'The Cellist'. Frances refrained from enquiring who it was for, and while he transacted the purchase she drank in the magic of her surroundings, the black silhouette of the Nikolai Church a proud backdrop for the illuminated booths and excited shoppers.

Occasionally throughout the day they had caught sight of other members of their group, but not until they all met up again for dinner at eight did they pause to compare their successes with the language, and share their worst faux pas. Even then, duty done, Charles guided Frances to a table for two lit by a single white candle. They were strangely silent amidst the ebbing and flowing of the surrounding conversations.

Intensely aware of Charles' scrutiny, Frances was glad she'd brought her favourite mulberry dress which enhanced the creaminess of her skin. She was grateful too for the protection of the veil of hair hanging over her cheek.

'What are you thinking, Fran?' he asked softly, leaning across the table towards her. Something somewhere deep down inside her melted. It was new today. Fran. Fran in Frankfurt. Only her brother had ever called her Fran before.

'Is this really me? Here in Frankfurt – in this magical place – is this my Thursday evening self or my other self? Who am I today? Tonight?'

'And is your other self so different from your Thursday evening self?'

'Oh yes.'

'Do you want to tell me about your other self?'

She shook her head.

'Well, your Thursday evening self is lovely. That's enough for me.'

'Do you believe we can be different people?' she asked, turning her glass so that the wine swirled rhythmically.

'I certainly do. I'm a different person at the hospital from the one I am at home. I'm different in a social setting from a professional one. I'm different with you compared with anyone else.'

Her eyes dropped before his again. She focused on her fingers playing with the stem of the glass.

'I don't speak appalling German to anyone else!' he said lightly.

She smiled.

'Your German's improving enormously. I like to hear you saying things – sort of carefully and deliberately.'

'If it *is* improving, it's thanks to you. You've made it fun.'

'It was good, wasn't it, trying it out for real today? And nobody asked us to repeat what we said. We got by with it.'

'And we got the *right* things. The worst bit was when they jabbered something back and I didn't understand a word they said!'

The moment had passed. They were back in the comfort zone.

After the meal it was Frances who made the suggestion of going out to see the city at night.

'Good idea. May I join you? I'll never sleep with all this rich food lying heavily in my stomach. A good shakedown is just what it needs,' Charles said.

It was a crisp dry night.

'I just want to saturate myself with the sights and sounds and smells of it all so I remember it for ever,' Frances breathed as they set out, wrapped in thick coats, collars turned up against the plummeting temperatures, hands deep in their pockets.

'Until you come again.'

'I won't come again,' she said with finality.

They were walking slowly along looking up at the towering twin skyscrapers of the Deutsche Bank when it happened.

'You can see why they nickname it Mainhattan, can't you?' Charles said close to her ear.

Next moment there was a blur of movement and a screech of brakes as the cyclist saw them just too late. The wheels skidded, one knee scraping the pavement, before he leapt to safety. He hopped around on one foot clutching his knee. The tyres spun wildly.

Charles was back on his feet, instantly at the boy's side.

'I'm a doctor. Let me see.'

The boy backed away, jabbering something incomprehensible, shaking his head.

In carefully constructed sentences Charles tried again, this time in German. 'My name is Charles. I am a doctor. I come from Scotland. Please speak more slowly.' (That was one phrase he had off pat!) 'Tell me where it hurts. Please, let me see. I am a doctor for children.'

The boy protested that he was fine. Charles checked his leg anyway, smiling his agreement, apologising for having scared him. Man and boy, together they examined the bicycle. No damage beyond a bent light. Smart bike, Charles said. The boy clicked his heels, bowing slightly first to Frances, then to Charles, before mounting and riding off into the night.

Frances looked at Charles in amazement.

'Well done! You were fantastic!'

'Phwo,' he dismissed it with a lift of his hands reminiscent of Frau Shröeder. 'Eet eez nossing. Ve are – how do you say? – as natives, nein?'

'Fast approaching,' she laughed.

His face changed to one of feigned anxiety as he peered in different directions.

'But theez ez a place wiz grrreat dangurrrr, 'idden around ze corner. You must stay *vaairry* close wiz me.' He threw an arm around her in an exaggerated gesture and pulled her against his side.

'More Hercule Poirot than Gudrun Shröeder but hey, nobody's deducting points now!'

It felt good, close to him.

From the Iron Bridge they looked across at the city sparkling in the frosty air. They were standing side by side, not touching, not speaking.

She held her breath. Then took shallow snatches of the laden air.

With one easy movement he turned her to face him. His eyes were shadowed in the darkness enclosing them, his fingers under her chin tilted hers into the light. She willed herself not to blink.

'Fran. Is this part of the magic?'

She let her unwavering gaze answer for her.

His lips whispered over hers. She leaned against him, feeling his arms tightening about her, his quickened breath warm against her neck. His face felt cold to her touch. Feeling her trembling, he wrapped his coat around them both, drawing her into an embrace they had both known was inevitable.

It was their last morning in Germany. As she lay against the white pillows in her room, feeling his fingers softly tracing the line of her shoulder, she eventually broke the silence.

'Charles, you know this is just my Thursday evening self.'

'With a sprinkling of Christmas magic. I know.'

She had to make it explicit. But he'd known anyway. Later today they would return to their normal everyday lives. Next Thursday they would meet again, tentatively try out new words, new phrases, laugh at their mistakes.

And Frankfurt would be a magical memory.

It was easier than she'd expected. She used the excuse of unwrapping her purchases to avoid looking at Bill while she told him about the weekend. His responses were gratifying.

He exclaimed over the exquisite craftsmanship of the Christmas carousel; he couldn't see her withdraw into a secret world as they watched the wooden shepherds twirling unceasingly round the stable to the tune of 'Silent Night, Holy Night'. He fingered the polished and painted wooden tree ornaments – stars, bells, quaint elf-like figures – as if he too felt the magic. He didn't know that her imagination saw other fingers tracing patterns, marvelling at the magic of touch.

She played the carousel over and over again until Bill cried out for a break. Kevin and Euan clamoured for more stories of the fairytale land Mummy had visited where all these special gifts had been made, gifts they must always touch gently.

She was three months pregnant before she told Bill. She needed time.

He held her tightly to his chest and told her that it was a good omen, the start of a better phase in their lives. This new little shared person would bring them closer again.

When it turned out to be a girl Bill was overjoyed. She knew he had dreamed of a daughter. Vivienne Elizabeth was a fulfilment of all his hopes. But for Frances the birth signalled the start of a descent into depression which robbed her of her bloom and energy. It was Bill again who suggested she return to her German class. He hadn't understood why she'd stopped going when the pregnancy started to show.

Charles wouldn't have understood her sudden absence either. She'd attended faithfully up to the end of the Spring term. They'd laughed together, practised together just as before. But she'd given him no hint of her intention not to return after the Easter break. No explanation, no warning, she just vanished. It was better that way. Better that Frau Shröeder didn't know either, that way she couldn't divulge information.

Now Bill was right, she told herself, she should give it a go again. It was almost December – a year on from Frankfurt.

Charles made only one allusion to her absence: 'I've missed you, Fran. You OK? You look tired.'

'I'm OK.'

She had to work hard to catch up on the work she'd missed. And Herr

Kaiser had taken over this next level. He had different methods. He was more didactic. There was less paired work, more group activity. And Frances had to miss many weeks, Thursday evenings when Bill was away, or the boys were sick, or the baby needed her. In the end it was too much of a struggle to keep up.

SIXTEEN

On the surface, normality had been restored at The Home. Even the new security measures ceased to raise eyebrows, and simply became part of the routine.

But for Bill and Geoff another change marked further disruption. When the newest Saudi patient, Fatima Omar, was moved into the room beside Rhona's, things were no longer as they had been. The staff explained it made sense to have the three women in a persistent vegetative state all in the same area. Bill sympathised with that. Indeed, even before the rape, he and Geoff had found it helpful to compare notes occasionally, to share the frustration, commiserate over an occasional coffee. Since Viv's rape it had been good to have Geoff close by, discreetly available.

But there was no sharing with Fatima's visitors. They were a tight-knit group who looked for no solace outside their own ranks. And they became a force to be reckoned with, a source of some irritation in themselves. The corridor became a busy thoroughfare. The black draped figures circled and hovered, flitted in and out of the room, from early morning till late evening. Sometimes it looked as if the entire family was in attendance. Usually they closed the door to the patient's own room but the noise in the communal areas at times threatened Bill's patience and Geoff's temper. The voices were shrill, excitable and incomprehensible.

The staff placed signs strategically, asking for quiet. The sound of women hushing excited children became simply a different kind of annoyance.

In the end Alison Reed was forced to intervene, requesting they limit their number to no more than three at a time, and refrain from talking outside the room if possible. After that it was not unusual to see up to ten swirling figures coalescing out in the garden or in the waiting room, awaiting their turn with Fatima.

Geoff and Bill marvelled together at the family ties which kept these heavily guarded women attending day after day. Had they nothing else to do? How many of them were there? It was impossible to know. They all looked the same. And they made Viv and Rhona look underprivileged in the paucity of visitors they received.

The men in the group were punctiliously polite but made it crystal clear that Geoff and Bill should make no attempt to speak to any of their women folk. Their fierce gestures and the clipped precision of their voices were intimidating enough; no second warning was required. Bill and Geoff kept themselves to the confines of the rooms Viv and Rhona occupied. Was it their imagination, or did even the staff seem to attend less frequently?

When Geoff received the first note he was totally unprepared for it. It was unusual to have messages addressed to him at The Home but occasionally the staff left one if they needed to see him about Rhona, or to seek his permission for something, or if she needed more supplies of clothes or toiletries.

The plain brown envelope was propped against the vase on Rhona's bedside cabinet. It was addressed to MR GEOFFREY ARCHIBALD. Typed. Unexceptional.

Inside was a single plain A4 sheet of paper. The irregular letters caught him by surprise. They looked like something out of a cheap story. Letters cut out of newspapers, magazines. Awkwardly assembled. Different fonts, different sizes. Capitals, lower case. Not even properly aligned. At first it was like some impersonal exercise. His eyes just scanned the composition.

WHERE WERE YOU WHEN I WAS ENJOYING YOUR WIFE?

Then the words engaged with his brain. He froze.

WHERE WERE YOU WHEN I WAS ENJOYING YOUR WIFE?

His fingers seemed to be glued to the page. Was this some sick joke? He turned the paper over, looked again at the envelope. His fingerprints were now all over it. Damn!

His eyes widened as the thoughts cascaded through his head. 'Enjoying your wife'... did it mean ... ? Surely ... it couldn't mean ... Not Rhona too! Please God, no!

He stared down at his wife. She looked exactly the same. Honey blonde hair close to her head, flattened where she lay unmoving on the pillow. Pale skin stretched tightly over her high cheekbones, just a sprinkling of faint freckles over her nose. Blue eyes closed as if in sleep. The fair eyebrows and lashes almost colourless now, her lips only faintly tinged with colour. It was part of the change. In the past she'd always applied colour, using make-up to give the definition that had first arrested his attention.

She'd been a beauty then. She made you look again. Her fine bone structure, those alert eyes, the fairness of her, caught your eye, made you take a second look. After that you saw the lithe body, the elegance. When you got closer and heard the unusual low register of her voice, you knew she was different, knew you wanted to get to know this woman who could capture your interest without resorting to a single artifice apart from the light film of make-up.

Since she'd been unable to care for herself her face had been left as nature intended it. Less striking, less alive. He knew she would have hated that. She'd hated even him seeing her 'without her face on' at first. Said she felt too exposed. He'd reminded her he *liked* to see her naked, she was his wife. She didn't need outer adornments to make her beautiful in his eyes – besides, his love was more than skin deep. Gradually she'd come to accept that her vulnerability was safe with him. But even when they were alone in the house, she would never come down to breakfast before she'd applied her protection. And she was always uneasy if he left the bedroom light on.

She'd fiercely guarded her privacy in other ways too. He'd teased her about her insistence on keeping her bathrobe at the edge of the swimming pool so she didn't have to parade herself in her swimming costume out of the water. She'd tried to gloss over it – did he *want* other men ogling her then? If she was unwell she resisted going to see the doctor until there was absolutely no alternative – she didn't like people touching her, she told him. Even getting into a crowded bus or train was an ordeal for her. She would squeeze herself into her corner of the seat, move away abruptly if anyone jostled her. She never talked about her emotions to anyone else but Geoff, and not even he had understood the depth of her body-image anxiety.

It was only after the tragedy that he found the tell-tale signs. The weight charts, the books about eating disorders, the diet plans – they'd all been secreted away inside the drawer of her wardrobe. It didn't make any sense to him. He loved her just the way she was. If he'd known about her insecurity he'd have told her so more often, been more explicit. But he hadn't known. It was taken for granted. Surely his eyes, his whole behaviour told her he found her attractive with or without her clothes, with or without 'her face'.

After they'd found her unconscious and she'd been admitted to hospital he'd told her. Over and over and over again he'd told her how he felt about her. But it was too late. She'd retreated into a private world beyond his reach.

His eyes returned to the note still clenched in his hand. Did this mean her integrity had been compromised even further? The constant nursing care, the total reliance on others – strangers – for her every physical function, that would have been totally abhorrent to her. Now this. If the veiled reference meant what he suspected, it would be the worst of all possible violations. He sank down into the chair beside her and stared at the words.

WHERE WERE YOU WHEN I WAS ENJOYING YOUR WIFE?

Where was he? Who knew? He didn't even know when it was the note was talking about. Day? Night? Had he been sleeping? Had he been working late at the office? In court? In prison? Speeding along in the car? With his colleagues? With a client? With Angela?

He felt the hairs rising on the back of his neck. Angela. The new partner. She was the reason he was having to work so hard at keeping his allocated time with Rhona sacrosanct. She was the temptation to forget loyalty and commitment. Not a soul knew of his internal struggle over the past few months. No-one must know. But what if Rhona was pregnant too? What if they started checking up on him? Probing. Asking questions. Unravelling things.

He took several deep breaths, telling himself to stay calm. Nothing to be gained by panicking at this stage. He must think sensibly, logically. Like the lawyer he was.

He'd known he was vulnerable. Ever since he became a lawyer. Especially since he'd become a high-profile prosecutor.

OK. Now, take this one step at a time. First of all, who wanted to scare him?

Plenty of people! No mileage there. Anyone he'd ever committed to jail. Anyone he'd ever grilled in the courtroom. Anyone whose case he'd lost – and some he'd won too, but at a price, spilling sordid facts out in the process. Any of the villains he'd implicated. And a hundred and one other criminals out there who hated anybody who fought for justice in the courts – on principle. It was just part of being a barrister. You were bound not to please all of the people all of the time. Come to think of it there were probably innocent relatives or friends of the defendants, or even the plaintiffs he'd given a hard time to – unnamed, faceless people – who'd like to see him sweat a bit. Other lawyers even whom he'd mocked in the courtroom, whose cases he'd systematically demolished. It'd be like looking for a needle in a haystack.

But, of course, it might not be anyone he knew. It might just be some nutter who got a kick out of raping defenceless women. Maybe he'd been at it for ages. Maybe it was the same animal who'd made Viv pregnant, high on all the excitement he'd already generated. Maybe it lost some of its appeal if no-one even knew till after the event. Who better to goad than the husband? Geoff became aware of his teeth grinding.

Whoever it was wanted him to know. Was that all? Would he be satisfied now? Was it over? Or would he do it again? How had he evaded all the extra security? Or did his actions pre-date the special entry systems, the visitors' book, CCTV?

The CCTV! Would this creep be captured on the CCTV? But where did you start to look? They didn't even know what date he'd done it … whatever 'it' was. If anything. Maybe it was just some false claim – just to put the wind up him. Yes. Much more likely. It took only seconds to deliver a note, much longer to arrange and perpetrate a rape.

But the note – it had just come today. Who'd put it there? Was it the guy who did … whatever it was … to Rhona? Or had he given it to somebody else to put in her room?

Yes, that was a starting point. Find out about the note.

He went in search of a nurse. Suzi Renwick was taking care of Rhona

today but, no, she didn't know anything about an envelope. Was it important? Different people came and went and sometimes things were handed
in at the reception desk, she told him. She couldn't be sure who else had
attended to Rhona today, but she could ask those on duty. And Geoff
could try asking the clerkess at the desk.

Geoff kept his enquiry casual. He was just curious, he said. The note
hadn't been signed.

Nobody asked about the contents of the note. He didn't volunteer them.

His mind continued to whirl through the possible ramifications of telling anyone anything. Did he need to involve The Home? Did the police
need to be brought into this? He knew – only too well he knew – how
police questioning went. Could he sort this out himself?

He needed time.

SEVENTEEN

Fourteen days later he still hadn't told anyone. But at least Rhona wasn't pregnant. One less thing to worry about. He'd been slipping in and out of The Home more often, staying late, even taking work in with him during the day sometimes. Before he left he routinely checked that her window was properly secured. If anyone was watching for a chance, he'd know Geoff had got the message.

But he was finding it hard now to concentrate on Bill's concerns. His own questions swirled in amongst the older man's need for justice for his daughter. Were they the same thing? Geoff's anxieties about Rhona's safety crossed the bridge to meet Bill's paranoia about Viv's rapist. Frustration about the silence from the police had a double edge now. It taxed his patience repeatedly advising Bill to await information from DS Latimer, even as he considered withholding facts himself.

The second note came in a white envelope. He'd had a tedious day in court but ten minutes before the end, the defence had produced a witness whose evidence changed the line of argument substantially. Geoff had to go back to the office to collect some papers to work on that night in order to be ready for the prosecution in the morning. He'd grabbed a Chinese takeaway on the way home but still he didn't get to The Home until nearly eight.

Mr G Archibald, it said. Not 'Geoffrey' like last time – just 'G'. Lower-case letters this time, Chicago font, bold. Last time it had been upper-case, Times New Roman letters. The sort of range any computer could churn out.

Inside was one sheet of A4 paper again.

SHE LIKED IT LAST NIGHT.

Same mishmash of cut-out letters. Same higgledy-piggledy arrangement. As if it had been done in haste.

He felt physically sick. What had she liked? It was now at least twenty hours since 'last night'. She'd have been bathed, cleaned, several times since then. There'd be no evidence, surely?

He'd not been in to see her last night. He'd gone straight to the squash court from the office, stayed there until seven thirty in the evening and then worked on his case for the murder trial until one forty-five this morning. Did this creep know that? Had he been watching for his opportunity?

He'd go and ask the nurses if they'd seen anyone lurking.

Outside Fatima Omar's room a lone figure sat reading, the black head-dress falling densely around the bent head. The visitor didn't look up when he opened the door, and Geoff knew better than to try to make conversation with any female person from that family. He couldn't tell one from the other anyway, but it didn't matter. You had to treat them all the same. As non-persons. All you saw were those dark eyes, and they were always instantly dropped when he appeared. If he tried for even a normal brief civility it went unacknowledged. It was worse than being ignored actually – they actively hid from him. What a life, he thought, hidden away from society, governed by the menfolk. Rhona, Viv, how they would have rebelled against any such restrictive regime. Did these women ever rebel? This one just kept looking down until he'd passed. Resigned to her anonymity presumably, knowing nothing else.

He found a couple of nurses, asked the same questions. No, the nurses on duty hadn't been handed any notes. The receptionist hadn't seen anything untoward. The visitors had all signed the book. Could he look to see who had come to see Rhona yesterday evening? Yes, she supposed there was no harm in that. No name appeared for Rhona at all. It was noticeable against the list of undecipherable names for Fatima Omar. And there was Bill's signature. He'd been Viv's only visitor yesterday, for four hours in the evening.

Bill. Might be worth checking with him.

'Last night? I was here until eight,' Bill said.

'Eight fifteen in the book.'

'OK, eight fifteen then.'

'Sorry. Didn't mean to be pedantic. It's the lawyer in me,' Geoff apologised. 'Did you see anyone visiting Rhona?'

'No. Can't remember seeing anyone.'

'Was there anyone hanging around in the corridor that you noticed?'

Bill frowned in concentration.

'Not that I recall. Only one of those Arab women from next door. She wasn't there when I arrived but she was sitting on the chair outside the room when I left. Like they do. She was the only person I remember seeing.'

'No men anywhere?'

'No. I didn't see any. Not our end. A few in the car park when I arrived but not down by the girls' rooms.'

Geoff felt himself sagging.

'Something wrong?' Bill asked.

Geoff shrugged. 'Can you spare ten minutes?'

'Sure,' Bill nodded.

'D'you mind if we go outside?'

Geoff led the way silently along the corridor, out into the car park, into his car. Only when they were inside with the doors shut did he begin his halting story.

He saw the mounting horror in Bill's eyes.

'I don't believe it! Not again! It was bad enough knowing it had happened once – but a second time! In the same Home!'

'And with all these extra security measures in place,' Geoff added bitterly.

'I suppose we can't be sure he did actually – you know – actually …'

'Rape her. No, we can't. And I don't think he did. I think it's me he's after, not Rhona. But the fact remains he was in her room and left the note.'

'Or gave the note to someone else to put in her room?'

'It's a possibility. But I can't find anyone who knows anything about any envelope for me.'

'You've asked the staff then?' Bill asked sharply.

'Well, I've asked the nurses. It's awkward to ask everyone – it'll only start them speculating and I haven't told anyone about the contents as yet. Don't want to panic folk unnecessarily.' It sounded lame even in his own ears.

'Ye gods! You *have* to tell them, man!' Bill punched one fist into his palm. 'I mean, all the patients must be at risk if this lunatic's still lurking.'

'If it was the same man. But this feels different. You didn't get notes did you? When it was Viv, I mean.'

Bill shook his head.

'It just keeps going round and round in my head. But it feels as if this one is specifically directed at me,' Geoff said.

'Blackmail?'

'Not exactly. Revenge more like, I'd say.'

'Get a lot of that in your line of business, I guess.'

'Well, I don't know about a lot. Enough. Threats anyway. Usually insults bawled across the courts.'

'What *are* you going to do?'

'I don't know. The staff have got enough to do just taking care of the patients. I don't want to dump more on them if I can avoid it. And I certainly don't want to deflect attention away from the investigation about Viv's attacker. But I was wondering if – when you're around – you could just keep an eye open. Would you mind? It's a liberty asking, I know, but …'

'Of course. No problem. I could pop in to visit her sometimes, as well. So anyone watching won't know when to expect someone to be with her so much. If that's OK with you, I mean. And you can bet your life I'm going to be around even more if this animal is still lurking.'

'I'd be grateful. I've been coming in more myself since this started but I just can't put in the hours …' He'd almost said, '… you retired folk can,' but thought better of it. It sounded as if he looked on Bill as some pathetic chap with hours to kill, and nothing more important to do. He knew better.

'Shouldn't you tell the police, though? I mean, we can keep an extra eye open but they can probe much deeper. And they'll have the power to ask questions. Check stories out. They might even mount a watch.'

'Possibly. But probably not. Too expensive – on the off chance.'

'But hang it all, man. Don't you want to protect Rhona?'

'Of course I do. And that's why I'm telling you.'

'Then what's stopping you telling the police?'

'I don't want to drag them in – if it's some stupid prank. No point in raising a mighty dust and then finding it's just some guy trying to get a rise out of me.' Geoff avoided Bill's eyes.

'Some prank! Nothing remotely funny about this,' Bill rejoined acidly.

'Warped sense of humour some of my clients,' Geoff said lightly.

Bill shrugged. 'Nothing to be lost telling the police, I'd have thought. Hell, *I* want them to know! I certainly don't want Viv put at risk again, I can tell you! And you must be on pretty good terms with the local constabulary in your line of work. You'd probably get the top brass.'

Geoff shrugged.

Steven Wilkinson knew it had taken courage for Libby Sinclair to come to see him. But he couldn't keep the note of doubt out of his voice.

'I *saw* him coming out,' she insisted. 'With my own eyes.'

'And you're sure it was Rhona's room? You couldn't have been mistaken?'

'Quite sure.'

'But from the end of the corridor it's easy to mistake the doors. They all look alike.'

'I know, but I'm absolutely sure it was Rhona's room.'

'And where did he go after that?'

'Into Viv's room.'

'But there's probably a perfectly innocent explanation,' Steven said. There had to be.

'Maybe. But I thought you ought to know.'

'Yep, thanks. You did the right thing.'

Libby looked doubtful.

'Did you challenge him?' Steven asked.

'No. I thought it was better to tell you.'

'You know he was cleared in Viv's case? Beyond doubt.'

'Yes. We were told.'

'But you're thinking maybe there's a connection?'

'I'm trying *not* to think! I like the guy. I don't want to think any such thing. It feels obscene even saying anything that might lead anyone to think it might be a possibility. But after Viv, you said we should all keep our eyes open and tell you if we saw anything untoward – no matter how seemingly insignificant or improbable.'

'Absolutely. As I said, you're right to have told me.'

'But *I* couldn't say anything. Not to *him*! Good grief! I wouldn't want him to think I had any such suspicion. Not for a second. Not after what he's been through.'

'I know. Not an easy one. But leave it with me.'

Libby withdrew, leaving Steven wishing he were anyone else but himself at that precise moment. But he had no choice.

If he was surprised by the request to go to Steven's office, Bill didn't show it.

'Is it right that you went into Rhona Archibald's room this afternoon?' Steven asked, trying to keep his voice expressionless.

'Yes. That's right.' Bill was looking puzzled.

'Any particular reason?'

'Geoff asked me to keep an eye on her. I agreed I'd sometimes pop in to see her. Why?'

'So Mr Archibald knew you were doing so?'

'Well, he knew I was *going* to. I didn't say when exactly – so he wouldn't know it would be today.'

'May I ask what you did while you were in her room?' Steven asked mildly.

'I sat beside her and talked to her.'

'And that's all?'

'Yes. Why?'

'I'm trying to understand why you should suddenly start to visit another patient.'

'Because . . .' Steven noted the hesitation, the tightened expression. 'Because Geoff asked me to.' It was clearly not what Bill had been going to say.

'And why would he suddenly ask you to do that?'

'After Viv – we didn't want anything to happen to Rhona. And Geoff can't be here the sort of hours I can.'

It all sounded so plausible, Steven mused, looking steadily at the older man sitting in his office chair, but why now? Why hadn't they started this checking for each other as soon as they'd known about the rape? That he could have understood. And why did he get a distinct impression that Bill Faraday wasn't telling the whole truth?

'Is there a problem?' Bill asked, frowning. 'Have things been going missing or something? I didn't touch anything, I can promise you that.'

'Have you heard about a problem?'

'No.'

'It's curious, that's all – the nurses saw you going into Rhona's room. We wondered why.'

'Why? Like I said, I'm keeping an eye on Rhona for Geoff.'

'Uhhuh.'

'Seemed like a sensible idea. I'm here so much more than he is.'

'Isn't it a bit odd a man keeping an eye on another man's wife?'

Steven saw the colour drain out of Bill's face.

'You … cannot … be … serious!' He dragged every syllable out. 'You think …'

'We have to be vigilant on behalf of these vulnerable patients, Mr Faraday. I'm sure you of all people can understand that.'

'It was bad enough having the police doubting my word when it was Viv. They didn't know me. But you! You've known me all these years. And you think I'm capable of …' The blazing horror in his eyes made Steven cringe.

'I didn't say …'

'You didn't need to say! I can see you *thought* it.'

'I have to check. It's my job. I'm responsible for these patients.'

For a long moment the older man glared at the doctor. Steven tried a direct appeal.

'If a man came out of Viv's room and someone saw him you'd expect me to check, wouldn't you?'

Bill's anger faded as rapidly as it had risen.

'Of course. I'm sorry. I quite see that. And I ought to be glad everyone is being vigilant. Sorry. It's just such a …'

'An appalling suspicion to have levelled at you. I know. And for what it's worth I don't believe it. That's why it's me doing the questioning, not the police. But I have to check. I shall have to check with Mr Archibald too. You understand that.'

'Of course. Please do. Why don't you phone him now? Before I have a chance to contact him myself to compare our stories and feed him the answers.' The sarcasm was gently mocking but not hostile. Steven smiled wryly.

Geoffrey Archibald was not in court, but at his desk writing a report. He was able instantly to corroborate Bill's story.

'But what I don't understand is – why now? Why not months ago – after Viv's rape?' Steven queried.

'I've only just recently started to think Rhona might be at risk. I mean, just at first everyone was on the alert. The police were about. But they still haven't caught this rapist, have they? What if he comes back?' Geoff replied evenly, reasonably.

Steven could get no further satisfaction. It didn't add up but he was relieved to have Bill's story corroborated. He devoted his energy to soothing the feelings of the man whose integrity he had just challenged, a man who'd had enough suspicion already to last him a lifetime.

Geoff was abject in his apology.

'OK, OK. It's done. But for heaven's sake man, tell them. This isn't some footling little thing you can just ignore. Not after all that's happened,' Bill insisted.

'I know. And under other circumstances I might well advise the same thing. But I've spent all my working life looking at the activities of criminals, don't forget. This is a completely different modus operandi.'

'That's as maybe, but aren't you scared for Rhona, whether it's a different person or the same one?'

'Believe me, it's Rhona I'm thinking of most in all this. Well, Rhona *and* Viv.'

'Well, then.'

'If I really believed for one moment there was any real danger to them I wouldn't hesitate. But the more I look at it the more I'm convinced this is the work of someone who wants to give me a hard time.'

'Even so …'

'Don't waste your anxiety on me. I can fend for myself. Years of practice. And I really don't want to deflect attention away from the hunt for Viv's attacker. If it's a question of Latimer and his merry men chatting to some of my unsavoury clients or taking statements from people who know the creep who abused Viv, I know where my money goes. No question.'

'Well, it's your call, I guess. But I don't like it. I don't like it at all. And it's certainly putting the wind up me even if you aren't taking it seriously. Hell, I'm already having a hard time trusting anybody these days. And judging from Steven Wilkinson's grilling of me, so's he!'

'I'm sorry about that. It wasn't fair of me. I didn't think of it from their point of view.'

'Couldn't you at least tell the staff something so they keep an extra eye out for Rhona? I know they're doing it for Viv. When I'm not here.'

Geoff knew he was thinking of the difference between the number of hours they each put in at The Home.

'I will do. And trust me, if I see any reason to think these threats are serious, I'll talk.'

'Well, I hope you mean it,' Bill said grudgingly. 'You owe it to the girls, *I* think. There's a time for going solo and a time to call for help.'

If only it were that simple.

EIGHTEEN

But it took a third note to persuade Geoff this was a police matter.

It was a cold wet Thursday evening and he was working late to clear the backlog of mail that had accumulated while he'd been absorbed in a protracted murder trial. With no-one at home to complain if he was out late, he found it strangely comforting to be in his office alone at night. He could retain his professional identity, his sense of purpose, without the distraction or effort of having to relate to colleagues and clients. And there was a great feeling of satisfaction getting things done – so much more efficiently because he was uninterrupted – so that he could face the next day's list with equanimity.

He heard the letterbox snap, automatically glancing at his watch; eight twenty-five precisely. Late for delivery boys to be out feeding junk mail into innumerable doors, he thought idly. Rotten job on a night like this too. Not until he rose to make himself a fourth cup of coffee did he bother to go downstairs to collect the delivery. It wasn't the expected free newspaper or advertising leaflet, and he was casually curious as he stooped to pick up the slim plain white envelope. It was typed 'For the personal attention of Mr Geoffrey Archibald,' unstamped, and unexceptional. With his usual economy of action he slit the envelope with his thumb as he went back upstairs, his mind still on the document from the Law Society he'd just been studying.

The sight of the jagged ill-assorted letters took him completely by surprise, and he was still staring at the chaos of cut-outs when he lowered himself heavily into his chair. The single sheet of paper shook in his fingers, and he dropped it onto his desk, on top of the Law Society papers, wiping his hands on his trousers as if to rid himself of the contamination.

YOU THINK I'M BLUFFING? OK, LOOK INSIDE THE FRONT OF HER NIGHTDRESS. YOU'LL SEE I'VE BEEN THERE.

He hadn't expected this evil to sneak into his working life. It had been part of the compartment labelled 'The Home'. So this … this … well, whatever, whoever – call him X – obviously not only knew about Rhona, but also knew where he worked. And X'd been there, to his office, tonight – yards from where he'd been sitting working. Or his delivery boy had been. Geoff cursed himself for not having looked out of the window when the letterbox snapped. Would he have seen the guy, recognised him?

But how did X know where to find him? Was he being followed? Were all his movements known? Shades of the FBI! But if so, there had to be more than one person involved. X himself couldn't be at The Home with Rhona *and* following Geoff. Maybe X was just taunting him for not being at The Home.

Maybe he'd been surprised to find the lights on. Maybe the creep just expected him to find the letter in the morning and be racked with guilt for not having been with Rhona, or spooked by the realisation that the sender knew about his workplace. Or maybe he knew the partners all worked late some nights, the cleaners came in the evening too, so he expected to see signs of occupation. Did he know it was Geoff there tonight?

Icy fingers closed around his heart. All this analytical rubbish, trying to sort things out as if it was just another of his legal cases – and all the time Rhona ...

Grabbing his jacket, he raced downstairs, flung himself into his car and sped off to The Home. His blood pressure soared – roadworks, a diversion, delays in being admitted through the security doors, the receptionist calling him back to sign in – it was like living a nightmare, straining to reach her but his feet sinking into quicksand. With each minute his sense of panic mounted.

There was no-one around in the corridors until he came to Rhona's section. Three Arabian women sat in silence on the chairs outside Fatima's room. Three pairs of dark eyes lifted in unison at the sound of his running feet, watched him advancing along the corridor, but he didn't even nod in their direction. Swerving into Rhona's room, crashing through the door, he ground to a halt inside.

She was not alone. Two nurses were in the process of washing and changing her. He knew them both – Suzi Renwick and Betty Andrews. They looked up in surprise as he burst in.

'I'm sorry ... I didn't realise ... Sorry for barging in,' he blurted out.

'It's OK. We've nearly finished here.'

Her white nightdress lay discarded on the floor, and they were easing a new blue one over her head. They carried on expertly handling the unresponsive body, settling her, making her look as if naturally relaxing against the pillows. Geoff watched it as in slow motion. They brushed her fine blonde hair, squirted perfume against her neck, filling his nostrils with her unmistakable scent. The blue of her nightdress matched the blue of her eyes, eyes that were levelled straight at him. She looked so calm, so unruffled. Surely that scumbag couldn't have ... She wouldn't look so peaceful if she'd just been abused, would she? But of course she would. She didn't know, didn't care – whatever happened. It made no difference to her. The horror of her situation washed over Geoff with bitterness he could taste.

His breath came unevenly as he stood leaning against the door, watching.

Every instinct made him want to rush over to her, hold her close, tell her he was sorry, he'd protect her from now on, but the nurses' presence effectively stunted any emotional response. His eyes constantly returned to the crumpled fabric lying only yards from him. Would there be a note inside it? Had the nurses already found it? Should he just pick the nightie up, stuff it in his case? What explanation could he give? No, he mustn't act precipitately, better behave as normal. He'd look inside when he got her bag of washing to take home. His hands clenched into fists.

With Rhona comfortably settled back against the pillows, Betty picked up the nightdress, shaking it slightly as she made to fold it up and place it in the laundry bag. As she did so a small square of white paper fell out. She stooped to pick it up but not before Geoff had seen the cut-out letters. He couldn't stifle a sudden swift intake of breath. For a long moment the nurse stared at the paper, a small frown creasing her brow. Geoff watched, rigid, unmoving.

'What is it, Bet?' Suzi asked, peering across the bed.

'Some sort of note.'

'Let me see?'

They both frowned at it.

'Where did that come from?'

'Seemed to be caught up in her nightie.'

'Strange.'

'Looks like one of those anonymous letters you read about.'

'May I?' Geoff said in a strangled voice, taking a step towards them, holding out his hand.

Betty held the single piece of paper out to him. There was just one word: *SEE*!

He closed his eyes and inhaled deeply. His heart, still racing from his sprint along the corridor, now pounded uncomfortably in his ears.

'Does this make sense to you?' Suzi asked him.

'Partly,' he admitted.

The two nurses stared at him, waiting for some sort of explanation.

'I think this is a matter for Dr Wilkinson. Sorry. No offence. Is he still here?'

'I'm not sure. But I can check.'

'Please.'

Suzi left the room eyeing Geoff oddly as she passed him. Small wonder. What must they think, hearing him pounding down the corridor, bursting into the room as if seven devils were after him; seeing his agitation at the discovery of a note, his trembling fingers? Oh yes, they couldn't fail to know something had rattled him.

Strange, he'd not thought much about the image he projected in The Home. Here he was simply Rhona's husband. He rarely talked to the staff, certainly didn't share anything of his emotions with them. They knew he was a lawyer – probably even that he was a bit of a hotshot if they noticed the number of times his name cropped up in big cases in the papers. Maybe they even pitied him, only in his forties, married but not, saddled with a wife who wasn't a wife. But he didn't want their curiosity, or their pity. Best to stay aloof.

Betty carried on clearing up the room, putting Rhona's toiletries away in her locker.

'I'll take the nightie,' he said, holding out his hand for it. He held it with his fingertips, just touching the edge of the lacy top, folding it carefully, trying not to think what he might be preserving.

He wished the nurse would stop fussing with things, leave him alone. When she didn't he moved over to Rhona, touched her face lightly, then stood staring down at her, a sense of defeat fighting for mastery. Her vacant eyes remained unseeing, unknowing as ever.

When Suzi returned it was with the news that Steven was still in the building. They'd bleeped him; he'd be available in ten minutes; someone would come for Geoff when the doctor was free. Geoff merely nodded, too preoccupied to even thank her. The involuntary grinding of his teeth sounded deafening in his ears.

As soon as the two nurses had left the room he strode across to close the door firmly behind them. His hands were still trembling as he spread open the single piece of paper. The letters seemed to mock him. Got ya! Over a barrel, mate!

'Oh, Rhona. I am so sorry.' He stopped abruptly as his voice cracked.

It was still heartbreaking, even after all this time, seeing her so unreachable. But at least what he was about to do wouldn't harm her now. The reporters, the ghouls who took such malicious pleasure in other people's shame, couldn't touch her. And so what if business fell off for him, if clients stopped choosing him? What did it matter now? He had enough capital to keep Rhona here, well cared for. Better to lose out himself than subject her to any more from the jerk who was doing this to them. Yes, it was time to hand it all over to the police.

The promised ten minutes extended to twenty-five and by the time Suzi arrived to escort him to Steven's office, Geoff had accepted the inevitability of what was to come. As he rose to his feet he looked down at Rhona for a long moment, before suddenly, unexpectedly, stooping to kiss her. If Suzi noticed she gave no sign of it. They strode in silence down the corridor.

Steven was at his desk. Geoff thought fleetingly how much older he looked in the shaded light of the anglepoise lamp. It exaggerated the lines around his eyes, glinted in the silver in his hair. There was a weariness about him too, in the way he pushed himself out of his chair briefly and then slumped back into it.

Geoff sank down into the proffered seat opposite.

'What's going on, Mr Archibald?' Steven's direct approach robbed Geoff of the opportunity to lead into his story cautiously.

'I think … my wife may be … being raped.'

He watched the colour drain from Steven's face, his fingers suddenly still and tight around the pen in his hand.

'You … are … not … serious?'

Geoff nodded.

'You'd better tell me what's going on here.' Steven seemed to shrink down onto the arms resting on his desk.

'I've had three anonymous letters.'

'*Three*! Since when?'

'The first one was just under three weeks ago. The last one tonight.'

'Saying what?'

Geoff knew each one off by heart, but it was still incredibly hard to repeat the words to anyone else.

'The first one: "Where were you when I was enjoying your wife?" Second one: "She liked it last night." Tonight: "You think I'm bluffing? OK, look inside the front of her nightdress. You'll see I've been there." And inside her nightdress: "See!"' Geoff silently showed Steven the last one as he spoke the word.

'But why on earth didn't you tell us?'

'Personal reasons. To do with my work. I thought … I hoped … best to deal with them myself.'

'You thought you could deal with *rape – yourself?*'

'Not exactly rape, no. Other things. I thought the letters were just a ploy to try to scare me.'

'Do the police know?'

'Not yet. But they'll have to know now.'

'This isn't making any sense to me.'

'I realise that. But the less people who know the detail, the better. I know you need to know about the rape – well, possible rape.'

'I should have known from the outset. For heaven's sake, I'm responsible for these women – your wife included! Who knows what else this lunatic has got up to? I should have known. Especially after Viv. For goodness sake, you can't unilaterally decide to let something like this just slide.'

Steven had always been so polite, so courteous, almost deferential. Now he was frankly accusatory, looking at Geoff like a headmaster close to the edge of his patience.

'I know that's what it looks like. But I was only trying to protect her.'

'You call this protection? Knowing this criminal is roaming in and out of her room, doing goodness knows what, and you do nothing? You call that protecting her? Pardon my saying so, but it seems to me you've got a warped idea of what she needs protecting from!'

'It's a lot more complicated than that.' Geoff heard the defeat in his own voice.

'I think you've got some explaining to do, Mr Archibald.'

Geoff nodded dully. 'It'd be better if I told the police at the same time, I think.'

Steven nodded, reaching automatically for the phone. Geoff saw the sticker with DS Latimer's numbers, work and home, on Steven's phone. Of course, this would be just the kind of case Latimer would stick at. There were some crimes that crept under the thickest professional hides. Viv's rape would be one of them. Lower than sewer level, a violation of even the criminals' code.

Geoff heard as from a distance Steven's side of the conversation. His voice was level, giving nothing away, nothing of the fear and despair he must be feeling.

'Good evening. May I speak to DS Latimer, please? ... He said to contact him directly ... Dr Steven Wilkinson, Director of Chivenings Home in Mortimer Road ... It's about an incident here ... in The Home ... There's been a development ... Not over the phone, no ... No ... Well, he said he wanted to deal with it himself ... Yes ... He gave me his home number so I can phone direct myself if ... OK, I'd be grateful. Thanks.'

He replaced the receiver quietly before looking across at Geoff.

'They're going to contact DS Latimer. He's off duty at the moment. But either he or the duty sergeant will be here before too long. Can I get you a coffee?'

'Thanks. Strong, black, please.'

Alone in Steven's office Geoff sank back in the chair, his iron composure momentarily slipping. Events of almost eight years ago flooded in, as vivid today as they had been then. Even more painful for having been actively, deliberately suppressed for so long. If only ...

121

NINETEEN

It had been one thirty in the morning when Geoff let himself into their flat. In spite of the ninety minutes driving around to calm himself, he was still shaking.

Darkness enveloped him but he didn't switch on the light. Rhona would be dead to the world by now and he didn't want to wake her. She'd never coped very well with broken sleep, and tomorrow she wanted to be at her best for an important appointment with the managing director of her publishing firm.

He sneaked into the dining room and by the light of the street lamp poured himself a large whisky.

They were on the last lap now. If he could hold his nerve for a few more days this case would be in the bag and he could sever all connection with Marilyn Petersen for ever.

His palms were sweaty on the glass just thinking about the woman. She seemed to leer at him now, long red hair curling around a handsome if rather heavily made-up face. She'd been particularly saccharine tonight. His eyes closed against the sensations: impossibly long eyelashes, grey eyes welling with tears, yielding flesh pressed against him, long legs exposed as the black satin fell open beside him. No doubting what her intentions were.

He shuddered and took a gulp from his glass. One false move and the whole thing could blow apart.

Over so many years dealing with the criminal mind, he'd become somewhat inured to the machinations that went on behind the scenes when these high-profile cases came to court. To begin with he'd been an idealist, on the side of right, determined to pursue and punish wrong. But he soon learned: you were paid to win. It was about trumping your opponent, outsmarting the other side. And as time went on, he knew, he'd made the odd compromise, sunk to a bit of subtle manipulation himself. Undesirable maybe, but understandable. This, though, this was the closest he'd ever sailed to the wind.

Meeting his client away from the office in the first place had been a mistake but back then she'd seemed so genuine in her fear. Taking her for a coffee in a quiet restaurant ten minutes down the road had seemed like a sensitive response to a celebrity seeking to avoid publicity. And she'd been so much more forthcoming in the intimate environment. It had paid dividends. He felt he got to know her quickly, how far she could be pressed under questioning, where her weaknesses lay. Over dinner on the second occasion – all at her expense she'd insisted – she'd poured out her sordid story in a persecuted voice, the hyperbole of her expressions matched by the extravagance of her gestures. It was a familiar story, but the expensive wine and excellent lobster had made it all so much more civilised. It dulled the grating edge of her voice confiding just how hard it was to be recognised wherever she went, how people only courted her because she was an actress, how much she longed for someone to love her for herself. How her husband had only wanted the fame by association, how his callous disregard for her sensibilities had become tantamount to cruelty. She had appealed to Geoff to save her from a quite unendurable fate at the hands of this monster.

Before the senior partner had delegated the case to him, Geoff had never even heard of Marilyn Petersen. But then he'd never taken the least interest in TV soaps, even the most well known, and her role was only a supporting one in an off-peak daytime series. Of course, she assured him, it would lead to great things, the casting scouts were already promoting her for important films in the future. But she had traded on his very ignorance. Over and over again she gushed about how wonderful it was to be with someone who wasn't star-struck, someone who cared about her as a real person, who could see that in spite of all the glamour she was a poor downtrodden innocent.

He'd entered her apartments at the Royal Brittania Hotel, exhausted, just wanting to finalise the details for tomorrow and get home for some rest.

She'd rung at six, her voice thick and muffled.

'I'm so sorry, Geoffrey. It's flu. Feels like a steamroller ran over me. And I'm burning up. I don't think I could even crawl to your office tonight.'

He felt a rush of relief.

'Too bad. Don't worry about it. Just get to bed and make sure you're well enough for tomorrow.'

'But we need to go over things.'

'You'll be OK.'

'I don't feel confident. I needed that final briefing.'

'Fair enough, I'll take you through it over the phone.'

But she made heavy weather of every point.

'I think we should forget it. Just get to bed and make sure you're all right for tomorrow,' Geoff repeated, trying not to let his exasperation show. Surely nobody could be that dense! Even with flu.

'I need to see you. Face to face. I could take it in if I could see your expression.'

'I don't think …'

'Just ten minutes. Please? Then I'd feel confident about tomorrow. We must win tomorrow.'

He looked at the piles of paper he still had to shift before he left the office. She understood his workload, she'd coaxed, she could wait. Just come whenever. She'd rest until then and try to clear her brain. Just ten minutes. That's all it would take to ensure a consummate victory tomorrow.

He was totally unprepared for her change from victim to siren.

When he entered the dimly lit room, she lay draped over the couch, one hand pressed to her brow, the other patting the seat beside her. The histrionics of a born drama queen, he presumed, though why she should waste her talents on him he couldn't understand.

Perched on the edge of the seat, his back against the farthest arm of the settee, he took out the papers relating to her divorce case and started to go over the salient points. When he felt her leaning against his arm he drew back, murmuring that it was late and he must get home. The warning bells rang louder as she clung to him, whispering flattery against his neck, fingers clutching at his jacket, as he stood up and backed away. Protestations about abusing his privileged position as her lawyer went unheeded. She applied herself with renewed enthusiasm to her task, taking his hand in hers to slide it inside her satin housecoat. Beads of sweat stood on his forehead.

'Please. Stop this,' he stammered, pulling his hands away, retreating further. 'I'm your lawyer. We can't …'

'We can. You want to. I want you to.'

'No …'

'I'll have to tell them that you came to my room alone at night. You undid my clothes. You felt my breasts.' The words were silky, the meaning deadly.

Only then did he realise the trap had been set and was about to snap shut. His fingers *had* done those things – he couldn't deny it. No-one seeing her would believe she had *made* him.

Geoff had dealt with blackmail in his professional capacity many times before, but never before had he been the victim of an attempt. He cursed his own naivety. How could he, even though tired and preoccupied with more serious cases, have fallen for something as stupid as this?

Now safely in his own home Geoff swallowed the rest of his whisky in one gulp.

Marilyn had promised if he won her case she'd say nothing about to-night's 'little episode', as she called it. Just the possibility of it coming out made him sweat. It wouldn't matter how innocent a victim he had been, the publicity would be damaging, the mud would stick. Even in his own ears his defence sounded pathetic.

Yes, Your Honour, I am a qualified and experienced lawyer.

Well, sir, I felt sorry for my client.

Yes, I did believe her story about feeling achey and shivery.

Yes, I did go to her hotel room late in the evening.

Yes, I suppose she is beautiful and sexy.

OK, yes, she is.

Well, yes sir, I suppose I did touch her, but she forced me to.

Give me a break! He had himself made mincemeat of other men pleading more mitigating circumstances.

Rumour, speculation, innuendo, truth, fiction – what did it matter which was which? The whole sordid story would ruin his reputation, his credibility. And worse than that, it would hurt Rhona.

Rhona! She'd be tainted by association. He didn't want so much as a breath of this messy business to touch her. He just had to win this case and hope and pray – yes, pray as he'd never prayed before – that the wretched woman would keep her mouth shut.

He dared not risk waking Rhona tonight. His mind was whirling and his composure rocky. Besides she hated it if he smelt of drink. He slipped silently into the guest room and lay endlessly rehearsing his case. He must win. He absolutely *must.*

Sleep eluded him. His brain was still working on the case when he got up at five thirty to make a cup of tea. He tiptoed along the hall to the kitchen cursing Marilyn Petersen under his breath. Odd. There was a greenish glow under his study door. He didn't remember leaving the computer on when he'd finished work in there the night before last. And Rhona never touched his machine, knowing only too well the importance of keeping his work confidential. Very odd.

He pushed open the door with an irritated shrug of his shoulder. Yes, the screen was still glowing. He punched a key to move out of the swirling screensaver. It was replaced with an email. Strange. He never left messages open; indeed he was so meticulous in his filing of documents that Rhona had laughed when she'd seen the rows of folders precisely aligned in his storage compartments. But it was part of his modus operandi, what made him so efficient, being so attentive to detail, so confident about where everything fitted. No time wasted hunting for things.

He was on the point of automatically closing the file and the application when the sender's name jumped out and hit him foursquare. It was from Marilyn Petersen. She'd never sent him an email before. How did she even know his address?

Thank you so much for agreeing so readily to come to me at the hotel tonight. These intimate times away from prying eyes have come to mean such a lot to me. Understanding my need tonight was so typical of you, always so courteous and sensitive. You have restored my confidence in men and who knows – once this divorce is through … Well, I shall continue to dream. This week will mark a new phase in my life and I just know you and I will make a winning team. You will always be my knight in shining armour. You are the first man in my life to see me as a woman first, actress second. Yours, M.

What on earth? He'd only just returned from seeing the woman. When had she sent this? Six thirty last evening, the message said. Just after she'd phoned to say she was unwell. But he hadn't been home this evening, he'd gone straight from the office round to her hotel, so he hadn't been here to open his mail. So how …?

It could only have been Rhona. But why was she touching his machine, never mind opening his mail, his new mail at that? It was a tacit understanding: she didn't. So why break that rule? Why open this, and why leave it open so he'd know she'd been there? It didn't make sense. He hadn't even told her about taking the Petersen case. It was just run of the mill stuff, part of his bread-and-butter work, same old story, just happened to involve a public figure. Besides people sometimes tried to winkle information out of her when they saw his name in the papers, especially when well-known figures were involved. What she didn't know she couldn't talk about.

He re-read Marilyn's message. Typically florid language. The actress in her came out in her writing too. But why would Rhona open it?

The third time he read the words he felt the prickling sensation on the back of his neck. If you didn't know the history it could mean … Oh God! Let her not have misread this. Let her have left it open to remind her to ask him about it in the morning. *Please!*

His mouth felt parched and his fingers shook as he filled the kettle and made the tea. Even with his two hands cupped around the mug he still shivered. He'd have to tell her everything. Including tonight's little drama. Thank goodness the case was almost over. He'd win it – he had to. But would Rhona believe him?

Suddenly his late nights, his silence about this high-profile case, his trysts with his client in restaurants, his preoccupation with work, took on sinister undertones. Had Rhona seemed disturbed recently? He hadn't noticed if she was. But to be honest he'd hardly noticed her at all of late. The work just piled up and evenings were spent either at the office or in his study, working. Always working. He must make more of an effort. Give her more of his attention. Once this case was over he'd take on less work, delegate more. There was more to life than work.

When she didn't appear at six thirty as usual he slipped into the bedroom to wake her. She lay with her face half turned into the pillow, her blonde hair covering it, but there was no response to his soft calling of her name. He reached out and touched her shoulder. Still no response. He shook her gently.

'Hey, sleepy head. You're dead to the world. But Fat Alec won't be too chuffed if you roll in late this morning,' he chided playfully. It was a big moment for her; she expected to hear she was being promoted.

When she still did not stir he made to roll her over. It was her face that told him. It was blue and totally unresponsive. Her eyes were swollen.

With shaking hands he dialled 999. She was still breathing but something was terribly wrong, even to his layman's eyes. Nothing would rouse her. The paramedics worked swiftly, checking vital signs, administering oxygen, asking questions, securing her on the stretcher, slotting it into the ambulance. He'd follow in the car, he said. The ambulance swung out into the road, blue light flashing, siren screaming, taking Rhona away. He remembered nothing of the drive.

The endless questions seemed to come from a great distance as the doctors searched for anything relevant to explain Rhona's condition.

How had she been before she went to bed? He didn't know. He'd been out. Working.

Had she been under the weather lately? Anything? Not that he'd noticed.

Been under any strain lately? Nothing out of the ordinary. As far as he knew anyway.

Any history of medical problems? Hers? Or in the family?

When did he find her like this? Could he describe what she'd been like, what he'd done?

Did she take any medication? Could she have taken anything? Drugs? Anything?

Had she ever tried to take her own life before?

That jerked him fully awake.

'What d'you mean, *before*? She hasn't … has she?' He couldn't put it into words.

They told him as gently as they could. They'd found excessive levels of barbiturates in her blood. They'd pumped out her stomach, they were giving her antidotes, doing their best to counteract the effect. They'd get a psychiatric assessment, try to find out what had happened.

Geoff felt like an alien creature alone on a planet surging with strange creatures, all whirling round him, speaking in an unintelligible tongue, intent on what they were doing, treading well-worn paths, leaving him struggling to find his way out of the maze.

Yes, she'd had sleeping tablets prescribed once but she'd told him she didn't take them, didn't want to resort to drugs if she could find a natural way to cure her insomnia. The herbal remedies she'd taken had done the trick. She hated taking any drugs. She *wouldn't* …

At nine forty he knew he must leave her. He must get to court. He explained to the doctors he had no choice. They looked at him oddly. Today's case depended on him, he protested. They could reach him if there was any change, and he'd come back immediately the case was over.

But in reality it was a relief, in the face of the total chaos and the lack of control, to shower, go to his office, collect his papers, drive to court for the Petersen case. Now he was the one treading a familiar path.

The press were out with a vengeance long before the star of the show arrived. He saw in the evening papers later that day how Marilyn had acted out her part to perfection, looking every inch the wronged wife. They showed her on the local news playing to the cameras. Only the thought of the threat she held over him kept him close to her side. She must not suspect for a moment he would let her down. And when Rhona woke up he must be able to face her squarely and tell her the danger was over. It had all been a hideous mistake brought about by a scheming, amoral, would-be actress.

He played his part like a man inspired. The sympathy for his client was palpable. The court believed not only that the marriage was over but that her husband was a monster who abused her, took everything he could get, and showed not a shred of human decency. Not for a moment did Geoff himself believe her sobbing story. His sympathy was all for the husband, Simon Fenton, whose worst crime had been to fall for the charms of a woman who made him look as innocent as a babe in arms.

It was as a cameraman that Simon had first met Marilyn. He'd watched, through a prejudicial lens, as she'd enticed not only the media men, but all the male members of the cast. He too wanted her.

Only the cold light of day had revealed her to be a shallow mockery of a wife.

Geoff knew in his heart the man was well rid of her. He told himself his performance was as much to relieve Simon of an odious burden as to shut the mouth of the woman who threatened his downfall, and Rhona's peace of mind.

During each recess he rang the hospital, not daring to leave the court-room. He must keep Marilyn in his sights until this charade was over. No change, the nurse said, Mrs Archibald was still alive, but still unconscious. He promised again, he'd be there as soon as he'd finished in court.

There was no question; it was a resounding victory. Marilyn Petersen thoroughly and decisively trounced Simon Fenton in the courts. Or at least her lawyers did, thanks to Geoffrey Archibald. And in full view of the press she threw her arms around him and kissed him. The cameras whirred furiously, the men behind them purred sympathetically, envying the lawyer the perks of his job.

Geoff stuck rigidly to his lines. He too could put on an Oscar-winning performance. He would give her not so much as a glimmer of doubt as to his support of her cause.

TWENTY

At the hospital Rhona lay unmoving.

The sound of the ventilator swooshing was hypnotic after a while. Geoff felt himself being sucked down into a dark place which held only dread and condemnation.

Words choked in his throat.

All day he'd stuck beside a vain, superficial, ambitious woman out for every penny she could claw back from the man she had tormented for four years. All day Rhona had lain alone fighting for her very life, a life she had shared with him so generously and lovingly.

He stayed until eleven that night, so bone weary from a sleepless night and an exhausting day that he felt as if he would concertina to the floor if he stood up. In the end the nurses pressed him to go home and get some rest. They'd call him if there was any change.

It took all his courage to walk into the flat.

Was it less than twenty-four hours since he'd slunk in last time, sullied by the touch of that vile woman? Had Rhona been already unconscious then? If only he'd gone in to see her at once, maybe it would have given her a sporting chance. They'd have washed out more of the drug before it had obtained a paralysing hold on her.

What could have pushed her into something so drastic as attempting to end her life?

He forced himself to go into the bedroom. What was he looking for? Anything. Any clue as to why she'd done it. Had she left a note? A diary? Anything at all? He found nothing.

There remained only the email. Surely that alone hadn't tipped her over the edge. But why was she even looking at his mail? Had she been suspicious, looking for tell-tale signs, when he was out so much? When she woke up he'd tell her, his only sin was allowing work to overtake him. She had no competition, nothing to fear.

Had she meant to kill herself? Or was it simply a cry for attention that had gone badly wrong? Was she relying on him coming home in time to raise the alarm? Pray God he hadn't been too late. It was so frustrating being unable to ask her, reassure her. Now. Immediately.

In spite of his unutterable tiredness sleep eluded him yet again. He rang the hospital several times throughout the night. No change. No change. No change.

He was back at her side at seven in the morning. Her colour looked marginally better he thought, but otherwise there was no sign of her emerging from the coma as yet.

He went through the motions of going to the office, dealing with the mail, tying up the loose ends from the Petersen case. It was mechanical. He knew he was in no state to think or make important decisions. By lunchtime his white face and haunted eyes forced his colleagues to override him. They were adamant, united in their insistence that he take time off, they'd cover for him. His place was with Rhona.

But in the impersonal, high-tech environment of Intensive Care he was restless. It was impossible to sit doing nothing but think, hour after hour, just listening to every forced breath. The nurses' attempts to engage him in banal conversation irritated him.

He paced the corridor. He drank endless cups of coffee, willing the caffeine to keep him going.

He rang their family doctor's surgery. Could he have an emergency appointment with Dr Harrison? There had been a cancellation at four thirty, any good? Yes, he'd be there.

Dr Harrison was clearly horrified by Geoff's news. But Geoff saw his face close down when he asked for specific information.

'Rhona … has she been to see you lately? Do you know, has she been troubled by anything?'

'I'm sorry, but I can't divulge information about another patient,' Dr Harrison said quietly.

'But she's my wife!'

'Even so. Secrets of the surgery, and all that. You know how it is.'

'But she's at death's door, for heaven's sake!'

'I realise that and I'm desperately sorry to hear it. But I'm still not at liberty to say anything she told me in confidence. It's the way the system works.'

'But … I'm a lawyer! Of course I understand about patient confidentiality. Under normal circumstances. But surely … under *these* circumstances … any light you, as her doctor, can shed … it might make all the difference to her recovery.'

'I do understand, believe me. And I quite see your point. What I can do is contact the hospital and see if I can supply any relevant information to the consultant in charge of her. Who's she under?' He reached for his pen.

'Dr Trevelyan.'

'OK. I'll ring Dr Trevelyan at the end of surgery tonight. Promise.'

'Seems ridiculous that you can tell a stranger but not me!'

'I know. And I understand why you're feeling upset about this. I'd feel just as angry if I were in your shoes, believe me. But my hands are tied. I *am* at liberty to share confidential information with my medical colleagues, however, if it might influence the management of a case, and on that basis I'll pass on anything that seems relevant. OK?'

It wasn't 'OK' but Geoff realised the sooner he left the surgery, the sooner Dr Harrison would contact Rhona's doctors.

The hospital staff told him nothing of the conversation with the GP. He could only presume Dr Harrison had kept his word. Whatever – if anything – they knew, he must wait until Rhona could tell him in person. He could only devoutly hope that it had nothing to do with that email.

The days went by and still Rhona lay unmoving, unaware of his long vigils. Well, he *presumed* she was unaware although the staff told him he should talk to her about anything, everything. The more he could stimulate her, the better the chances, and the first sense to return was hearing, they said. He knew that. But it was easier said than done. Not knowing what had troubled her, he might inadvertently be making things worse. And, anyway, he'd never been one for idle chatter. He felt self-conscious, knowing he sounded stilted, and it was only when the nurses left him alone with her briefly that he really appealed to her, telling her of his love, his anguish at her action, begging her to wake up. He promised her things would be very different; he would cherish her as she had never been cherished before.

She first opened her eyes three weeks after the overdose. Geoff was there. Tears of relief fell unchecked. He renewed his promises. Her silence was unnerving, but he told her over and over again, he could wait. She must concentrate on building up her strength. He'd be there when she was ready to talk.

It was four weeks before he found the first piece of evidence of her hidden anxieties – the books on eating disorders, the piles of diet sheets, the weight charts. It felt wrong somehow to be poking into her private space looking for things she'd elected to keep from him when she had the power to decide these things. But he needed to know. If there was anything at all that helped to explain why she had chosen death to life, he needed to know it. Until he did he'd be haunted by guilt and dread.

To his chagrin his composure finally snapped in Dr Harrison's surgery. Never before had he wept like that. The great racking sobs tore through him uncontrollably. Perhaps because of Geoff's utter desolation, perhaps because of his own knowledge of what was to come, Dr Harrison relented enough to confirm Geoff's suspicion that she had deep-seated hang-ups about her body. Carefully, impartially, he outlined the medical facts about such obsessive tendencies.

Geoff looked them up on the Internet, searched for enlightenment in the medical library, sent away for literature, tried to understand. But surely Rhona *couldn't* have thought like that. She had a beautiful body. She must have known he thought so. Could she really have felt that insecure, that unsure of his devotion? Was that why she had looked on his computer, looked for evidence that he had turned elsewhere? Was finding that email the final straw – confirming her fear that she had lost her appeal, telling her that he was having an affair with Marilyn Petersen, that he might even leave her?

It was too appalling. He had to blot such an idea out of his head. He must try to keep an open mind until Rhona could tell him what had gone on inside her head. All he could do was tell her over and over again what she meant to him, how he'd never been tempted to stray, how all he wanted was for her to return to him. It was marginally easier now the nurses weren't constantly in attendance.

The weeks passed. Months.

The doctors started to sound a note of caution. Geoff noticed they had started to say '*if* she regains consciousness' instead of '*when*'. The longer it went on, the more reticent they seemed about committing themselves to any prognosis.

Geoff dragged himself through each day at work, spending hours sitting beside Rhona, holding her hand, searching for a glimmer of recognition.

It was a full fourteen months before three doctors conferred and told him about the condition of persistent vegetative state. Outwardly he took it stoically; it was only what he had come to suspect himself. Inwardly he rebelled, screaming, *No!* Rhona, beautiful, elegant Rhona – the girl he loved – could not be equated with a vegetable. Never. It was too grotesque a thought. He would not accept it.

Again and again he reassured her. He would not rest. She meant too much to him for him to give up on her. But the faces were grave, the evidence overwhelming. He knew. Deep in his heart he knew they were right.

Two years after he had found her lying in their bed alone that fateful morning, he finally accepted it, and told the family. Only then did he break down in the privacy of her room and tell her exactly what had happened with Marilyn. In some small measure it was cathartic telling her – every little detail, not only what they had done but how he had felt. Honestly, no holds barred. He told her he wouldn't talk about it again, no point in risking other people overhearing; there must be no hint of scandal attached to her through him, nothing to taint her. He would see to that. He had been offered a partnership in another firm and he'd be moving to take up this new position at the end of the year. It'd be a clean start. It would take care of the tiny risk that remained.

TWENTY-ONE

As he waited now for DS Latimer, Geoff re-examined his own actions since the notes had started.

It had been a shock to meet Marilyn again unexpectedly a few weeks before the first note arrived. She was more blowsy, more coarse, than he remembered. The big break hadn't come, she'd lurched from one bit part to another, life had dealt her a bad hand, she told him.

It seemed too big a coincidence getting the letter so soon after that encounter. He knew the hellish fury of a woman scorned. The suspicion had been strong enough to prevent him contacting the police.

He told himself it was simple malice. Nevertheless doubts niggled. How had she known about Rhona? Had someone followed him, watched him going regularly to The Home, seen that no-one else went in and out of his flat? Surely she hadn't personally got the brains or the patience or the dogged persistence to follow such a careful investigation herself? Had she hired someone else to watch him? But why should she? He'd spurned her advances certainly but if she'd been going to hold anything against him surely she'd have used the threat she'd issued at the time. There was no demand for money, no threat of exposure. Did she just want revenge, to hurt him because he had hurt her? It was possible. Yes, that's all it was – a frustrated female lashing out at anything in its path.

The doubts hammered hardest in the small hours of a sleepless night. What if it was nothing to do with Marilyn? Had he misjudged this whole thing and put Rhona at risk of some other lunatic who might indeed have been violating her? Should he have told the police from the outset, left them to decide whether there was any substance to these claims?

What if this wasn't even a personal vendetta against him? After all Viv had been raped. But then, why the letters? It wasn't the same modus operandi. What if it was opportunistic? Maybe the scum had just heard what had happened to Viv, capitalised on it to dream up this new insult. These things had a way of leaking out.

It was a relief, having his hand forced. He'd talked himself out of telling anyone for too long already. Even if it was someone gunning for him personally, they weren't giving up. Perhaps his lack of response would provoke them to go further. Yes, he'd been right to give in now. Rhona, Viv, Fatima – all these vulnerable women needed police protection. What was his reputation against their safety? He'd give the police the whole sorry story. And Rhona's nightdress. Maybe it held incriminating evidence. Whatever it took. This villain must be put away.

DS Latimer listened in silence. What a treat hearing evidence from a trained lawyer. Especially one of this calibre!

Methodical, coherent, consistent. It must have cost him to talk about his wife's hang-ups, about his own failure to notice anything was wrong, about finding her like that, poor sod. And sharing that stuff about the crazy actress.

But he seemed armour-plated. Only when Geoffrey Archibald made an impassioned plea to him to save Rhona from any hint of scandal, if he could, did the policeman see any emotion. And it was clearly genuine. It wasn't anxiety about his own reputation; his only concern was this woman who knew nothing, felt nothing. Protect her, he said, if you possibly can. Was it possible? Only time would tell.

For the moment Brian Latimer had two paramount concerns, he told Geoff: to prevent any further crimes against these vulnerable patients, and to identify the scumball who'd perpetrated these crimes – whatever they were. Internally he registered a flickering light: after all the blind floundering in the search for Viv's rapist, the precise and logical mind of this lawyer was offering new hope. His involvement was potentially invaluable. With his intimate knowledge of the facts, he'd already pieced together the picture: dates, possible connections, potential logistics. He'd noted that the creep was getting bolder, playing more cards, making his timing more explicit. This latest letter wasn't referring to a time in the past or even yesterday – it was *today*. I've just done it! Now see if you can catch me!

The nightie might help. Having his DNA would be a major step forward. Geoff took some persuading but DS Latimer insisted: they must take swabs from Rhona this time.

Brian Latimer went straight to his office. No point in going home now; he needed to get his head around this case. He'd instructed Dr Wilkinson to lock the doors at Chivenings and admit no-one apart from validated staff, step up the patrolling.

Meanwhile he'd work out a strategy. They'd need it immediately. And it had to be foolproof. He'd get straight onto it.

It was with heavy steps that Geoff returned to Rhona's room. The police knew it all now. It wasn't his responsibility any longer. Why then this weight in his heart?

He sat silently holding Rhona's hand, stroking the soft skin, willing her to understand why he'd had to do what he'd done.

Unexpectedly tonight the sight of her inert figure brought him close to tears. He swallowed them fiercely. That was the last thing he needed. No-one, absolutely no-one else but Rhona should see what this all cost him. He'd intended staying late tonight. Instead he left The Home precipitately, passing without a word the security man posted at the end of the corridor, nodding curtly at the uniformed official at the main door, hung about with keys and badges, peaked hat pulled low over his eyes.

Back at the flat Geoff flung himself into the leather swivel chair in front of his computer. He closed his eyes, imagining Rhona sitting in this exact spot in his study, reading that ambiguous email.

What had she suffered? And would he ever be able to right the wrong he had done to her so inadvertently?

Two years after the tragedy, in a frenzy of activity, trying to adjust to the futility of her prognosis, he'd got rid of the old computer and invested in a sleeker, faster model. He'd personally taken the old one to the dump and thrown it as hard as he could, glad when the smashing glass and crunching metal put it beyond salvaging. Normally he'd have shipped it out to a country in the developing world but he'd suffered nightmarish thoughts of it polluting distant deserving causes. Better for it to be relegated to non-existence. The action smacked of impotent teenage rebellion he knew, pointless and illogical. But it was symbolic. So much was now out of his control.

Scalding tears ached against the back of his eyes. Control, choice. What choices could Rhona make? None. Absolutely none. Not even the tiniest, most inconsequential fraction of a decision. She had no say in whether he ruined her reputation, whether the police guarded her, which nightie the nurses put on her. Nothing. Even a pet – a cat, a dog – chose what they ate, and when they slept, and who they liked. But not Rhona.

Was that why they called it 'vegetative' state? Oh yes, the doctors sanitised it. It referred to there being only vegetative functions left, they said. But the expression still made him cringe. It always made him think of cabbages. But the police wouldn't protect a cabbage. No-one would care if it got damaged or destroyed.

For the umpteenth time Geoff's mind struggled with the concept of Rhona's choices. What was it that made people like Viv and Rhona persons with special rights? His legal brain endlessly toyed with the arguments. Somehow, because it was Rhona, he couldn't accept things that had seemed perfectly acceptable before.

Was human life, as distinct from other life, intrinsically of more inherent value? As far as Rhona was concerned his every instinct told him it had to be. No doubt about that. But if all human life was so sacred and special how come so many thousands of lives were aborted every year and society – and he – condoned it? Just like he'd approved of Viv's abortion. And why didn't people object to grossly deformed babies being allowed to die? He had himself, in the High Court, argued a case successfully against the parents, on the basis that society had no right to impose suffering on a helpless infant.

His mind raced through the landmark legal cases where adults' lives had been in debate: Tony Bland, Janet Johnston, Annie Lindsell, Diane Pretty. He'd always had a peculiar interest in these cases where terminally ill or progressively incapacitated patients, or their families, were pleading for the right to die. They intrigued him. The law, the legal constraints, society's reactions, attitudes to death – the arguments were fascinating. They'd challenged him to examine his own values and beliefs. That is, until Rhona became one of those incurable patients. Now he rarely allowed himself to dwell on the pros and cons. It was too close to home. But tonight he was feeling strangely vulnerable and introspective.

There had to be something fundamentally inviolable about human life that made people instinctively recoil from ending it. Life was sacred – period. Once you started to blur the edges of what was permissible it became increasingly hard to uphold the law, and he was a staunch supporter of law and order. Of course. He was a lawyer. A successful lawyer. But he'd always harboured a sort of grudging respect for the families who scoffed at the law's intransigence. Knowing nothing much about the ways of the legal profession, but with their backs against the wall, they spent precious years, dug into their sparse resources often, to battle with the courts because life to them was not worth living at all costs. Life – biological existence – wasn't absolutely sacred. Not in their cases. He had to admire their courage and their tenacity.

And now? Would he personally fight for Rhona's life to be ended? How she'd have hated the indignity of it all. No. He wouldn't. He knew beyond doubt he wouldn't. But it was not on principle; it was because he couldn't bear to let her go. Intellectually he knew her life was of no interest or value to her; she neither knew nor cared. But *he* cared. In spite of the changes, she was still Rhona. His living wife. She still looked like Rhona; she felt warm and soft to his touch. Good luck to others who appealed against the law, but it was not the way for him. Crazy really. He'd be more at home in the courts finding loopholes, arguing his case, than any other relative he'd watched fighting that particular battle. But he just couldn't do it.

Tonight he sat immobile in that chair, staring at the blank screen in front of him, and his unfettered thoughts ranged over the arguments he might have considered. He almost heard his court voice pleading the cause, defence and prosecution rolled into one …

'One of the most basic qualities that differentiates human life from other forms of life is the capacity to communicate and be communicated with. The appellants, Viv Faraday and Rhona Archibald, have been fully participating members of the human race on those terms, with aims and aspirations, hopes and dreams to share. We, their families – Viv's father, Rhona's husband – we know what they liked, their preferences, their opinions, their beliefs. But now? Neither woman can communicate anything. Nor will they again. Ever. Are they still fully persons with all the rights that persons in our society enjoy? Or have they slipped into a legal, ethical, twilight zone?

'And then there is the capacity to form and maintain relationships. Ah, relationships. In the past both these women were able to form intimate rewarding relationships, such special relationships that their menfolk keep visiting year after year, no matter the completely one-sided relationship they now have. But if their relatives stopped visiting them, would they be of any less worth? Hardly. They'd be the same. The father, the husband, they'd be the poorer. It is precisely because of the value attached to their former relationships that they continue to visit and care as they do.'

Geoff shuddered to a halt in his defence. Tonight he was being brutally honest. It had been a struggle to maintain this constancy. A bigger struggle for him than for Bill, he suspected. He'd been tempted to slacken his attendance, worn down by the futility of it all; Bill never wavered. Was what he offered enough? Marriages ended for less. It was too painful. Deliberately he dragged his mind away from this dangerous line of thought, back to the detachment of the court.

'Let's look more closely at Bill Faraday. Love of his child has kept Bill visiting every day, year after year. You can't just dissolve a father-daughter relationship. Viv wouldn't cease to be a daughter if he stopped visiting. But then you could argue that it is only his effort that is sustaining the relationship in any meaningful way. Until the rape, her brothers were making a pretty good job of ignoring her status as a sister. They rarely if ever saw her. But then suddenly Viv is in trouble. And they leap to her defence. They find they do care. Deeply. She is after all still a valued person. Still a loved human being. And she's in need of protection. Would they react in that way if it was their pet cat being violated? Or the cabbages in their allotment? No. I submit that there is something about a human relationship that is special. Unique. Does that uniqueness transcend the persistent vegetative state? Yes. I believe it does.

'Then what about self-awareness? That is one of the basic attributes of personhood. We see it developing in babies at an early age. On that basis Viv and Rhona now score zero. They have no awareness of anything, certainly not of themselves. No, they do not possess that criterion of personhood. Is that enough of itself to invalidate their rights? To de-value them?

'We move now to a sense of responsibility. Ah, how often we lawyers turn to this feature of personhood to make our case! Diminished responsibility. Again and again we hear it. We use it to lessen the enormity of a crime. We use it to appeal for leniency of sentencing. Even in hideous crimes we sometimes use it to soften the edges of our indignation and revulsion. If he wasn't at that time fully aware of what was right and wrong, what he owed to the victim, to society, we must excuse his behaviour to some extent. We lawyers know it's something of a legal device. But outside of the courts we all know what responsibility really means, don't we? And these two women had a sense of responsibility. Until they were overtaken by the tragedy of their insentience, they were fully paid-up members of the human race where responsibility was concerned. Much more so than the criminals we defend in our courts every day.'

He closed his eyes, gritting his teeth. Rhona had always taken her responsibilities very seriously. She'd been a thoroughly conscientious employee at the publishing firm, as committed to supporting her juniors as to advancing the good of the company. She'd been gentle with new authors, kind to agents, fair with the competition. She'd been an attentive daughter caring for her mother right up to her death from congestive cardiac failure. Whatever she took on she'd applied herself with commitment and integrity. And she'd taken her responsibilities as a wife so seriously that …

Geoff got up abruptly and left the study, slamming the door hard behind him. It didn't bear thinking of.

But the thoughts wouldn't be dismissed so easily.

Give him a wig and gown, stand him in front of the top six judges in the land, and would he be able to argue a winning case for Rhona and Viv still qualifying for full membership of the human race? To his chagrin he still wasn't sure.

He poured himself a third glass of Glenlivet, knowing he was only temporarily stilling his doubts, and diverting the pervasive sense of helplessness. But he must get some sleep.

His subconscious mind was relentless. He awoke unrested and the troubling thoughts continued to seethe as he drove to work the next morning.

The leading question pounding against his brain wasn't new: how far should someone else be able to make decisions on behalf on the mentally incompetent? Incompetent. It seemed an insult to use the word for Rhona – with her fine mind, her sensitivity, her well-thought-through opinions about things. Just because she couldn't use these capacities at the moment. 'Present incapacity' sounded nearer the mark.

The cross-examination continued.

'OK, let's take the present crisis. There is a real potential danger of these girls being raped. Until the perpetrator …' – no, it was too refined a word for this animal – '… until this criminal is found and locked up, would it be a wise precaution to give them prophylactic contraceptive pills?'

'No, sir, it would not! It is a revolting suggestion.'

'But what these women don't know won't trouble them. Shouldn't we attempt to limit the damage here? The damage to the women themselves. And the possible denting of public confidence in our healthcare?'

'Stuff public confidence! There's only one legitimate reason for giving Rhona Archibald contraceptive pills and that is if her husband wishes to have sex with her himself.'

'And would it be acceptable to make that decision on her behalf?'

'No, it would not. Without her consent, even with her husband, sex is too close to rape for comfort.'

'Even though she consented for all the years before she was struck down in this way?'

'Even though. Yes, sir.'

'I return you to the scenario we were considering before, Mr Archibald. The rape of your wife. If she did indeed become pregnant in the same way that Miss Faraday did as a consequence of being raped, should you as her husband be able to decide whether or not to terminate that pregnancy?'

'Legally, I know I'm not entitled to. But emotionally I feel I should be.'

'And why is that?'

'Because I know better than anyone else what my wife felt about these things. And I am the person most nearly affected by the outcome of the pregnancy.'

Geoff knew the answer already. He'd faced it when Bill had talked to him about Viv. He'd insist on an abortion. No way would he bring up the child of a rapist. And he knew Rhona would have said the same.

'Well, Mr Archibald. You sound very sure. But how do we know your marriage was a strong one? That you are really representing your wife's views? How do we know that your interests reflect hers? You might have your own agenda here.'

'True. I might. But I know what she would have said.'

'And did your wife actually tell you what she would wish to happen in exactly these circumstances? Did she envisage a situation where she was in a persistent vegetative state and raped and now pregnant?'

'No, of course not.'

'Then I submit that you cannot say with any certainty what she would have chosen.'

Damn you!

Geoff felt a cold hand clench round his stomach. How often had he impassively, systematically, overruled families? How often had he cocooned himself against the human elements of the case, maintained his legal precision, beaten down their arguments, legitimate, deeply felt opinions about what was right? What arrogance! His careful summations, his clever words, his neat quotable phrases – were they just a feature of such arrogance?

Rhona's circumstances had shown him. Human life, tragedy, you couldn't parcel them up neatly. Real life was messy, illogical, unfair, indiscriminate. Woe betide any advocate, any judge, who presumed to tell *him* what was in Rhona's best interests!

His persecutor was back on the offensive.

'Mr Archibald, you say that you would insist on an abortion. Consider, if you will, the outside possibility that one day your wife will recover. What would she say then, do you think, if she knew you'd authorised her being given contraceptive pills, or you'd killed her baby? She might never have a chance to have other children. Would she want that one, conceived in that way?'

'No. She would not.'

'Would she be grateful to you for robbing her of the chance of mother-hood?'

'Under those circumstances she wouldn't see it in those terms.'

'You're certain of that?'

'I'm certain.'

'I return then to your wife's present condition. She knows nothing. She is not distressed by the rape. She will not know one way or the other if she has a baby or not. Why waste valuable courtroom time and taxpayers' money debating this case? Isn't it better to worry about the fully mentally competent girl who's physically restrained and raped? One might argue that *she* is in no fit state to make a decision regarding termination of pregnancy either. She has been mentally traumatised as well as physically violated. She is severely distressed by the whole business. And yet we often leave her to decide without the benefit of legal counsel. Isn't her right to support in decision making of a higher level than your wife's?'

'Arguing from hard logic we might protest many things, sir, but every decent feeling screams against abandoning the most vulnerable members of our society. Their complete inability to help themselves seems to me to place an even greater burden on the decision makers.'

'And that's why you left your wife vulnerable to being raped rather than involve the law in protecting her, is it?'

Geoff screeched to a halt as a pedestrian stepped out onto the road without warning. Papers shot off the back seat. The driver behind leaned on his horn and made a threatening gesture.

Geoff shook himself mentally. He switched on the radio, resolving to still the questioning.

The news item bombed his brain.

'A forty-five-year-old woman is taking her case to the European courts in an effort to win the right to end her life when she chooses. Greta Down suffers from motor neurone disease and has been unable to do anything for herself for two years. Her daughter has appealed on her behalf for the right to assist Mrs Down when the time comes but the case has already been dismissed by the House of Lords.'

Was there no escape?

Geoff shuddered. Legal minds might debate the age of consent for minors, the rights of individuals to choose the time of their death, the whole notion of respect for autonomy, but what were these arguments in the face of raw human tragedy? Real-life tragedy.

Of course, you couldn't run the system on gut instinct. Individual decisions almost invariably impinged on the rights and duties of others. And, besides, you had to prioritise to some extent. After all, babies, young children, the dementing elderly, the mentally disabled, you couldn't attach the same importance to their stated preferences as you could to a fully mentally competent adult, could you? But it was perfectly conceivable that on certain subjects some of them might be better able to choose for themselves than the people who decided on their behalf. If you'd never had a mental impairment how could you know what someone who had would want? Weren't their own perceptions what mattered here? Besides, who really knew about the unfathomable parts of the brain?

He swung the car left into the car park. For a long moment he sat with his fingers clenching and unclenching on the wheel, his eyes tightly shut, as he willed himself to regain his professional composure.

He had come full circle. How could he ever be one hundred per cent sure that he made the right decisions for Rhona? He was probably in a stronger position than anyone else to do so, but he wasn't Rhona; she hadn't always seen things as he did.

And he couldn't even be sure he wasn't doing some of this for himself. It wasn't possible to separate out himself from her – not completely. They were in some ways two parts of a whole unit. He couldn't make decisions on her behalf without considering their impact on his own life. It was his responsibility to consider them both. Ahh, but he could now make decisions for himself which wouldn't affect her one way or another. Would that be irresponsible, an abuse of his autonomy?

Autonomy. Now there he could defend his position.

'Your Honour, it seems to me the notion of autonomy is being used too narrowly here. It's commonly taken to mean the individual's right to choose for him or herself. I prefer to qualify the concept. I believe it devalues the whole notion if one ignores one's responsibilities and chooses from entirely selfish reasons. The right course of action may not always be the one that best promotes one's own personal interests. No, autonomy is more properly a *responsible* use of one's freedom to choose.'

Aha! The judge's attention was arrested now.

'Tell me more, Mr Archibald.'

'Being competent to decide means seeing things in the round. And in a way it's more of a compliment to the individual to give them that sort of autonomous choice. It shows you think they're capable of weighing up all the arguments and making wise judgements on behalf of all those concerned.'

'And you consider you are capable of that sort of decision making on behalf of your wife, do you? Wise, responsible decision making.'

'I think I am, yes.'

'You only "think" you are?'

What evidence was there for greater conviction? Hadn't he put the risk of scandal ahead of the risk of rape? And hadn't he swithered, changed tack himself? Only now speaking up – after three anonymous letters. Only now perceiving the risk of physical abuse to exceed that of psychological trauma. Whose interests was he really serving?

He groaned aloud. Only Rhona could tell him if he'd got it right. Would she have wanted him to talk about her secret fears, about her suspicions, about the Petersen business, to the police today? She'd so jealously guarded their private lives. She'd have hated any grubby innuendo, any hint of impropriety. She'd rather have suffered in silence. Was that what she had done, what had brought her to the point of suicide?

If only he could ask her, set her mind at rest.

Would the sense of guilt and the uncertainty never end?

TWENTY-TWO

Steven was at The Home ahead of DS Latimer.

The policeman arrived on the dot of six o'clock next morning, looking as if he hadn't been to bed at all. He was apologetic. Much as he would like to have the place crawling with officers, resources simply didn't stretch to it.

To Steven it felt like a body blow. Ever since Viv's rape, he'd increased security with a round-the-clock janitor or security officer patrolling the corridors. But it hadn't prevented the breaches. There was a limit to what he could implement.

They had to face the facts, Latimer said. No-one had any idea when – if ever – this guy would appear again. And there was no concrete evidence that he had ever actually harmed anyone.

Steven did a double-take on that.

No, Latimer pointed out, there had been nothing on Mrs Archibald's nightdress or her swabs. She didn't seem to have been raped yesterday.

Yes, they had the DNA sample from Viv's fetus but it didn't match with any of the sex offenders they had on record. And there was a strong possibility that that rape was quite unconnected with this latest business with the anonymous letters, anyway. Whoever had assembled those letters had worn gloves, and they'd used plain water to stick down the envelopes.

It was just too expensive to mount a guard on such a flimsy pretext. He'd arrange sessions to give the staff some guidance on what to look out for. And of course, anything suspicious and the police would be there instantly, he promised.

Steven was not impressed. One definite rape, a pregnancy, three anonymous threatening letters, a lawyer involved who perceived the danger to be real … good grief, what did it take to make the police suspicious?

He had graphic visions of his Home emptying rapidly as public confidence was eroded. The staff too, they wouldn't want to stay with a sinking ship, and he couldn't blame them.

DS Latimer made the right noises. He understood. He agreed. He would do more if he could. But Dr Wilkinson knew what staff shortages were like, didn't he?

They'd come like a shot if any of the staff was in the least bit suspicious. Just ring.

It didn't help having Bill Faraday agitating all the time. What were they doing? Were there any developments? Why wasn't there somebody watching Viv's room? When were they going to take these crimes seriously?

Steven found it increasingly difficult to maintain a patient understanding with the man. Didn't he have any idea of what this whole business meant for The Home?

What else could he do, Bill argued. If *he* didn't keep up the pressure, would the police lose interest all together?

'I know what it is,' he fumed to Geoff in the car park one evening. 'Viv, Rhona, they aren't high enough up the list. If it was some famous face – royalty, film star, politician's wife – *then* they'd do something. If it was a vote-catcher. But they know these girls can't give them bad publicity. Who cares about a Home full of incurable folk? Just a drain on society.'

Geoff heard the bitterness.

'I don't think it's like that actually, Bill. I mean, you and I, we could raise a dust on their behalf. They know that.'

'Do they? We aren't, are we? Raising a dust, I mean? Not even you. And they know you've got clout.'

'No. I guess not. But that's only because we want to protect the girls. Or at least that's why *I'm* not. Rhona would absolutely hate having her name dragged through the papers.'

'Well, exactly. We don't court publicity. Not like these high-profile people do. So the police know they can just let it ride. OK, they pretend to listen to our case, but they don't take it seriously. I mean, you can *see* they don't. They don't even have an officer watching the place!'

'They don't have the manpower.'

'They would have – they'd bloody soon find it if it was some famous person in here, or some politician's wife!' Bill snorted, slapping his hand down on the roof of his car.

'Have you talked to DS Latimer? Told him what you think?'

'You bet.'

'And?'

'Same claptrap. Not enough resources. Not enough evidence. As if a pregnant patient isn't enough evidence.'

Bill opened the door of his Rover, but the movement was arrested by Geoff's next words.

'But in fairness there's nothing to suggest this guy has come back here.'

The door was slammed shut again as Bill stared at Geoff in astonishment.

'How can you say that! You of all people. Hell, you're a cool customer and no mistake. Anonymous letters coming out the woodwork and you say there's nothing to suggest he's back.'

'I'm sorry. It must seem illogical to you. Blame my legal training, my warped way of thinking. But I still think these two things aren't connected.'

144

And I think it's careful thinking and attention to detail that'll trap these criminals. Not an outward show of strength.'

' "Careful thinking?" *Careful thinking?* Bloody hell, man. You don't need to think carefully to know my daughter's been raped. Or your wife's been threatened. And some swine's out there laughing up his sleeve at us both,' Bill hissed fiercely.

'Believe me, I understand your frustration. But I do honestly think Latimer's doing everything he can. I'm as concerned for the girls' safety as you. Honestly, I am. I just know, perhaps, a bit more how things work. It takes time to carry out these investigations and they have to be meticulous. At every stage. No merit in going off at half-cock. Only takes a little loophole and these criminals slip through the net. For good.'

'Huhh.'

'No disrespect, Bill, but it doesn't speed things up if the relatives distract the police from the enquiry.'

'Huhh. A distraction. That's all I am these days. A distraction.'

'No. Everybody understands. I've often thought it's harder in some respects for the relatives of a victim than for the victim themselves. And in this case I know it is.'

'Ye gods – if I could only get my hands on that ... that ...'

'I know. It's natural. Anything civilised seems too tame for him. But try to hang on, Bill. Let Latimer get on with his job. You want to see this guy locked up, yes?'

The eloquence of his appeal was as much in Geoff's calm manner and steady look as in his words. The man obviously believed in the system. And he should know.

'As long as they throw away the key – to use a pathetic cliché,' Bill grunted.

'They'll throw the book at him. Believe me.'

'If they ever find him.'

'They will. They've got his DNA. Incontrovertible evidence. It's the best there is.'

'And your bloke – think they'll get him too?'

'If I have anything to do with it.'

'Well, I hope you're right.' With that Bill flounced into his car and swept out of the car park without so much as a wave.

But Geoff's own confidence took a nosedive five days later.

The envelope was tantamount to a red rag. He'd only been to Cath's Canteen for a coffee, but in spite of all the extra vigilance, in spite of all the precautions, someone had managed to get a letter onto Rhona's locker in that small window of opportunity.

It beggared belief. He'd actually been *in the building* and whoever it was had brazenly taunted him.

145

I'm here! I can get access to your wife whenever I want it. Don't think for a moment you can stop me with your security locks, your CCTV cameras, your patrolling.

As soon as he saw the brown envelope lying on the bedside locker he knew.

MR GEOFFREY OLIVER ARCHIBALD

So X even knew his middle name.

He felt physically sick opening it. The same ragged assembly of letters confirmed his dread.

SHE'S MINE WHENEVER I WANT HER. DOWN TO THE TINY MOLE ON HER RIGHT HIP BONE.

His eyes travelled instinctively to Rhona's curled-up body. Who could possibly know about that? The only mole on her entire body. He knew, of course; she'd once laughingly told him, 'Grandma said it was the touch of a fairy godmother.'

He'd lightly touched the dark spot with his little finger.

'Fairy godmother must have had chocolatey fingers,' he'd teased.

That was before he knew how fragile her sense of self-worth was.

The nurses, maybe some of the doctors, would know about the mole too. And probably some of her therapists, the ones who worked with her body to stop it stiffening up and becoming distorted. They worked hard at that here, and all the exercises, all the careful skin care, had paid dividends in preserving her shape, stopping contractures, pressure sores. Surely … *surely*, none of those people who worked so tirelessly year in and year out would stoop to this outrage.

But it would explain the easy access, the intimate knowledge of her body …

The thought made him grit his teeth. It was a step too far. Only Rhona's privacy mattered. He could not sit back and allow this animal to take advantage of her vulnerability, touch her, know her … He had to hand this over to the police. Insist they protect her.

And how could he leave Rhona here, with this criminal on the prowl? He'd have to get her moved to a place of safety. It had gone on too long.

He reached out to touch her as she lay immobile against the bank of white pillows but as suddenly snatched his hand away before making contact. He'd just finished freshening her up before he'd gone for that coffee.

She'd always taken good care of her hair, brushing it vigorously every night, and he'd taken over that role of late, finding the sweeping movements soothing, loving the feel of it in his hands. Her hair was as sleek as he'd left it, no sign of disturbance.

The nurses had helped him get her into bed from the chair and her arms lay across the top fold of fresh clean sheet exactly as he'd placed them. He'd gone through her routine physiotherapy methodically just as they'd trained him to do, carefully positioning her legs with one bent higher than the other to keep her slightly over on her side, the bolster behind her holding her secure.

Yes, she was in exactly the same position.

He began to breathe more easily. There was no way she had been disturbed, never mind raped. No, whatever had happened in those thirty minutes he'd been gone, Rhona had been unmolested.

But someone had been there. And this time they knew precisely when.

If it was an outsider he'd surely taken a huge gamble; he could so easily have been discovered. They'd have to check the CCTV footage of course, but even if X had managed to slip through security at the door, and evade the cameras, he'd had less than twenty-five minutes, because there'd been no-one at all in the corridor when Geoff went to the canteen, no-one there when he returned. Bill had been next-door with Viv; Fatima's women friends were in the end room; any of them might have come out at any time.

And there was no other means of entry. The window in Rhona's room was open about three inches but it was exactly the same now, and it had a device on it to stop it being opened any further except from the inside.

No, it had to be an inside job. Everything pointed to it being a member of staff. And that sick person was here, in the Home, now. Roaming free. Unchallenged. Free to do whatever he liked to these unknowing women. Geoff felt a wave of cold anger sweep through him.

For only the second time in six years he rang the bell to summon a nurse. This time his vicious repeated pressing on the buzzer brought running footsteps. In spite of his pent-up emotion he knew a moment of relief when a familiar face appeared, someone who knew about the anonymous notes. Betty needed the minimum of information to agree to stay with Rhona while he went to find Steven and call DS Latimer. Neither was on the premises but Alison Reed rang them both.

They came in immediately. It crossed Geoff's mind fleetingly he must tell Bill about the swift response.

Behind closed doors in Steven's office, notes scattered across his desk, the three men watched the surveillance videos in silence, the entrance and foyer, the main corridors, each in turn.

Steven could identify every member of staff, every visitor that afternoon and evening – apart that is from the six veiled women who were visiting Fatima Omar. But they stuck close together in two bands of three, taking it in turns to visit or remain in the waiting room. Every so often the two black clouds would merge and then separate again as the shifts changed.

Geoff hardly dared voice the question.

'Do you think … it could be … an inside job?'

He was unsurprised by Steven's swift look of annoyance. Morale was only just beginning to recover after the suspicions about Viv's rape. If they started to investigate the staff again, a lot of them would seek jobs elsewhere. Nobody wanted this kind of slur hanging over them.

'Well, I think we'll need to tread very carefully here,' DS Latimer said quietly, leaning back and linking his hands behind his head. 'Nobody wants to start accusing anyone before we've got some facts together. Now we've got a couple of time-frames to start us off. Should help to narrow the field a bit. There was the time when the note was inside your wife's nightdress. We could get a list of everyone on duty for the period of time she was wearing that nightdress – well, *could* have been wearing it anyway. And then today. The note must have been put in her room during that thirty minutes you were in the canteen. We can check everyone in the building on both occasions and see if any names match, for a start. Presumably you have rosters or a record somewhere, Dr Wilkinson?'

'I don't personally, but Alison Reed will have. I could ring her and get the files for you.'

'Please,' the policeman said. It would be a start.

Mrs Reed brought them herself. Her lips were set in a thin line, and she said nothing as she handed over the files to DS Latimer. She didn't look at Geoff.

There were two doctors, four nurses, two kitchen staff, one cleaning lady, and the evening receptionist who had been on duty during both periods of time. Only three of them were men but then, as Latimer pointed out to nobody in particular, it didn't need to be a man to just deliver a note.

'Nothing to say it was someone on duty though,' Geoff mused. 'If they were known faces, knew their way around, anyone could come in, no-one would challenge them, would they? I mean, you don't keep tabs on other people's rosters, do you?'

He saw both Steven and Alison Reed stiffen again, their faces inscrutable masks. You couldn't blame them. Between them, he and Bill must seem like the relatives from hell, bent on destroying The Home. Especially probably Geoff, with his suggestions, his questions, his probing. As if it wasn't bad enough that his personal threats had crept into The Home. Now he was wanting to antagonise every member of staff.

He knew Steven had been reluctant to have Geoff watch the CCTV footage with them, but DS Latimer had overruled his objections, arguing that it might jog his lawyer's memory, or there might be someone he knew in some other context, someone who might just bear him a grudge. Fair enough, Steven had agreed, but reluctantly. It was understandable. Geoffrey Archibald might be a lawyer in his other life, even a hotshot lawyer, but here he was a relative. Just a relative. A wronged relative, a frightened relative maybe, but just a relative. *He* didn't stand to lose if the whole staff were antagonised. *He* wouldn't be around to bail The Home out if it collapsed around their ears, would he?

'Let's not jump the gun,' DS Latimer said quickly, his eyes flickering between them, sensing the tension. 'I think we should start with the staff on duty. If we draw a blank there we can spread the net wider.'

'And how much will you tell them?' Steven asked. 'We've got a Home to run here. Morale plummeted with the last episode. The last thing the team need is more suspicion.'

'I understand. And I'll certainly do my best to make sure they all think we're only asking them as important potential witnesses, helping us with enquiries. We want to know if they saw or heard anything, because they were on duty. No need to mention rape, I think. Not at this stage. No evidence of any disturbance of Mrs Archibald this evening, you say, sir?'

'None that I could see. Not this time anyway,' Geoff said.

'And nothing to suggest rape when we tested the clothes and bed-linen and swabs last time,' DS Latimer said soothingly. 'No, I'm hopeful this is a threat rather than a promise ... Sorry, sir. Not meaning to be flippant. But at the moment it looks more like an invasion of privacy rather than any actual bodily harm. Best make it a question of who saw anyone who might have put a note in Mrs Archibald's room. Straightforward breach of security, I think we could say.'

Steven was nodding. That sounded much less sinister.

Geoff could only hope it was the truth. He rose to his feet and made for the door.

'And no need for anyone to know about the precise contents of the notes either,' Latimer added. 'I'd be grateful if you'd both continue to keep that information to yourselves. Don't want anyone confessing to something they didn't do. Just slows up the investigation getting red herrings.'

Geoff needed no persuasion on that.

TWENTY-THREE

Though secure in the knowledge that The Home was today crawling with plain-clothes policemen, and that all the staff would know that the investigation had been notched up, Geoff was reluctant to keep his appointment with the bank manager. He shuddered, remembering the painful conversation about Rhona's financial affairs he'd had three years ago. He'd been in no hurry to repeat it, but Mr Hardcastle had been persistent, urging him to return to discuss investments. Geoff had pleaded pressure of work but even to his own ears the excuse sounded improbably flimsy. Even so, it was certainly not part of his thinking to tell Hardcastle about the anonymous letters. He was already far too vulnerable for comfort.

Moving Rhona's money around, trying to gain as much as possible in the process, smacked of self-interest. If anyone were to benefit from her investments, it would be her next of kin. Geoff. He told himself sharply, the bank manager was only doing his job, making wise decisions which gave the best returns. There was nothing unseemly in that. And it was the bank not Geoff urging action. But he still hated it.

The personal assistant – Pattie, her badge said – was smilingly courteous.

'I'm so sorry, Mr Archibald, Mr Hardcastle has been unavoidably detained. But he's just phoned in to say he'll be no more than ten minutes late for his appointment. May I bring you a coffee?'

It was light and airy in the anteroom to the main office. Geoff, his mind on the task ahead, idly watched the staff through the glass partitions. Odd having so much glass in places handling so much money. Ideal you'd think for prospective burglars. Suss out the place, plan their crimes.

From where he sat he could see directly into four different offices. Not Mr Hardcastle's, of course, that was hidden behind a big wooden door, and he'd be glad of the privacy when his turn came to go before the top man, he knew. But these lesser minions, they had to suffer public scrutiny. Did they feel it conveyed a sense of openness and honesty? Was it actually designed to give them the maximum chance of detecting potential trouble, stopping and apprehending would-be bank robbers? No-one seemed in the least bit interested in his activities anyway.

Pattie was back in her office next to Mr Hardcastle's, her neat black suit and impeccable grooming giving an aura of business-like efficiency. And she certainly looked efficient, at her computer, even answering the phone without stopping the lightning dashes around the keyboard.

Nothing like his own laboured two-finger typing. Rhona had tried to persuade him several times to learn properly but he'd stuck to his argument that it would take years to get up the speed he'd acquired with his own ungainly methods. And no amount of practice would ever acquire for him the kind of speed this woman had at her fingertips.

He watched mesmerised as the frosted pink nails flew effortlessly down the pages.

A sudden movement in the adjoining office drew his attention sideways. Geoff amused himself by noting every detail as if he would be required to give a detailed eyewitness account. It was a trick he'd developed in his student days when he was bored. And he was easily bored.

Three people seated in a parallel line, all with their backs to him, worked on three parallel screens. The one on the left had curly black hair and a vivid magenta top hugging her curves, tight black skirt well above her plump knees. An older woman occupied the middle position, short, cropped white hair tinted vaguely mauve, a grey cowl necked sweater, darker grey wool trousers, shiny black patent loafers. The one on the right wore a crisp, blue shirt, black trousers smartly creased, long brown ponytail curling down to the waist, secured with a plain red rubber band.

Geoff stared again at the rubber band. It was strangely incongruous amid such understated elegance. There was no attempt to upgrade it with a ribbon, a clasp, or a scrunchie. Had the girl been in a hurry getting up this morning? Had her last decent clasp broken in her haste? Or had one of her children secreted it away somewhere? It would make a rather intriguing title for a whodunnit: *The Red Rubber Band*, Geoff thought. But nobody seemed to be caring about it in this office. Far too busy no doubt. And it'd be a brave boss who'd criticise an employee for something so minor. She was probably terribly hard working and utterly dependable.

It was the movement of the lady in grey which had caught his attention initially. With one deft push from her feet and hands she'd gone into motion. The castors of her mobile seat spun her straight back, then down to one side where she lifted a file from a filing cabinet. Geoff saw her say something, her mouth moving but no sound penetrating the proofed glass. She laughed at something the magenta girl said. His mind supplied the conversation. Then into reverse, sideways, straight forward, returning to her regular slot. Once more three backs hid the daily grind from Geoff's eyes.

Did these people ever wonder about the lives of the people whose money they dealt in? Did they take as much interest in what made them tick as he, Geoff, took in his clients' motives and predilections? Or as Steven Wilkinson took in the lives of his long-term patients? Or as DS Latimer took in the workings of the criminal mind?

He watched the three backs curiously. What did three women lined up side by side all day in a bank talk about?

The ponytail swung loose as the blue shirt stretched widely, easing cramped muscles, a gold link bracelet falling over the cuff, catching the light as it moved. The curling hair oscillated as the seat spun around and …

Geoff started. The other side of that glossy head sported a neatly clipped beard. He watched the young man rise to his feet and walk across the office, saying something to the two women as he opened the door and vanished.

At that moment Pattie appeared.

'Mr Hardcastle will see you now, Mr Archibald.' She smiled.

The meeting was every bit as painful as he'd anticipated. Not that the bank manager would have known; Geoff's façade never slipped throughout the whole encounter. By the time he left, Rhona was in line to make a lot of money on a block of shares Mr Hardcastle had recommended. Geoff had in his pocket a handwritten list of worthy causes to whom he might safely, ethically and anonymously transfer the proceeds.

Not until he was back at The Home did the incident with the ponytail return to his mind. For some reason it disturbed him. He was sitting beside Rhona, stroking her hand automatically with his thumb, when the thought struck him.

He sat motionless, his back rigid, his eyes staring unblinkingly into the staring eyes of his wife. What if … ?

DS Latimer was cautious about his idea. It was infuriating how slowly he responded at times.

'It's only a hunch, I know. But it's possible. Isn't it?' Geoff ventured again.

'Maybe.'

'Worth pursuing?' Geoff was doing his best not to be too pushy. After all Latimer was probably wishing he'd thought of it himself.

'We could look at the CCTV videos again.'

Yes, yes, yes. Come on. Get on with it. Contact the interpreters, find someone who can read Arabic. Why didn't the guy see the urgency? Talk about Mr Plod … ! No wonder Bill got agitated.

They skimmed through the film on fast speed until they saw the first black-draped figure. Rewind. Normal speed. Freeze-frame. Geoff peered closer. It was the nun.

'Bill Faraday's ex-wife,' Geoff said. 'Viv's mother.' Move on!

Latimer zoomed in on her face, confirmed his identification, returned to full frame. They watched Frances walk sedately down the corridor and vanish from the screen. Latimer fast-forwarded to her return, checked her face again. They watched her leave The Home. She didn't reappear. Ever.

Her solitary appearance was in stark contrast to the usual mass of robed figures visiting Fatima Omar. Always in twos or threes, sometimes more, grouping and regrouping, huddled together, always together. Day after day. Every day. Latimer gave up zooming in. Only the eyes were visible.

Anybody's eyes. Anonymous eyes swathed in black.

Seeing it now, the sight of a solitary black figure seemed to jump out and hit Geoff. He sucked in his breath. He should have been more observant earlier.

'There!' he shot out.

Rewind. Normal speed.

They both leaned forward, eyes glued to the screen. The figure moved confidently into the foyer, approached the reception desk, wrote in the visitors' book, glided off down the corridor. Steven Wilkinson appeared from the other direction. The head dropped; the figure slid past him. All unexceptional. Except … the figure was alone.

Several times Latimer zoomed. Geoff gritted his teeth. It was perfect. Only the eyes visible. Just like all the other anonymous eyes.

Latimer fast-forwarded through the film, stopping only where the Arabic women appeared.

The next appearance of a single figure made both men stiffen, the tension in the room palpable. Once past the desk the figure suddenly halted, turned on its heel, and left the building precipitately. Seconds later three Arabic figures were seen coming down the corridor, leaving The Home.

'Ahhah! Couldn't risk being spoken to by the *real* visitors,' Geoff hissed.

But it was coverage taken several days later which Geoff pounced on. This excerpt showed a solitary figure walking slowly along towards the occupied rooms, pausing occasionally to look or listen. At the end of the corridor it made to turn and pass out of sight but suddenly stopped, returned rapidly to the waiting area, and sat down. The head frequently turned to look back along the corridor.

Ten minutes later Geoff saw himself walk into view, talking to Bill. They must have been standing in the corridor. As if on cue the figure rose and hurried away along to the rooms where Rhona and Viv lay, head downcast demurely. Walking within inches of them!

Geoff felt the sweat gathering in his palms.

'Can you rewind back to the waiting area?' he urged, not taking his eyes off the screen.

The black drapes again flowed down the corridor, paused and returned. The figure seated itself to one side of the corridor, occasionally leaning forward to look along it. At one point it shuffled on the seat and remained in one position for longer.

'There! See!' Geoff shot out, stabbing his finger at the screen. 'Freeze that, can you?'

'See what?' Latimer stared at the frame.

'See how he sits? Women don't sit like that. Especially not *these* women!'

DS Latimer let out his breath in a low whistle. The figure sat, legs spread wide, elbows leaning on knees. A male stance.

'Play the next bit again – slowly,' Geoff said.

They watched as the figure suddenly shrank back, head down, arms lightly in its lap, knees and feet trimly together. Bill and Geoff approached. The figure rose decorously, sidled past them, and moved without a backward glance towards the rooms they had just vacated. To where Rhona and Viv lay. Unsuspecting. Out of sight of the camera.

Geoff felt waves of nausea wash over him as he stared at the film. How long would that animal be? Was he in Rhona's room all this time? Was this the time when … ?

He kept his gaze fixed on the screen, the bitter taste of bile in his mouth, until the black figure walked confidently past the reception desk and left the building under the eye of the camera.

It was a full eighteen minutes since Geoff had left his wife. The swine!

Dates matched. Times fitted. Those *were* the times when X had left Geoff mocking notes. He *had* been with Rhona. Who knew what he'd done?

DS Latimer was in overdrive.

The interpreter was at The Home within the hour. Yes, she'd be happy to look at the visitors' book. But what was she looking for?

'Just see if you notice anything odd or unusual,' Latimer said, keeping his voice even, handing her the book.

She scanned the signatures carefully. Her tracking finger stopped suddenly.

'This signature. It isn't a proper signature.'

'Meaning?'

'It's just a scrawl. Sort of mimicking the earlier entries. But nothing like a name.'

'OK. Can you show me when that same kind of scrawl appears?'

Latimer jotted down dates and times. Even without consulting his notes he knew. Yes, they all matched with the dates of the anonymous notes. Clever beggar, Archibald. The net was closing.

But wait a minute. The latest note – yesterday's note – there was no false entry. None all day. Who had delivered that? Had he slipped in without signing the book? Or did this guy have an accomplice?

They studied every inch of the CCTV footage. Steven Wilkinson and the girl from the reception desk watched it with them. Between them they could identify every person on the film. Every one had a legitimate reason for being there. And there was no appearance of a solitary figure swathed in black.

Two weeks passed. Geoff, Steven, Mrs Reed, everyone was constantly on the alert. Geoff worked more from The Home than his office.

He confided in Bill. Yes, he'd keep an extra eye open, too. He could put in even longer hours. And he would. Anything to nail this creep.

'No heroics now, Bill,' Geoff said urgently. 'If you see anything just tell the staff. We don't want to frighten this guy off.'

The Home seethed with vigilance.

But ... nothing. No sign of that isolated Arabic figure. No notes. Nothing.

The police enquiry fermented somewhere unseen but DS Latimer could only reiterate: call us if you see anything suspicious.

Did X know the net was closing? Had someone tipped him off?

TWENTY-FOUR

It was seven o'clock in the evening. Geoff was at home, engrossed in writing a review of a book on medical jurisprudence. He'd had three reminders from the journal editor already pointing out the deadline he'd ignored.

He was irritated by the interruption of the phone.

'Archibald,' he muttered automatically, still reading.

'Archibald. Yes. Husband of the delectable Rhona Archibald.' It was a low male voice.

'Who is this?' Geoff asked sharply.

'I think you know who it is.'

'What do you want?'

'Your wife.'

'Leave her out of this. Just deal straight with me. What d'you want?'

'You owe me, Archibald. You took my wife. I'll have yours.'

'Who ...'

The phone went dead.

Geoff instantly dialled 1471.

'The caller withheld their number.' Damn. Damn. Damn.

His hands were trembling. Beads of sweat gathered on his brow. He had to think.

The voice. Was it familiar? No.

Was it disguised? Almost certainly.

'You took my wife,' he'd said.

Whose wife?

DS Latimer came in person. Geoff took him straight into the study as if something of the caller might still linger in the air.

'This looks promising. Narrows the field,' Latimer said, rubbing his hands together, his eyes taking in the rows of legal books, the neatly ordered papers, the framed picture of Rhona Archibald as she must have looked in her other life. 'Gives us a motive.'

'Motive nothing! I've never taken anybody's wife.' Geoff spat out. But he knew there was no escaping the questions.

Yes, it was the first time the man had called. No, he didn't recognise the voice. No, he didn't know who it was. No, it didn't make any sense. He hadn't taken anybody's wife.

He didn't like the insolent way Latimer looked at him. Or was it his fevered imagination? It was true, he hadn't. Whatever the man on the phone said. Not that he hadn't been tempted. Since Rhona ... Especially since Angela ... But he hadn't.

But no amount of protestations of innocence could still the surging questions in his own brain. There must be something. Think, man, think.

'Let me know if anything comes to mind,' Latimer said. 'No matter how seemingly unimportant. You know what these jokers' minds are like.'

Indeed he did. Unfathomable half the time.

OK, *he* knew he hadn't taken anybody's wife but what *had* he done that might be interpreted in that way? To a sick mind. Or a criminal one. If there was anything, it had to be in his professional life. That at least he knew.

His mind trawled through cases he'd dealt with involving women, his hand jotting down names, crimes, possible links. Haphazard, jumbled. Blacklock, divorce; Adams, divorce; Davidson, Lee, blackmail; Christie, Koepleman, Abdul, murder; Jackson, Greenaway, grievous bodily harm; Stewart, Hope, Fleetwood, Franks, rape. He could sort them later, look at each one to see if it could be reinvented to fit this accusation.

He groaned aloud at the size of the task, the waste of time. But no, it wasn't a waste of time, not if it would mean Rhona was safe.

Pertwee, Mansfield, divorce; Gray, Underwood, Carlton … The jumbled lists grew. His methodical self took over; he organised the information systematically into lists: rapes, murders, divorces …

Driving to The Home, sitting beside Rhona, his mind constantly working, the lists grew. It would be a start. He could go through the files in his legal office tomorrow. But this was a start.

'I didn't, Rhona. You have to believe me. I didn't take anybody's wife. I never have. I swear it.' He found he was clutching her hand so tightly the fingers were white.

By the time he went to bed he'd covered two whole A4 pages with names. He didn't stop to dwell on the details of each one. Better not to trust to memory for that. He'd consult the files tomorrow.

He woke with a start at two forty-five. The room was in total darkness. Names seethed and twisted in his brain. Faces – contorted, leering faces – hung disembodied in the gloom. The tramp of boots, advancing, pounded in his ears.

He swallowed another sleeping pill, buried his head under the pillow and wished for the day.

But the daylight brought nothing more reassuring than a severe headache. It was a relief to get to the office and begin the disciplined task he'd planned. The list was still formidable. Every wronged husband, every convicted one, any man whose woman had got away, might perceive him as the thieving accomplice. Not one of them stood out as a prime suspect. The police would have their work cut out sifting through this number of interviews. *If* they bothered to pursue this line of enquiry. He jotted down his own shorthand ideas as to guilt or innocence, potential for revenge, capacity for plotting it. There were some people you just knew couldn't do anything as tortuous as this.

DS Latimer whistled when he saw the lists.

'Very helpful, Mr Archibald. Very helpful indeed. And of course we won't divulge our source, as you say. Any front runners in your mind?'

Geoff shook his head. Any one of the names on his shortlist could have written a few letters, made one phone call. Any one of them could have dressed up as an Arab woman. A little make-up, coloured lenses.

'Presumably you'll be able to eliminate some pretty easily – the ones that have died, the ones still in prison.'

'Takes time. Takes time.' Latimer was running his eye down the lists.

'And the exceptionally tall or small ones, I guess,' Geoff added.

'Mmmhm. If he did it himself.'

Point taken. Back to motive.

'Anything jump out at you from this lot?' Latimer asked, flipping Geoff's careful list with his hand.

'Not so far. I've marked the ones who might have a legitimate grievance but a nutter like this doesn't need right on his side.'

'True. What do these squares mean?'

'They're the women I represented but didn't believe myself. Their husbands, boyfriends, might have a grudge against me, but I wouldn't necessarily know about it.'

Latimer looked at him oddly.

Geoff shrugged. 'Just doing what I'm paid for,' he said defensively.

'Stinks sometimes though, eh? Bit like our job sometimes.'

It was curiously comforting.

It had taken Geoff two days to draw up the full list of possible cases.

DS Latimer immediately assigned three of his men to checking the names, tracking, phoning, visiting, interviewing. They'd be discreet, he'd said, but it was still unnerving knowing they were out there, raking up old scores, starting with the ones with an obvious grievance. Who knew what that in itself might unleash?

Geoff left the answerphone on but still jumped every time the phone rang.

He spent the evenings with Rhona, taking papers to work on, books to read, to try to distract his mind, not let his routine work lag behind. She didn't mind. He was there with her, wasn't he? And it took him away from the phone, helped to calm his jittery nerves for a few hours. And she had to be safe while he sat there … didn't she?

It was a surprise when one of the nurses came to tell him there was a phone call for him at the reception desk. Was there no escape, even here?

It was DS Latimer. Fair enough.

'Sorry to bother you at The Home, Mr Archibald. But have you seen the local evening paper?'

'No. Never see it.'

'I think perhaps you should tonight.'

'Why?'

'There's an article about one of your cases.'

'Which one?'

'Marilyn Petersen – the one you told me about.'

It felt like a physical blow in the solar plexus. Geoff leaned heavily against the desk.

'Mr Archibald? You there?'

'Yes, I'm here. What does it … say?'

'Well, I'm afraid there's a photograph of you kissing Ms Petersen.'

'But I never kissed …' Geoff's voice tailed away.

No, but *she* kissed *you*! In the full glare of the cameras.

'And there's stuff here about your wife.'

Geoff closed his eyes, his hand clenching on the phone.

'Damn her. Damn her,' he ground out under his breath.

'I'll come over. This might be relevant,' Latimer was saying.

It was what he had dreaded. It was now only a question of how far she had dredged?

He waited for Latimer in the interview room. Someone brought him coffee in the white china cups he'd grown to hate, three garibaldi biscuits on a matching plate. The intimacy created by the softened lights seemed to mock him, teetering as he was on the brink of public exposure.

Latimer spread the newspaper out on the coffee table facing Geoff, and took a seat opposite, leaning back as if to watch him squirm.

In the photograph, draped in Marilyn Petersen's arms, her pouting lips on his cheek, Geoff seemed to be smiling. And there was enough truth in the text for him to know it had come straight from her. Oh, of course it was distorted, sensationalised – he could almost hear her saying it – but the kernel of accuracy made it the more persuasive.

The investigative journalist had dug deep for this one. It was all there: Rhona being rushed to hospital the night before, in a coma ever since; Geoff a kind of grass widower, young, handsome, alone.

Marilyn was quoted supposedly verbatim, suggesting there was a relationship between them. They'd reported some of his court pronouncements word for word too, out of context, implying a personal agenda. Various other sources – all unnamed – spoke of his clever tongue, his reputation for winning cases whatever the rights or wrongs of the situation. More by insinuation than by direct comment they'd managed to portray him as an unscrupulous but highly successful lawyer, who could twist anything to his own advantage.

Geoff felt physically sick. How long before they ferreted out where Rhona was, about the rape, the threats, the breaches of security.

'Can you embargo anything more?' His voice sounded hollow.

'I've already spoken to the editor. Done my best,' Latimer said, casting him a look of sympathy.

'Surely patients' privacy has to be protected.'

'We're doing our best.'

'What a bloody awful mess,' Geoff ground out, more to himself than to Latimer.

'I'm sorry, sir, not a good time, I know, but … could this be the connection? With the letters, I mean.'

'Mmmm?' Geoff mumbled vaguely, not listening, the nausea threatening to overwhelm him.

'This case. Could this be the one?'

'One what?'

'Where you took a man's wife.'

'I didn't take her … Ahhh, I see what you're driving at. Sorry. Mind's gone crazy.'

'I know. Understandable.'

'Marilyn Petersen. I only met the husband in court. Felt sorry for him, though, I can tell you.'

Geoff found his eyes kept straying to that incriminating photograph. He leaned forward and folded it out of sight.

'But you found *for* the woman?'

'Well, yes. She was my client.'

'So he came out of it badly?'

'I suppose so. I don't remember the details.'

'You've marked it as a possible query for the bloke having a legitimate grievance,' Latimer said, his finger tracing the line of text in Geoff's typed list of clients.

'Did I? Well, he would have. Bitch of the first order.'

'But you …?'

'Yep, I'd have made *him* into the villain. It's my job.'

'So he might want revenge.'

'He might, I suppose. I don't know the guy. But *she's* the one spilling this stuff. Making out there was something going on. Which there wasn't. There most definitely wasn't.'

'What can you tell me about the husband?'

'Nothing much here. But if you care to come back to my office I could dig out the file.'

Even there the details on Simon Fenton were sketchy. DS Latimer would have to do his own digging.

But it didn't add up. Surely Geoff had done the guy a favour? No-one would want to hang on to a leech like Marilyn Petersen. And after four years living with her Fenton must know what she was like.

TWENTY-FIVE

Brian Latimer took DC Mary Hobart with him. From what Geoffrey Archibald said, he'd need female protection for this one.

Marilyn Petersen kept the safety chain on until they'd shown her their identity cards. When she did open the door it was with an extravagant flourish, oozing towards them, all apologies for her *'obsessive* precautions'.

She fitted Latimer's stereotype to perfection. Her lurid pink blouse and tight black slit skirt were calculated to reveal enough flesh without being rated precisely indecent. Latimer wondered fleetingly how much the taut skin of her face and cleavage owed to the knife, how any head of hair could be that red, remain that rigid in movement. He stared for a fraction too long at the display of sharp nails held permanently extended as if she feared piercing her own palms.

'I'm *so* sorry,' she purred, moving in, pawing at his arm as she ushered them through into the sitting room. 'But one can't be too careful. Especially in my line of work. Fans can be *so* obsessive. I mean just look at what happened to poor dear Jill Dando.'

Out of your league, dearie, Latimer thought.

'Now, how may I help you, Officers?' she gushed, indicating seats opposite hers.

'It's about this newspaper article,' he said without preamble, opening the paper and spreading it on the floor.

'Ahh *that*,' Marilyn sighed, leaning forward to peer at the picture. 'So long ago. *Soooo* long ago. I'm surprised they wanted to print it now. It's so … such *old* news.'

'You didn't have anything to do with getting it printed?'

'Me? Why ever would *I* want to do that?'

She spread both sets of pink talons against her matching chest as she opened her eyes wide at him, her extended lashes blinking in slow motion.

'I'd like *you* to tell *me* that, Mrs Petersen.'

'Ms, please. Ms. But do call me Marilyn. Ms Petersen sounds so *formal*, don't you think?'

'So why *did* you talk to the press?' Latimer repeated, not calling her anything.

'Oh, I only gave one tinsy *winsy* interview this week. Such a *nice* reporter, he was. *Soooo* anxious not to intrude, not to bring back all the pain. *Sooo* anxious. He really didn't stay more than two minutes. He could *see* how upsetting it was for me. And really there was nothing more to tell. He had it all. They covered it *then* you see – it was big news then, of course, during the actual divorce. Then they were *all* there, wanting to know how it had gone, all the details. Geoffrey – he was my lawyer, you know – he was so wonderful, so supportive, so *clever*. He deserves all the credit. Not me. He was so strong, so masterful. One does so like masterful men. Only the paper hasn't been exactly nice to poor Geoffrey. I don't know why anybody would want to give somebody like him such a hard time. Poor man. So clever. He doesn't deserve it.'

She opened her eyes wide at Latimer again, holding his gaze, slowly uncrossing, re-crossing those long legs.

'And why would the press want to resurrect this story at all now, d'you suppose,' he asked conversationally.

'I can't for the life of me imagine why. Unless …' She dropped her eyes.
'Unless?'

'Well, one hesitates to sound boastful. But you know the public is always *so* interested in famous people. They just love a little story about someone they see on their screens. Brings a little colour into their rather dreary lives, I suppose.'

Latimer didn't dare look at DC Hobart.
'And this story, how much of it is true?'

'Well, of course, I only *skimmed* it. I don't actually *read* that kind of paper. And one can't possible keep up with everything they write about one. One would never do a stroke of real work!' She tittered in a high affected voice. 'But my agent rang me and told me it was in. I just skimmed it, you know. Just to see what they're saying about me, really.'

'And?'
'And, Inspector?'
'It's Sergeant.'
'Oh, how very formal. What's your real name, Sergeant?'
'Sergeant Latimer.'
'And your first name?'
'Detective.'

She twittered at him directly, as if he had just said something flirtatious. Out of the corner of his eye he saw DC Hobart grinning fleetingly, but he kept his eyes firmly on Marilyn Petersen.

'Ah, I *do* so like a man with a sense of humour. Well, Detective *Sergeant* … oh, I'm sorry, what was your question? You are such a *fascinating* man, I've forgotten now what you asked me.'

'How much of this article is true?' Latimer surprised himself by the evenness of his voice.

'Well, it's difficult to say really because, of course, I didn't write any of this myself. And everyone sees the world through their own eyes, don't you think? I mean, the way *I* see *you* will be different from the way *your colleague* here sees you. So if we were both to write an account of this meeting we would write it quite differently, don't you think, Constable?'

'I'm quite sure we would,' DC Hobart said, the quiver so slight as to be barely discernible.

'But, in your perception, is what is written here about Mr Archibald an accurate account?' Latimer persisted.

'Well, of course, I know nothing about his poor unfortunate wife being in a coma. I mean, we didn't talk about things like that. The press must have found out about that.'

'You didn't know?'

'Not until I read it here. No. Poor, poor man. What a waste.'

'You're quite sure you didn't know it before?'

'Absolutely sure. Why would you doubt that, Sergeant?' She was looking straight at him, a small frown hovering between her eyes, not evolving into a full crease.

'What *did* you and Mr Archibald talk about then?'

'Why, my *case*, of course. My divorce. My home circumstances. That was why I was meeting him.'

'And was there ever any suggestion of anything personal between you?'

She shot him a suddenly alert look. In an instant it was transformed into a coy, embarrassed half-smile, the eyes fluttering, dropping before his steady gaze.

'Well, not on *my* part. He was simply my lawyer. A very good one. But still my lawyer.'

'And on his part?'

'Well, you know how it is, Detective Sergeant, boys will be boys.'

'Meaning?'

'Well, he was a *man*. A man in his *prime*. And now I understand he was probably not a very ... how shall we put it? ... a very *fulfilled* man.'

'So what are you saying?'

'Well, I don't wish to give you the impression that men find me irresistible – *so* unpleasant that kind of trumpeting of one's own charms, don't you think? But I do know that Geoffrey ...' She shrugged eloquently, casting her eyes down again demurely.

'And what exactly gave you the impression that you had engaged Mr Archibald's interest?'

'Well, he was so insistent on ... being intimate ... close ... private. And he so much hung upon one's every word. You know.'

'Can you be more precise?'

'Going over and over the story – just wanting to hear my words – over and over, over and over. Going to quiet little restaurants, coming to my hotel room – instead of his office. Going over and over the facts – as if he just liked the sound of my voice.'

'And these venues were his idea ... not yours?' Latimer fixed her with a bayonet stare.

She looked down at her hands, glossy nails erect, twisting in her lap, conveying discomfort in a stage-whisper.

'Not the last one I must admit, Sergeant. Oh, it's all *so* embarrassing. It was all my fault. But you see, I was feeling *sooooo* ill. Aching, shivering, headache. Too ill to move.'

'And?'

'So it was my idea that he came to the hotel to see me – the night before the hearing. I wanted *so* much not to be a nuisance, you see.' She looked up at that point with swimming eyes. 'It would have been so *dreadful* for him if I'd delayed the case. After all his hard work. And my evidence was *crucial*. I mean, *absolutely crucial*. And he needed to go over it, fine-tune it. You know. How they do. I was too ill to move, so he came to me. In my room at the hotel.' There was a long pause. The eyes were again downcast. 'But that was a mistake.'

'A mistake?'

'Yes. It was *my* fault. I take *full* responsibility. You mustn't blame him. But I was *so* ill, you see. I just … didn't think what effect it would have him seeing me … in my negligee, late at night, alone.'

'And what exactly did happen, Ms Petersen,' Latimer said, the steel bands round his voice taut and unyielding.

'Well, he … touched me … you know … and he obviously wanted … you know … but of course, I couldn't allow it. He was my lawyer.'

'So did anything take place at all?'

'No. I wouldn't *let* it.' The words were muffled in the handkerchief dabbing gently at her mouth and eyes, but the upright back conveyed the moral outrage.

'Ms Petersen, where is your ex-husband?' The complete change of subject surprised her into raising dry, wary eyes.

'Which … which one d'you mean?'

'How many are there?' It was involuntary.

'Three. Well, I suppose … almost – no, of course that'll still be three.' Latimer swallowed hard.

'I mean Simon Fenton. Which number was he?'

'He was my second.'

'And where is he now?'

'Well, he's … he's actually back with me now.'

'You mean – here? In this house?'

'Well, not at this exact moment. He's at work. But yes, he lives here. With me. I'm just waiting for my divorce to come through from my third.'

'And where does your … Mr Fenton work?'

'At one of the hospitals – the City, I *think,* although we *never* talk about it. I've never been very good about those kinds of things, you know. I couldn't *bear* to hear about those sick people. Saving lives is wonderful, of course, and I *so* admire him but …'

She gave an eloquent shudder, and pressed the handkerchief to her mouth for a long moment.

'And in what capacity does he work at the hospital?'

She rushed into the first part of her answer as if all the words were joined together: 'Well, he's a nurse at the moment, but, of course' – the pace slowed to half the speed – 'he's *much* too clever for that really and once we get ourselves sorted out he's going to do a university degree and he'll eventually become a plastic surgeon. That's what he *wants* to do. There's something so … *exciting* about plastic surgery, don't you think, Constable?'

DC Hobart choked something incomprehensible.

'He has *such* an eye for beauty and symmetry. It's exactly right for him,' Marilyn gushed, not noticing, her eyes playing to Latimer's gallery.

'So he's on duty just now? Saving lives.' Latimer knew it was unworthy.

'Yes. He will be.'

'And what time do you expect him home?'

'By about six this evening. He's taking me out tonight. He is *such* a romantic. And soooo protective. He chooses such *wonderfully* secluded places. It's rather sweet – him being just a little bit jealous of my admirers, don't you think? After all this time. Very sweet.'

'And which ward does he work on?'

'It's Ward – oh, I can't remember the number exactly. In fact, I don't think he ever told me. We don't – you know – talk about those kinds of things. He is *so* protective of my artistic sensibilities, you see. But I do know that it's with all the old dears. You know, he says he couldn't *bear* to work with younger people because he'd always compare them to me. Sweet, isn't it? Not that I'm anything special. Not now. But to *him*, you know …'

Latimer rose to his feet suddenly. Marilyn stopped in mid-flow, eyeing him warily.

'Thank you, Ms Petersen. You've been most helpful.'

'Have I, Inspec – I mean *Sergeant*. *Detective* Sergeant. One always wants to help the police – such a *noble* calling I always think. But I'm afraid I live a very quiet life now and I can't imagine you'll be the least bit interested in *my* doings. Why did you need to talk to me? In what connection? I do so hope poor dear Geoffrey isn't in any trouble.'

'Just routine enquiries. Routine. Thank you. Sorry to have disturbed you.'

Latimer kept on the far side of Mary Hobart as they moved out of reach of those clawing nails.

TWENTY-SIX

'Simon Fenton?' the girl at the reception desk said, frowning, her plain unvarnished nail tracking down the list of names. 'Nope. No-one of that name here, sir.'

'Working on a geriatric ward? Or at least one that takes old folk.'

'No. Nothing here. Shall I call the Director of Nursing Services for you? She might be able to help.'

'If you would. Thanks.'

Beatrice Affrick took them away to her office.

'Now, Detective Sergeant, before I release any information I need to know what this is all about.'

Latimer looked at her with new eyes.

Short and bordering on the stout, she nevertheless exuded authority. Her hazel eyes, beneath heavy, unplucked brows, met his squarely, her rigid posture behind the desk telling him unmistakably she would go nowhere, do nothing, until he gave her answers. Chivenings could do with a bit of this, he thought unexpectedly.

Without so much as a change of expression she listened to his selective account of the need for this information. Even in his own ears it felt flimsy, not knowing the ward or even the hospital with certainty. But she must have been convinced because she eventually reached for the computer mouse.

'I can't think of anyone of that name, but I'll check just to be sure.'

'Thank you.' Latimer watched her scrolling down through the names to 'F', looking carefully at the 'Fe's, then all the 'F's. In case.

'No, there are no Fentons in my hospital.'

'You're sure?'

'I'm sure, Sergeant.'

'Any Simons?' It was a long shot. But he didn't want to have to go through all this again.

A longer scroll. Lots of pauses. Presumably all the 'S's.

'Yes, two.'

'Nurses?'

'One a nurse, one a care assistant.'

'And their surnames?'

'Aintree and Hassan.'

'But not Fenton?'

'No, Sergeant, not Fenton. As I've already said.'

'Sorry.'

'Which one is the nurse?'

'Simon Aintree.'

'And does he work with old people?'

'Some of the time. He's on a medical ward. They have a good number of old people. But it's not a geriatric ward per se.'

'And the other one?'

'Working on an orthopaedic ward. That's bones and things, Sergeant.'

'Yes, thank you. I did know that.' He couldn't resist it. Good grief! Did she speak to everyone like a headmistress? You couldn't imagine her ever being a nurse, caring for people.

'Will that be all? I'm very busy.'

'Sorry. But could you tell me which wards these two nurses work on?'

'You are *not*, I hope, planning to visit the wards.' He almost saw the bristles protruding through her severe maroon jacket. 'These are busy people working in extremely trying circumstances, Sergeant. Resources are already stretched to capacity and I will not have my staff harassed by extraneous business during working hours.'

'I didn't intend harassing anyone, Ms Afflick.'

'Rick. Aff*rick*.'

'Sorry, Ms Aff*rick*.'

'Is it vital that you see these two men? Even though they're not called Fenton?'

'I think we have to establish they are not the man we're looking for, yes.'

'That might take just minutes then?'

'Probably, yes.'

'In that case, Sergeant – I have no wish to obstruct you in the course of *your* duty – so I will call these men to my office. One at a time. That is, if they can be spared from their wards for a *few minutes*.'

OK, OK, I hear you, loud and clear, Latimer thought.

'Thank you. I appreciate it,' he said humbly.

Simon Aintree was a giant of a man, well over Latimer's own six foot four, and getting on for twenty stone by the look of him. A human crane. Ideal for lifting heavy patients. A shock of fair hair sat incongruously on top of this walking mountain; the vivid green eyes were genuinely bewildered by the summons to see a policeman.

Ms Affrick looked like a dwarf beside him, glowering at Latimer as she said, 'A few minutes, Sergeant,' before stalking from her office.

It took no more than two minutes to eliminate him. Simon Aintree ambled out, the slight frown never having left his brow.

Latimer played with his pen as he waited for the second Simon.

'Do you mind, Sergeant?' The irritated voice broke into his thoughts.

'Sorry?' he said, puzzled by Ms Affrick's glacial glare.

'The pen, Sergeant. Do you have to keep flicking the end in and out?'

'Sorry.' He put it away in his pocket.

The light tap on her door seemed undeserving of her cross, 'Come in!'

Latimer felt a wave of sympathy for the man who entered this frosty atmosphere.

'This is Detective Sergeant Latimer. He has a couple of questions to ask you. Routine. Nothing to worry about.'

The words were more reassuring than the tone. Latimer wanted to tell the man, she's cross with me not you.

'A few minutes, Sergeant!' She stalked from the room again.

'I'm sorry to bother you, Mr Hassan. Just a couple of quick questions. May I ask you where you live?'

'King George Terrace.'

'And do you live alone?'

'No.'

Latimer waited. Simon Hassan stood looking at him.

'Do you know a Marilyn Petersen?'

'Yes. I … She's not … has there been an accident …?'

Latimer saw the dark eyes dilate, the hands clench against the pale grey tunic.

'No. She's fine.'

'Then what …?'

'Mr Hassan, I must ask you to accompany me to the station. I have reason to believe you're in a position to help us with our enquiries.'

'What enquiries?' The tone was even, the eyes watchful.

'It concerns your wife − ex-wife − future wife − Ms Petersen. Might be best in a more private place, don't you think?'

'Sergeant, you *said* … !' Ms Affrick had bristled from a hedgehog into a porcupine.

'I know, and I'm sorry. But information which has since come to light makes it necessary to extend those few minutes to an indefinite period. I'm afraid I must ask you to release Mr Hassan from his duties.'

The two men drove to the station in silence. DS Latimer asked Mary Hobart to accompany him for the interview.

'If it's half as entertaining as the Petersen chat it'll be worth it, Sarge,' she grinned.

'Just control yourself, Mary. And just spare a thought for the poor blighter who *lives* with her!' he retorted with feeling.

'You make your bed, you lie in it.'

Simon Hassan was edgy but met his look without flinching.

'Hassan, Fenton. Which is it?'

'Both.'

'Meaning?'

'Outside the hospital I'm Fenton. Inside, Hassan.'

'Any reason for two names?'

'My mother's name was Hassan. She died. I took it. She'd have liked that.'

'Hassan. Sounds Arabic. Yes?'

Latimer watched his face. Impassive.

'Israeli.'

'Was your father Israeli too?'

'Half Arabic.'

'Ever live over there yourself?'

'No. I was born and brought up in this country.'

'D'you speak any Arabic?'

Still no emotion.

'No.'

'Can you write it, read it?'

'No.'

'You used to be a photographer, didn't you?'

'Yes.'

'Why the change?'

'I was fed up with the rat race – wanted to do something worthwhile. No crime in that.'

Latimer felt a wave of sympathy with his disillusionment photographing the Marilyn Petersens of this world.

'None whatsoever. None whatsoever. If that *was* the reason.' He levelled a direct look at the man, taking in the olive skin, the black brows and lashes, the dark eyes. 'Mr Hassan, does the name Archibald mean anything to you?' Try for a surprise attack.

'Archibald? There was a kid at my school called Archibald. Poor sod. Got bullied to death for it.'

'And Archibald as a surname?'

'Rings a vague bell. Can't place it.'

'Archibald as in lawyer?'

'Archibald. Lawyer.' He pursed his lips, shaking his head, musing.

'Your wife's lawyer. At the time of your divorce.'

'Ah. *That* Archibald. I remember now.'

'Did you ever meet Mr Archibald yourself?'

'Not personally. No.'

'And how did you feel about him?'

'He was just a lawyer, doing his job.'

'Bit of a hatchet job though, eh?'

Another shrug.

'Did you see the article about him in the paper last night?'

'The evening rag, you mean? Briefly, yes. Marilyn showed me. Why?'

'What did you think of it?'

'I didn't really think about it. Usual stuff. I never do take much notice of what the papers say. They make it up as they go along.'

'You thought it was all made up, did you?'

'I don't know. I didn't really read it.'

'Just skimmed it, I expect, eh?'

'That's right.'

'Like Marilyn. She's in it, photograph, quotes, details. But she just "skimmed" it, too. Funny thing, that.' Latimer considered the point gently for a long moment. 'So you wouldn't have had anything to do with its being printed last night then?' he said, conversationally.

'Me? No. Why would I?'

'Would it surprise you to learn that the paper told us that a man answering your description – a man who described himself as just a friend of the family – gave them a lot of information about this same Mr Archibald just two days ago?'

'There are plenty of men answering my description, Sergeant.'

'But not plenty of men who know details about Marilyn Petersen *and* Mr Archibald *and* Mr Archibald's wife, Mr Hassan.'

The dark eyes stared unblinkingly. Hassan shrugged.

'They'd have had most of that stuff in their reports from the time. Photos. Comments. They keep stuff like that,' he said.

'Oh, of course. They're always interested in stuff on famous people. Isn't that right? Marilyn told us that,' Latimer explained softly.

Hassan shrugged again. 'Maybe. I never thought about it.'

'So why contact the newspaper now?'

'I told you. I didn't.'

'Was it to stir things up? Did you think it would destroy the man's career?'

'I don't know what you're talking about. I told you I only skimmed it. I didn't have anything to do with it.'

'How did you find out about *Mrs* Archibald, Simon?' Latimer engaged a more friendly tone, leaning forwards across the table.

'I don't know anything about her.'

'Oh, I think you do. More than you should, don't you?'

'I don't know what you mean.'

'You hated Mr Archibald, didn't you? He'd helped Marilyn to leave you, hadn't he?'

Still the dark eyes held his. Unfathomable. He was a cool customer, give him that.

'And did Marilyn tell you what he tried to do? Did she tell you about the intimate dinners, the meetings in her hotel room, his advances? Did she tell you all that? Did it make you jealous? Did it make you want revenge on this man who *stole your wife*? Did it? Hhhmmm?'

Another pause. Still no response.

'Did she tell you how she liked it, being seduced by a hotshot lawyer? She likes powerful men, doesn't she? She thinks you're going to be a hotshot too, doesn't she? A plastic surgeon. Wow! Famous. Helping her stay for-ever young. You've spun her a fine tale, haven't you? Such a fine tale. What was that all in aid of, I wonder? Did you think it'd make her stay with you? What would she think if she knew you weren't even a proper nurse, do you think? Never will be a doctor. Will I tell her, or will you?'

Beside him Latimer felt Mary Hobart tense. Hassan said nothing.

'Has it ever occurred to you, Simon, that *she* has been spinning tales to *you* too?'

Latimer heard DC Hobart's swift intake of breath. OK, OK. He'd been young and idealistic too, once. Didn't want to upset people, destroy trust, break up homes. But this creep deserved a bit of upset. Latimer had met Viv. And Rhona. He'd watched Geoffrey Archibald struggling to hang onto his sanity. He'd seen the look in Bill Faraday's eyes. Mary Hobart hadn't. Come to think of it, he should probably take her to The Home.

'Oh yes. Your *famous* ex-wife. The *delectable* Marilyn Petersen. Was that why you took her back? Because she convinced you it was all Mr Archibald's fault; she was the innocent victim. Huhh? Was it?'

He waited, watching. Then he leaned closer to Hassan, dropping his voice to a conspiratorial whisper.

'She made it all up, you know. All that stuff about Mr Archibald fancy-ing her. Yes. It was all lies. But Marilyn can't bear to think men don't find her irresistible. She couldn't cope with his rejection. So she had to turn it into something else. She trapped him into thinking she'd print scandal-ous things about him. And why? Why did she go to such lengths, d'you think?'

He paused again for a long moment.

'To – get – away – from – *you*.' Latimer spat each word across the table, stabbing his finger at Hassan as he said 'you', and then leaned back slowly to watch the effect.

The dark eyes narrowed slightly.

'It's true. She was that desperate to escape from you. She begged Mr Archibald to do everything he could to get her out of the marriage. She basically forced him to go along with her lies about you. She put the fear of God into him, if you want to know. But then *you* know how … *persua-sive* Marilyn can be. But this was a new experience for Geoffrey Archibald. He was afraid of what she'd do to him, his career. He knew it was all lies, of course, but he also knows how mud sticks. I dare say he went a bit over the score. Did he? Exaggerate what a bad husband you were? Make you into a monster? Did you see him as the villain stealing Marilyn away from you? Huhh?'

Silence.

'Can you blame him if he did exaggerate? It was him or you. And his job was to get his client – Marilyn – her divorce and a good settlement. But you *did* blame him, didn't you? All those cruel things he said about you. Rankled that, I expect. Can you remember what he said, Simon?'

No answer.

'Shall I remind you? We looked it up. They keep files you know. Makes amazing reading. Want to hear it again?'

'No!' The word shot out.

'No,' Latimer said softly. 'Painful, hurtful things, weren't they? Made you into a real villain of a husband. You, whose only crime had been not being able to give Marilyn all she thought was due to her. You weren't a villain, were you? Not back then. Just a weak man. A weak man manipulated by a scheming woman. Funny thing, you know, Mr Archibald thought he was doing you a favour. Ridding you of her. Can you believe that? He did. He saw himself as on your side.'

Again Latimer paused to let this truth sink in.

'Nice man, Mr Archibald. Thoroughly decent bloke. So I repeat, how did you find out about his wife?'

The dilated eyes swivelled from him to Mary Hobart and down to the table.

'Hassan – we know about the anonymous letters, we know about the abuse, we know it all. So you might as well start talking.'

Latimer saw the hesitation.

'She's not worth it. She won't wait around for you when she knows about your real job, about how long you'll be gone. Now, let me see. What are we talking about here? Blackmail – three years. Perverting the course of justice – another three. Rape of a defenceless woman – ten, fifteen. If you're lucky.'

'I didn't rape her!'

'No? Why don't I believe you?'

'I didn't. Whether you believe me or not.'

'The blokes in jail won't believe you either. They'll crucify you. Know what they do to scum who rape defenceless girls? Imagine the worst and multiply it by ten. And you needn't expect help from the screws either. Oh no. They're very good at turning a blind eye in these kind of cases. They don't hear the screams. They'll swear in court they saw nothing, heard nothing. Prison's too good for vermin who abuse defenceless girls, they think. It's rough justice I know, but that's the way it is. No, you won't *want* to come out of there alive.'

Latimer leaned back slowly in his chair. He looked steadily at Hassan, linked his arms behind his head and pursed his lips.

Sweat stood on the olive brow. The dark eyes darted from place to place, haunted, imagining.

'I didn't, I tell you. I didn't do it.'

'I'll let you into a secret. I've seen a lot of rapists in my time – the ones that go for little girls, old ladies, handicapped youngsters, pregnant women – but you're the first one I've had who raped a woman in a persistent

172

vegetative state. And you know what? I think those prison officers have a point. I think I'd turn a blind eye in their shoes.'

'I didn't rape her.'

'And I tell you what makes it worse. You pretending you went into nursing because you wanted to do something worthwhile. Now it would make sense if you told me you really went into the job because you wanted to perv on women. Yeah, I could follow that. Or if you told me Marilyn wanted you to give up the old job because she didn't like you photographing other women – beautiful women. Yeah. That'd make sense. But you – *caring*? I mean, you see my dilemma? I'm trying to picture it. One minute you're helping some old biddy eat her lunch, have a bath, go to the loo. The next minute you're busy raping a patient who's in such a bad state she doesn't even know you're there. You ever had schizophrenia, Hassan?'

'I didn't rape her. I didn't.' The words slid through gritted teeth.

'What was it like, eh? Doing it with somebody who wasn't there?'

'I didn't. I *couldn't* ... do ... something like that.'

Latimer watched the walls crumbling. In silence. It was a long time before anyone spoke.

'I didn't.'

Very slowly Latimer leaned back in his seat, hitching both thumbs into his belt.

'Convince me.'

'It was only to scare him. I only *said* it. I didn't *really* do it. I didn't do anything to her. You've seen her, haven't you? You *couldn't*!'

'Some men could, Hassan.'

'*I* couldn't.' He shuddered. 'Great balls of fire, man ...'

Latimer believed him, but he wasn't going to let him know that. Not for a long time.

'You sent the letters.'

'Yes. I admit that. I did send him letters. I wanted to make him sweat too. Like he made me.'

'Only it wasn't his fault. He didn't have a choice. It was Marilyn's fault. So you owe him the truth – at least give him that, eh?'

'Maybe. If he really is innocent. Like you say.'

'Believe me. He's innocent.'

'Like you said, he made me mad. All those things he said about me. They were lies. It wasn't like that. I never bullied her. Never. I never lifted a finger against her. It was just ... well, she just wanted things. More and more things. Things I just couldn't give her. I just ... wasn't enough. I wasn't grand enough. I didn't know all the right people. She could have had anybody. But I never hurt her. He said I did. He convinced them that I did.'

The pain showed. There was a long silence. Latimer didn't move.

'After the divorce, I didn't see her again for ages. I saw in the paper she got married again. But I didn't *see* her until about a year ago. Then I bumped into her. By accident. She was in a hell of a mess. Weeping all over the place, begging me to help her. Said she didn't have anybody to turn to. The new bloke had just gone off. Well, I felt sorry for her. Hell, I knew what it felt like being dumped. Well, she told me how people kept taking advantage of her generous nature.' Latimer felt rather than heard DC Hobart stifle a snort. 'And then she told me about Archibald seducing her. It was the first I heard about it. I felt sorry for her. And the new husband abusing her. And ...' He shrugged his shoulders, suddenly silent.

'So you took pity on her,' Latimer said gently.

'She said Archibald had poisoned her mind against me. How she'd been taken in, believed his lies. But how she knew now she hadn't really stopped loving me. Well, I'd heard the lies he'd told about me in court myself.'

'Lies she'd told him,' Latimer corrected quietly.

Again the shrug.

'Whatever. But I believed her. It wasn't hard to believe her. I guess I wanted it to be true. I wanted to hate him. I wanted him to be responsible for ruining our lives.'

'So how did you find out about his wife?'

'By accident. I was doing a care course. You have to do training to do what I do. And there was this bloke on it. He worked at that Home – you know, where Archibald's wife is. We talked, shared stories, you know like you do. In house. And he told me about this top lawyer's wife. Of course, he didn't know I knew Archibald.'

'And did he tell you anything else about that Home?'

'He told me about the rape of the other girl.'

'And it gave you the perfect idea for getting back at Geoffrey Archibald.'

Latimer leaned forward to scribble something on his notepad. He made it deliberately illegible.

'Only I didn't really do it.' Hassan's eyes flicked from the notepad to Latimer's face, back and forth, back and forth. 'I just wanted to put the wind up him. Give him a dose of his own medicine. Look, I'm pouring my guts out here and it's the truth. I didn't do it.'

'So why did you need to get into The Home then? You could have just sent the letters.'

'He'd soon have twigged. He's not a fool. I needed it to look like I *had* done it. And I could have done. He knew that. *Somebody* had been in her room.'

'How did you think up that disguise? How did you find out about the Arab women?'

'I stayed in touch with the guy from The Home. We met for a drink after work sometimes. And one weekend when it was quiet, he took me to show me round where he worked. I got him to show me where the cameras were, where Mrs Archibald was. I saw those women all milling about.

It was dead easy. Even with the cameras it was easy enough to get in, dressed like that. Nobody expected those women to speak.'

'We saw you on the CCTV footage. But the last time? How did you get the note in then?'

Hassan smiled slowly.

'You didn't twig?'

'No. Tell me.'

'Grabbers. Long-handled grabbers. The kind they give to orthopaedic patients who can't bend down to reach things. The window was open enough. I just reached in with the grabbers and put it there when Archibald left the room. I figured it'd kill him to think I'd done it while he was in the building.'

'You're a sadistic blighter, aren't you,' Latimer said. 'You sure you didn't rape her?'

'Word of honour. I did not. For crying out loud, you *must* have done swabs and things. I figured you'd soon know I didn't really do it.'

'And you used gloves for the letters – I guess you'd have a ready supply of surgical gloves in your line of work.'

'That bit was easy. No fingerprints. But I always knew I wouldn't get away with it for long. Beats me why the guy didn't put you onto the letters way before he did. Why not?'

'How d'you know he didn't?'

'They didn't beef up the security for ages.'

'Hmmm.'

'So why didn't he?'

'Mr Hassan – *I* ask the questions around here.'

'So?'

'That's for me to know and you to wonder. So that's the letters scam – now then, why the newspaper article?'

'I knew I couldn't keep up the pressure with the letters. But he was still carrying on pretty much like normal. I wanted to ruin him for what he did. Mud sticks. It was easy – he's a big guy in the courts. I just pointed the reporter in the right direction.'

Latimer shook his head slowly. Revenge served cold. It had a cruelty of its own.

'This other care worker, the one from The Home, what's his name?'

'Here, I don't want to get him into strife. He was only being a mate.'

'Just want to corroborate your story. It's not a criminal offence to talk to your colleagues. Your professional organisation mightn't like the breach of confidentiality, but that ain't no concern of ours.'

'You mean it – just corroborate my story?'

'Unless he turns out to be another criminal like you. In that case we'll arrange for him to have the cell next to yours, shall we, and you can amuse yourselves by swapping nursey stories. Now come on, man, what's his name?'

'Bernard. Toby Bernard. Lives near Chivenings. That's all I know. But they'd be able to give you his exact address. I used to ring him at The Home.'

Toby Bernard had the grace to look embarrassed.

'Yeah, I did take him in once. Harmless visit. He was dead interested in our kind of work, said he fancied specialising in something like that. Something where the nursing care really counts.'

'Oh, that's right, he was interested. Particularly interested. Asked a lot of questions, I expect.'

'Yeah, he did.'

'And did you give anyone else a private conducted tour of your place of work, Mr Bernard?'

'I don't remember anyone else …'

Latimer knew he was lying.

'Think very carefully, Mr Bernard. It's a criminal offence to obstruct the police in their enquiries, you know.'

Bernard shifted uncomfortably in his seat but kept his eyes averted.

'Was it just before Viv Faraday was raped?' Latimer probed, his voice soothing. 'Tricky one that. You couldn't tell anyone, of course. Not supposed to take anyone in without permission, are you? Specially you just being a care assistant. Dr Wilkinson would blast you from here to eternity. Mrs Reed would probably fire you. Probably had a few sleepless nights, huhh? Worrying about them finding out. So tell *me*, Toby. Tell me. *I* know you're not a criminal. I can smell them a mile off. *I* know it's just because you're proud of what The Home does, proud of your special skills with these people. You want people to know what a superb job you all do. I can understand that. I'm dead impressed myself. Fantastic stuff. Me – I couldn't do it, but I admire men who can. And these blokes were really interested, weren't they? It'd be good to let them see for themselves; they'd spread the word about the excellent care these patients get. I can see that. So go on, tell me.'

He leaned forward encouragingly.

Silence.

'It'll be a weight off your mind. Who else did you take in? We only want to talk to them – we're talking to anybody who knew anything about The Home. Just a little chat with them and we can eliminate them from our enquiries. Doesn't need to go further than that. You'll be helping us to find the guy who actually raped Viv all the quicker. That'd be good, huhh? Knowing you'd helped put away that scumbag.'

'It was only one other bloke. Honest. Just the one. An agency nurse. I met him at the Sick Kids' Hospital. I sometimes do extra shifts over there – nights, you know. Helps pay the mortgage. Only, well, they wouldn't like it – at Chivenings – if they knew.'

Latimer shook his head.

'I'm not interested in your moonlighting, Mr Bernard. But I do need to know about anyone you took into The Home. So tell me about this agency nurse.'

'Well, this bloke was on with me one night there – at the Sick Kids' Hospital. Staff nurse. He was dead interested in persistent vegetative state. He asked me about how we stopped them getting all seized up, and getting infections and everything. And he wanted to know if I could show him some of the equipment and everything. It was only the once. And I swear, I never took anybody else there.'

'Nobody else, eh? You certain?'

'Just the two. Simon Hassan and Ernest Johnson.'

Only!

'And where might I find this Staff Nurse Johnson?'

Bernard knew only his hospital connection.

TWENTY-SEVEN

Latimer was tireless. His team grew edgy. Everyone recognised the signs. They knew what to expect; it was always the same when the net tightened. The boss didn't sleep and they took the brunt of his irritability.

It had been a blow finding Johnson's DNA didn't match. So near and then so far. But it had to be the connection. It *had* to be. Bernard, Hassan, Johnson. All so-called carers. All interested in these unconscious patients. All linked in some way to Chivenings. But how were they linked with the rapist?

Both Bernard and Johnson were grilled so relentlessly they'd probably have confessed to anything just to get some peace, Latimer thought. Johnson even knew a sex offender personally. But it didn't smell right. It just didn't fit.

Latimer ordered more interviews.

'Find out where Johnson's interest in persistent vegetative state comes from.'

'See who he drinks with.'

'Lean on Toby Bernard. See who else he talked to about his work.' The DC on the receiving end of this barked instruction paled visibly. What – *all* of them?

'Put the pressure on. See if he took anybody else into The Home on one of his little excursions.'

'Get a list of every hospital Johnson did agency work for.'

'Look for anything. Links. Leads. Coincidences. Anything.'

Latimer sorted, sifted, saw what everyone else saw, tried to think what no-one else thought. Relentlessly. Day and night his brain worked on it.

'We're on his trail,' he reported to Bill. 'The net's tightening. Can't give you chapter and verse – not till we've finally nailed him – but the trail's red hot.'

Conflicting emotions dulled Bill's responses. Deeply as he desired the criminal to get his just deserts, he did not want to see the face of the man who had violated Viv.

Geoff, now that his own tormentor was out of harm's way, listened more patiently to Bill's fears.

'Will they have to bring all our family story out in court?'

'Can we keep Viv's identity secret?'

'Will they have to know she had an abortion?'

'Will we all have to testify?'

'Frances even?'

'Where do Viv's rights come in all of this?'

He did his best to be reassuring.

Geoff's file for the case grew visibly thicker. It would be a delicate prosecution to handle, given the sensitivities he could name, never mind the unspoken ones he sensed. And Viv's privacy was as dear to her father as Rhona's was to him. He must keep that in the forefront of his mind. This was no place for flaunting legal skills.

The name Harry Franks came up twice. He'd taken a specialised course on the care of comatose patients and he worked for the same agency as Johnson.

Ernest Johnson was back on the rack. When? How? What? Where? Yes, the two men had met. Johnson recalled the name but couldn't remember anything about Franks. Had he talked about The Home to this man? He shrugged. Who knew what they'd talked about? He was a friendly chap, easy with folk, made him good at relating to his patients and the relatives. Franks was a colleague – in the business. You talked. Nothing specific, you understand, just facts, no names or anything.

Damned loose-lipped lot, these nurses – or whatever they were – Latimer thought. Funny idea of confidentiality. Considered themselves discreet if they just avoided names. Rapists didn't need names.

The agency knew surprisingly little about either man. The paperwork was in order. Qualifications were verifiable. Latimer checked them himself just to make sure. And the agency double-checked – no, there'd been no complaints against either, no criminal record, no hint of suspicion. None of the hospitals they'd worked in had anything recorded either. Squeaky clean.

Franks' mother had Alzheimer's. No joy there. His father hadn't been seen since Harry was three. There were no siblings, no women in his life. Latimer's team had a job finding anybody to tell them anything about the man. Neighbours rarely saw him. A loner, they said. Pleasant enough if you met him in the street, but essentially a loner.

A loner without a story – now *that* Latimer liked.

'Bring him in!'

Franks was morose, answered in monosyllables. You didn't need to talk to comatose patients, Latimer thought wryly. Ideal for the Rhonas and Vivs of this world. And if the agency sent him to different places he didn't need to bother about forging relationships. Fill in the hours, get back to his own private world. Anonymous almost.

Things were looking decidedly hopeful.

Latimer ratcheted up the pressure several notches. DC Hobart sucked in her breath audibly several times. Latimer ignored her.

Franks didn't crack.

179

Latimer lost his cool first. The creep had the nerve to smile faintly, watching him cursing and threatening. But he didn't crack. Polite, monosyllabic, but in control.

Perversely Latimer believed his innocence.

Needing an outlet, Latimer went straight into another session with Toby Bernard. OK, the man wasn't the rapist. OK, he might be next door to a saint to work with. But something wasn't right. What was it?

Alison Reed had begrudgingly shown him Bernard's file. Exemplary. Reliable. Hard working. Good attitude. Maybe rather lacking in ambition but an excellent employee. Nobody had a bad word to say about the guy. Even Steven Wilkinson, who'd admitted finding the man slightly odd, couldn't pinpoint a fault. He'd even been commended by Bill Faraday – and, heaven knows, *he* hadn't been at all easy to please recently.

Good at his work he might be but Toby Bernard had to be the weak link in this chain. He *had* to be. OK, point one: he wasn't above cheating – doing a fair bit of moonlighting from all accounts. Point two: when it came to security – well, wasn't he every policeman's nightmare! Two strokes against him already there. Three scores and you're out, matey! Just who else had he smuggled in the back way? And why was he protecting them?

Time for some serious pressure.

By the time he sat facing Bernard again Latimer was past caring how much his bad temper showed. He'd had enough of the whole bang-shoot of these wretched nurses. For some reason the sulky look on Bernard's thin face added fuel to his fire.

'You look after the women patients as well as the men?' he asked without preamble.

'You know I do.'

'Ever do it without a chaperone?'

'No. It's against regulations.'

'Chivenings' regulations?'

'Yes.'

'Why's that?'

'To avoid any possibility of trouble.'

'Irk you, that?'

'No. It takes two to do most of the work with these patients anyway.'

'You a queer, Bernard?'

Latimer knew a surge of begrudging admiration for the man opposite. No flicker of emotion. No hint of irritation.

'No.'

'Pansy job for a bloke, isn't it? Looking after folk like that.'

'No.'

'Your mates think it's sick?'

'Not that I know of.'

'Have mates, do you?' Latimer sneered. 'Or d'you just hang out with the women?'

'Both – men and women.'

'Which d'you prefer?'

'Neither.'

'Your girlfriend mind you working with a lot of female nurses?'

'No.'

For the first time Bernard moved. He ran one forefinger across his upper lip. Then it was back to the same rigid impassivity.

'Not a nurse herself though, is she?' Latimer asked.

'No.'

'Remind me again – what's she do?'

'She's a travel agent.'

'How long d'you say you've lived with her?'

'Three years.'

'Talk to her about what you do?'

'Sometimes. Not the detail.'

'Did you tell her about letting your mates in?'

'No.'

'Tell her about the rape?'

'No.'

'More discreet at home than in the pub, eh?'

'I didn't talk about it in the pub either.'

'Oh no, I forgot, you just do guided tours.' Again Latimer's scorn was blatant.

Bernard glared back at him. Latimer fixed him with a baleful stare.

'Ever take any women round the place?'

'No. I told you.'

'Oh, you told me a lot of things, *Mr* Bernard. You told me you took Hassan round. You told me you took Johnson round. Blokes. Blokes that like unconscious people. Like you. What is it you guys get out of that, eh?'

Bernard shrugged.

'Why only two blokes? Weren't the women interested?'

Another shrug. 'If they were they didn't ask to see round.'

'Male thing, eh? Guided tours?'

'Not particularly.'

'Any of your female colleagues do it?'

'Not that I know of.'

'They care more about the patients as real people, eh? Not a spectator sport to them, p'rhaps.'

Another silent glare.

Latimer leaned forward on the table.

'So tell me who else *you* took round.'

'I told you, nobody.'

'Why do I get the feeling you're not telling me the whole truth, Mr Bernard?'

Silence. Bernard met him stare for stare.

'What did you think when they told you about Vivienne Faraday's rape, Bernard?'

'How d'you mean?'

'Did you instantly think about those guys you'd taken round? Did you think it might be them?'

'No.'

'Why not?'

Bernard shrugged again.

'Didn't look like rapists, eh?'

'They were in the job. Interested in the work.'

'Know what a rapist looks like?'

'You and me.' Insolent beggar.

'So why didn't you suspect them?'

'I just didn't.'

'Because you know who really did it?'

'No.'

'Who else did you take round, Bernard? Who else? You know who it was, don't you? You know who raped Viv Faraday. Shielding him, aren't you? Think you'll put us off the scent telling us about Hassan and Johnson. You think we'll think you're a dead honest chap, leave you alone.'

Silence.

'Well, let me tell you something for nothing. We won't leave you alone till you cough up. I know you're hiding something. Like I told you, I smell these things. So if you want a bit of peace you just tell me who else you took round The Home.'

Nothing.

'Still afraid for your own neck, eh? Moonlighting *and* bringing unauthorised personnel into The Home. Your boss isn't going to like that, is he?'

'You've probably told him already, anyway.'

'You reckon?'

Another baleful glare.

'So if they already know, why not give me the name – or names? Nothing to lose.'

'Because there wasn't anyone else. Like I told you.'

'So who else did you *tell?*'

'Tell what?'

'About these women lying there asking to be raped.'

'Nobody.'

'Oh, come off it! You can't tell me you spun a story so interesting to two blokes that they wanted to see inside, but you didn't talk about it to anybody else at all.'

'I'm not saying that.'

'What exactly *are* you saying?'

'You know perfectly well what I'm saying.'

'You get smart with me, matey, and you'll live to regret it!'

Bernard curled his lip slightly, giving his face an insolent defiance.

'OK, have it your own way. For what it's worth I haven't actually told Dr Wilkinson about your moonlighting, but I think I'll just pay him a visit this afternoon. I think he'll be mighty interested in what I have to tell him.'

Nothing.

Again Latimer leant closer, confidingly.

'You do realise that when we do eventually nail this creep it'll go against you that you withheld information? Penalties are stiff for raping these kind of women. Anybody harbouring jerks who do it – the courts don't like them either. Guilt by association. Not the sort of thing your colleagues will like either. A care assistant protecting an animal like that? Phwww. You'll be lucky if you ever work again.'

Bernard just sat, a blank face, cold eyes. It was like trying to rake over dying embers.

Latimer felt bone weary.

Steven Wilkinson shrugged when Latimer told him about the moonlighting.

'Of course I don't condone it. But I understand it,' he said. 'I mean, d'you know what these assistants get? It's a pittance. And a loaf of bread costs the same for them as it does for you or me.'

'What else d'you know about this bloke that I haven't been told?'

'Well, I did tell you that he had money troubles, when you asked about him last time. I know I did. He was honest about that. Asked for extra shifts. Alison gave him some occasionally, but we have to be careful. Regulations and all that. But we didn't know he was working at Sick Kids. So I couldn't tell you that. Presumably they've no complaints. If he was working long hours his work here didn't seem to suffer.'

'Fair enough.'

'Ahh. There was one other thing. It's probably nothing but since you're asking, I remember vaguely, something about being off sick for a month some time back. Alison Reed would be the one to fill you in.'

'Yes, he was off for a few weeks, about eighteen months/two years ago,' Mrs Reed confirmed. 'Had a funny turn at work. It was genuine. We got sick notes from his own doctor, but we didn't know the details. I suppose he could have been moonlighting then. Some sort of psychological trauma, the notes said. But no details. I gave him a chance to talk when he came back. But he didn't. Not my place to probe something like that. Like I say, he's a solid kind of worker. As long as it doesn't affect his work, the past's the past.'

Maybe not your place, Latimer thought grimly, but it could just be the lever we need.

TWENTY-EIGHT

The constable standing stiffly in front of him kept his eyes rigidly ahead.

'You told us – anything at all suspicious, tell you, Sarge.'

'Yeah,' Latimer said.

'Well, I don't know if this is something or nothing.'

'Spit it out man, I haven't got all day.'

'The care assistant at the Home, Bernard?'

'What about him?'

'Girlfriend – name of Gillian Jones – says she hasn't seen him for a couple of days.'

'Working shifts, I dare say. Or moonlighting. Does she know he moonlights?'

'Says she knows he does sometimes but he always writes it on the calendar so she knows where to contact him in an emergency.'

'And there's nothing on the calendar.'

'No, Sarge.'

'Maybe he's just left her.'

'They haven't had a row or anything, she says.'

'Anything at all different?'

'Not as far as she can recall, Guv.'

'She worried?'

'Says she is. She came here to report him missing.'

'She know he's been talking to us?'

'Only that – she doesn't know what about. He told her it was just a routine thing at work apparently.'

'Huh. Discreet when it suits, eh? And you didn't enlighten her, I presume?'

'No, Sarge. Not my place.'

Funny how often people seemed to know their place these days.

'Good. She still here?'

'Yeah, Duty Sarge said best tell you before we let her go. In case.'

'In case what?'

'In case – well, he thought maybe – in case somebody's trying to silence him.'

'Silence Bernard. Hmmmm. Interesting. What gave him that idea, I wonder? OK, I'll see her. What's her name again?'

'Gillian Jones, Guv.'

'Give me five minutes. And get me Bernard's file,' Latimer roared after the retreating back.

It was frustrating how little Gillian Jones knew about the man she'd lived with for three years.

She was prettier than Latimer had expected. Why had he expected anything? OK, he had his stereotypes like the next man. And he didn't expect a pretty girl to fall for a wimp like Bernard. Average height, nicely rounded in the right places, shoulder-length fair hair permed tightly. The grey eyes would have been engaging too if they hadn't looked so haunted. She spoke with a slight lisp and kept putting her hand up against her mouth. Clear polish, neatly trimmed nails – not like those dreadful talons.

'On Wednethday – he went to work jutht like he alwayth doeth. Morning thhift.'

'Working where?'

'Chiveningth.'

'You saw him before he left?'

'No, he geth up at half patht five.'

'I thought he lived near The Home.'

'Not when he thtays with me. I live out of town. He'th got a flat near Chiveningth though.'

'So you didn't see him before he left.'

'No.'

'But he was definitely there with you that night.'

'Yeth.'

'Sure?'

'Yeth.'

'Couldn't have just gone to his flat?'

'Not unleth he got up in the night and went.'

'So how was he that night – last time you saw him?'

'Jutht … normal.' She shrugged her shoulders, spreading her hands out briefly.

'You didn't notice anything unusual at all.'

'No. Unleth …'

'Yes?' Latimer pounced instantly.

'Well, he wath a bit quiet maybe. But he goeth like that when he'th got thingth on hith mind.'

'And did he have anything special on his mind that you know of?'

'No.'

'Money worries, anything like that?'

'No.'

'Everything all right between you two – getting along OK?'

'Yeth.' Her hand fluttered to her mouth fleetingly.

'So he was quiet but not unusually so.'

'Thatth right.'

'And in the morning he'd gone, but you assumed he'd gone to work.'

'Yeth, and I know he did – I phoned to check and they thaid he'd been there, normal time.'

'That was at Chivenings … you mean?'

'Chiveningth, yeth.'

'So when did you start to think something was wrong?'

There was a moment's pause while she frowned in thought.

'That evening. He thaid he'd be home by half patht five. He'd do the meal. I work late thome nighth. We had training that night.'

'So you got in when?'

'About quarter to nine.'

'And was there any sign of him having been home?'

'No.'

'Perhaps he just went to his own flat.'

'I thought that. But I rang and there wath no anthwer.'

'Maybe he didn't want to talk to you.'

'No. He wouldn't do that.'

'No problems then? No arguments, not cooling off?'

'No.'

'What day was this – Wednesday, you say?'

Wednesday. Bad day Wednesday, Latimer remembered. The day Franks had riled him. The day he'd lost his temper with Bernard.

'Yeth.'

She pressed a shredded tissue to her nose but, seeing its state of disintegration, hastily stuffed it back into her pocket with an embarrassed, 'Thorry.'

'Did Toby say what else he had on on that day?'

'No.'

'Did he tell you he spent a chunk of it with us?'

'No. I haven't theen him tho he couldn't have, could he?'

Corroborating her own story, huh?

'Did he tell you about the other days he spent with us?'

'Well, he told me you'd athked him quethtionth. But he didn't thay what about.'

'And weren't you curious?'

'He thaid it wath to do with work. Jutht routine. They're not allowed to talk about a lot of thingth they do there. Confidential thtuff. I don't athk.'

'Maybe he's been doing extra shifts elsewhere.'

'He alwayth tellth me. Where he'll be, I mean.'

'So you knew he was working ridiculous hours?'

'Thometimeth.'

'Sometimes you knew, or sometimes he worked ridiculous hours?'

Again a quick frown of concentration as if she was intent on being precisely accurate in the detail.

'I knew he thometimeth workth ridiculouth hourth. But it wath only now and then he did it. Jutht to make a bit ecthra.'

'Why didn't you report him missing yesterday morning?'

'Becauthe the polithe don't take it theriouthly – not adultth going mithing. Do they?'

'Depends.'

'Anyway Toby'd have been upthet if he'd come home that day and found I'd reported it.'

'Done it before has he?'

'Wunth.'

'Tell me about that time.'

She took a deep breath and paused as if considering the wisdom of confiding the detail.

'He wath away all night. Went to work necht day. Didn't come home that necht night. I rang everywhere, friendth, hothpitalth and everywhere. I wath frantic. I thought thomething bad had happened.'

'How long ago would that have been?'

'Oh, I can't thay. Five month – thicth. Thomething like that.'

'And where had he been?'

'He wouldn't thay. Jutht out. Needed thpathe thometimeth, he thaid.'

'Did that happen often – him needing space?'

'Not often, no.'

'Does anything in particular upset him?'

'Not thpethially. Not that I can think of.'

'Know much about his past, do you? Family, childhood, that kind of thing?'

'Not a lot, no. He never hath talked about himthelf much. He'th jutht a quiet, private thort of perthon.' She shrugged her shoulders.

'Got family, has he?'

'Hith mother died when he wath little. I know that. Hith father'th thtill alive but Toby doethn't thee him. From what he thayth, hith Dad wath a bully. And thatth one thing Toby doeth hate – thatth bullieth. He'th a thenthitive perthon himthelf. He hateth violenth or anything like that.'

'And had there been anything like that – recently – to upset him? That you know of?'

Had Toby told her about the police pressure?

'Not that I know of.'

Latimer saw that her eyes were wide and scared now.

'So you don't know of any reason why he might have gone off – to get some space, as you say?'

'No.'

'Is there anything else you can tell us – any leads that might help?'

'I'm thcared.'

'What of?'

'I think he'th frightened. I don't know why he'th talked to you but – but – ith thomebody threatening him?'

'Has he been different – since he started talking to us?'

'Yeth.'

'How different?'

'On edge. Thitting jutht thtaring. Going out for walkth. Quiet.'

'And what does he say when you ask him?'

'I daren't athk him. I don't want to invade hith thpathe too far.'

'Hmmm.'

She searched in her sleeve and then in her handbag for a fresh tissue, and blew her nose noisily.

'So ith there? Ith there thomebody after him? Ith he a witneth or thomething? Could he jutht be hiding? Or hath thomebody got him?'

'I don't know. But I intend to find out. You were right to come. Now I need you to wait here and I'll get somebody to come and take a statement. And don't worry, we'll be right onto this. I promise you.'

'That meanth you think he'th in danger.' The hands fluttered up to her face, back to her lap, up to her mouth again.

'I don't know, like I said. But we'll keep you posted.'

They found Toby Bernard in the garage adjoining his own flat. Two streets away from Chivenings. He was still hanging from the beam.

The garage was locked from the inside, no sign of forced entry or exit. Looked like suicide while the balance of his mind was disturbed, the police told Gillian Jones.

'You give him a hard time, Latimer?' the Superintendent asked, looking at him keenly.

'Only verbal pressure, sir. He was a link man. Introduced Hassan – the man who threatened Geoffrey Archibald – to Chivenings. Seemed to be hiding something. I suspect he took somebody else into The Home – our rapist.'

'Didn't drive him over the edge?'

'I don't think so, sir.'

'We're not smelling too pretty with this one as it is. We do not want, nor do we need, an almighty stink here. Not with this lawyer fellow ferreting around.'

'No, sir.'

Latimer kept sniffing the air. Checking. It was a bad time to lose a key informant.

Why had Bernard done it? Why now? Was he scared of what they'd find? Who *was* it he'd taken into The Home? Had Latimer been too heavy-handed? Would Bernard have confided if he'd been softer, not let his temper get the better of him?

It kept on niggling. There was no closure with this sudden death. There was no-one to fill in the gaps.

Somehow he couldn't let it rest. He continued barking orders, sitting for hours himself going over the amassing data.

'Find out about his childhood. What was his father up to? Where is he now? What skeletons are there in the Bernard cupboard?'

'Who did he see when he was off sick for that month? Find his doctor. Make him talk.'

'Bernard was checked for the rape in The Home so we've got his DNA. But look again, will you? Check it against any unsolved crime for the past five years. If you draw a blank, make that ten years.'

'See if he had any dodgy pals.'

It was a long shot, but he'd smelt Bernard's unease. He'd had something to hide. Latimer was sure of it.

The phone call came when he was at home, spreadeagled over the settee, listening to Johnny Cash crooning *A boy named Sue*, letting his thoughts wander over the facts, searching for clues.

'Sarge – something's come up.'

'Uhhuh?'

'Bernard's DNA – looks like there's some confusion.'

'How come?'

'Matches a guy called Colin Warner.'

Latimer swung his long legs off the settee, sat bolt upright, straightened his shirt.

'What d'you mean?'

'Like you said we checked other crimes and this came up. Warner was had up for robbery with violence six years ago. DNA's the same.'

'As in same person? Or changed identities? Or what?'

'We've only just found it, Sarge. Haven't started following it up yet. Thought you'd like to know.'

Colin Warner cringed when Latimer presented his identity card, protesting his innocence before the accompanying officer had even closed the door, repeating it all the way to the station. He huddled into himself as if expecting a beating at any second.

Latimer kept the preliminaries short and essential. To be honest he could think of no possible explanation for Warner's DNA being on file with the staff at The Home. But that wasn't going to stop him drawing blood with this lowlife. This was no time for niceties.

At first Warner denied all knowledge of Chivenings.

But Latimer was sick of all the lies, all the time wasting. The pock-marked face, the darting eyes, the nervous scratching, all irritated him beyond reason. He racked up the torture several turns at a time.

Warner broke more easily than he'd expected.

'OK, OK. I heard tell of it. I know a bloke what works there.'

'Name?'

'Toby.'

'Toby what?'

'Dunno. Toby … Toby Brown, Bingham … B somethin'.'

'Toby Bernard?'

'That's it! Toby Bernard.'

'How d'you know him?'

'Met 'im on a train coming back from London one time, didn' I? Me and 'im got talkin'. Give me a lift from the station, 'e did.'

'And?'

'Bumped into him once or twice since. Same pub. Fings like that.'

'Did he know about your record?'

'Nah. Not first off anyways.'

'Did you know what he did?'

Warner shot a sudden sharp look at Latimer. 'Whatcha mean?'

'Did you know where he worked, what he did by way of employment?'

'Sort of.'

'What? What did he do?' Latimer barked.

'Looked after these folk what can't look after theirselves.'

'Did you ever go there – to The Home where he worked?'

'Nah.'

'You sure?'

'Sure I'm sure. Why would I go there?'

'To see Toby. See where he worked. What he did.'

'Nah.'

'When did you last see Mr Bernard?'

'I dunno. Few weeks ago maybe. Maybe longer.'

'Did he ever talk to you about The Home.'

Latimer's eyes gimleted into the weathered face in front of him.

'Nah. Wouldn' want 'im to.'

'So what did you talk about?'

'Football, darts – that kind of fing. And when I tellt 'im about bein' inside – a bit about that.'

'You told him you'd been inside then?'

'After a bit. It just kinda come out.'

'So you told him about prison life, did you?'

'Bits and pieces.'

'Ask anything specific, did he?'

'Can't recall.'

'Did you like him, Warner?'

The man shrugged indifferently.

"E was OK.' It sounded guarded.

'But you weren't interested in what he did at The Home.'

'Like I tellt yu', no.'

'Ever seen somebody in a coma, Warner?'

'Once, yeah. Bloke inside, went into a diabetic coma.'

Warner's eyes and voice were suddenly animated.

'And how did that make you feel?'

'Sick. Scared actually. Fought the screws'd fix it on me.'

'Ever seen somebody in a coma but looking at you?'

Warner shuddered.

'Nah. They don't.'

'You ever raped a girl?'

'Nah, never. Not my style, rape.'

'I think you have, Warner. I think you've raped a girl who's in a coma but has her eyes wide open.'

'Nah. I never 'ave. Never.'

'So what were you doing up at The Home where Toby Bernard worked?'

'I never went there. I swear I never did. You can't pin nofin' on me. I never done nofin' like that. Never.'

Latimer heard the lapses, saw the control slipping.

'Well. That's where you're wrong. We have.' He leaned forward until his face was inches from Warner's as he hissed out the two words. *Your DNA.*

'Never. You're makin' it up.' Warner tried to back away. His back was already to the wall; there was nowhere to go.

'Am I making it up, Constable Phillips?'

'No, Sarge.'

'No, indeed. Cast-iron proof. DNA.'

Warner's pallor was sickly.

'You know, don't you, Warner, what they do to lowlife like you inside?' Latimer lowered his voice to soft, gentle, sympathetic.

'I never. I never did nofin' like that. I swear.'

'So how come we've got your DNA on our files in connection with a rape?'

'I dunno. It weren't me.'

'Ever had your DNA done?'

'When I got done for that there robbery. They done it then.'

'Any other time?'

Warner shook his head.

'Never had a swab taken from your mouth?'

Latimer saw the sudden arrested expression. He sat waiting.

'This 'ere Toby Bernard – 'e in trouble?' Warner asked.

'He's dead!'

Warner whistled.

'No kiddin'?'

192

'No kidding.'

''Ow'd 'e die?'

'Topped himself.'

'Well, in that case – I guess … Only I ain't no grass.' Warner glared at Latimer for a long moment.

'No. You're too smart for that kind of malarkey. So?'

'Well, I did it for 'im, see? Return the favour like.'

'What favour?'

''E gives me a lift from the station, I stand in for 'im. Weren't no 'arm in it. Just 'elpin' out a mate.'

'How d'you mean, stand in for him?'

''E says to me, 'e says, "I gotta work in that other 'ospital" – Sick Kids, 'e calls it. "Only," 'e says, "The 'Ome I really works at, they don't know I go up there as well, like," 'e says. Well, seems they was needin' to check everybody what works in The 'Ome. For infection like. Routine stuff. Just in your mouth, you know. Says 'e knows 'e's clear – been done up at the Kids' 'Ospital. Can I just be there, let them take the swab fing from me instead. Just in and out. Done and dusted. Just give 'is name. Open my mouth. That's all like.'

'So you pretended to be Bernard.' Latimer let the words out slowly. Very slowly.

'Aye. But I never done that other fing. I swear I never done it.'

'You know what, Warner, I think for once you might be telling the truth.'

TWENTY-NINE

Bill Faraday slumped down in the chair, staring up at Brian Latimer in silence.

'One of the nurses?'

'Care assistant actually.'

'Someone who … looked after her?' It was incomprehensible.

'Well, to be fair, he was only ever assigned to look after Viv personally once. But yes, he did look after the patients generally. Very well from all accounts.'

'Why? Why would anyone who works in this kind of place – someone who cares – like that – want to …?'

'I wish I had the answers.'

'So what *do* you know?'

'We know his name and that he did it. DNA matches. And we know that he's dead. Almost certainly by his own hand. Suicide.'

'And is it … anybody I know?'

'I'm afraid it is, Mr Faraday. I'm sorry. This will be painful, I know.'

'So … who …?'

'Toby Bernard.'

'The chap who … You're kidding! You have to be kidding.'

'No, I'm afraid I'm not.'

'But he went out of his way …'

'So I've heard. Doesn't make sense, does it?'

'Nothing about this makes sense. But, I mean, he *talked* to me about it – he offered his help. He seemed genuinely upset about it. I nearly told him … I don't believe this.' Bill's eyes were widely dilated, remembering. 'I told Dr Wilkinson …'

'Incomprehensible, I know. We can't fathom it out yet either. But we're working on it. We'll keep you posted.'

'Has he done anything like this before?'

'Not that we can establish. Nothing on file. Doesn't match any other unsolved crimes.'

'And did he … touch Rhona? Any of the others?'

'We don't think so.'

'Why Viv? Why Viv?' It was rhetorical.

Latimer respected his silence.

'What happens now?' Bill dragged out. It was mechanical. Did he care? It was done. Nothing could undo it.

'It'll be reported, filed. But of course there won't be a trial.'

'No.'

No, there would be no tidying up of ends, no sense of justice being done. But there could never have been justice for what had been done to Viv. Never. Not even if this man had lived to face the consequences. There was no adequate punishment for what he had done.

'It'll save dragging Viv into this – publicly – won't it?' Latimer was saying hesitantly.

'Hollow comfort that, Sergeant.'

'Sorry.'

But it was true. Viv's name wouldn't be bandied about. There'd be no danger of other stuff coming out – family stuff, things best left buried.

And he, Bill, wouldn't ever have to look at the swine who'd violated her. He wouldn't have to dread seeing his face in the streets when they let him out. He'd gone. For ever.

'You'll keep us posted?'

'If anything else crops up. If we can help in any way to make sense of this you can be sure we will. I can't tell you how sorry we are.'

'Thank you.'

'I expect you want to be alone just now. It's a shock, I know. I'm sorry.'

'Thanks. And thanks for all your work on this, Sergeant.'

Latimer inclined his head briefly.

'It's my job.'

'Thanks anyway.'

'For what it's worth, this has been one of the most painful cases I've ever handled. Seeing your daughter ... I'm sorry.'

And he was gone.

Sitting beside Viv, Bill was silent for a long time.

'Viv, darling ...' He couldn't say it. Not until his voice was steady anyway. But she ought to be the first to know.

'Viv, they've found the man who ... raped you. He was one of the care workers here. Nobody knows why. Seems he was a good worker. Nobody suspected. They don't know if it was just a sudden ... urge ... or whether he planned it. Nobody knows. They only know he was the one.'

The pictures threatened to overwhelm him. Toby Bernard on top of Viv. Bernard the father of his grandchild. Bernard walking around The Home afterwards, coolly, caring. Bernard evading the traps. Bernard sympathising with him.

He buried his head in the blankets over her knees, his whole body shuddering.

'But he's dead now. He'll never hurt you again, my darling. Nobody will ever hurt you again.'

The amber eyes were open. A tiny dribble of saliva oozed from the side of her lips.

'I'm struggling with this, Viv. I'll be needing you. This whole thing – it's been eating me up. Now it's sort of over. But I'm struggling. I want to get back to how we were. But I can't, not with all this burning inside me. I want to scream and kick and *kill* somebody! But old Bill Faraday doesn't do that kind of thing. So I need to shout in here, Viv – shout in whispers. You've been good at that. Listening to me shouting. I need you now.'

He sat in silence for a long moment staring at the impassive face, the fixed unseeing eyes.

'I want to think the guy was so racked with guilt about what he did to you that he couldn't live with himself. They can't say either way, of course. There was no note. Maybe he just didn't want to be found out. But I want to believe it was remorse. I might need you to listen to me when I'm having a hard time believing it. Your mother … tells me … I'll never move on until I learn to forgive. I don't know if she's right. Grit your teeth for me, Viv.'

The tunnel was impenetrably black ahead today. He knew there'd be many more dark days.

'And I want you to remind me to hang on to the thought of his family. I know he had a father, and a girlfriend – imagine what it's like for them. I can't, Viv. I can't imagine what they're going through. But one thing I know – and I can say this to you – I'd rather be me than *his* father. And *we've* been to hell and back – no, not quite back yet, still a long way to go – we've been to hell with this. But we'll survive it, Viv. You and me. I really think we're through the worst. There'll be good times again. And we've always got each other. His family … well, I couldn't live with that.'

The dribble hung sparkling from her chin. Bill wiped it away gently.

'I'll tell the boys tonight. It'll be hard for them – knowing he's dead. They'll feel cheated. They love you, Viv. They'll never forgive him. Never. They never met him but they won't ever forgive him. It's a funny thing, you know, darling, but it's helped them see how much they still love you. That's good, eh? And I know they've been coming to see you. I'm glad. They'll be here for you when I'm gone.'

Was he glad? Yes, it was true, he was. Things had changed.

'I'm going to contact your mother, too. I owe her that. I don't know what she'll do – but she ought to know.'

His voice cracked. He took long quivering breaths.

'I'm sorry, Viv. I am so, so sorry.'

Blindly he reached for the latest book he'd been reading her, Tolstoy's *Anna Karenina*. It fell open at a page towards the end. Through a sea of tears he skimmed the bottom lines silently: 'Levin was several times so near to suicide that he hid a cord he had lest he should hang himself, and he feared to carry a gun lest he should shoot himself.' Was that how Bernard had lived? Until the noose tightened?

He closed the book with a snap.

'Forgive me, sweetheart. I can't. Not today.'

The small office seemed overflowing – Steven Wilkinson, Alison Reed, Bill and Geoff in a semi-circle around Steven's desk, DS Latimer perched on the edge of the desk, one leg swinging loose. The policeman had changed into a light grey suit; he looked as if he'd just stepped out of the shower, fresh, invigorated, his ginger hair darkened by the water.

No-one interrupted his monologue. It was time, he said, to give them the full picture – or at least all they had. And he had to admit it was unlikely that they'd ever uncover more. The case would never come to court but he felt they were owed some detail.

The story – all the fragments pieced together – was beyond fiction. He did his best to convey the reality: Toby Bernard's abused childhood, his fears, his desire to care for others weaker than himself. But Latimer could offer no plausible explanation for what he had done to Vivienne Faraday, beyond the probability that it was a one-off aberration. It didn't fit with the rest of the profile. They'd probably never now make sense of it.

They listened in silence. Of course, they knew Latimer had told it carefully; he had his own confidences to preserve, his own code to follow. But it was still strangely unreal. Scarcely believable. Except that the pieces fitted together with the reality they knew. Except that they had lived this nightmare.

Geoff, relieved of the responsibility for building a case for the prosecution, had the luxury of space and distance. He'd been intrigued by Bill's account of developments and glad of the invitation to attend as his lawyer. The criminal mind had ceased to amaze him long ago but it helped to close a case, tying up the loose ends.

His eyes went from one face to another, looking behind the silence.

Bill, huddled in his seat, his face set, grey, defeated, struggling to blot out the pictures, fighting the aborted murderous rage. Knowing that no amount of explanation could undo the wrong this man had done to his daughter. Geoff knew a sudden secret surge of relief. Rhona would have been so thankful that she had been untouched.

Steven, his own eyes surreptitiously flicking from the policeman to Bill, to Geoff, probably wondering how far they would press for compensation, how much of this sordid business in his Home would become public knowledge, what future there could be. But outwardly in control, leaving the murky details to the police.

Alison Reed, impassive, but her spirit crushed by the revelations, the actions of trusted colleagues. The epitome of desolation, Geoff thought, would be an apt caption.

Latimer, suddenly years younger, the frown gone, crisply recounting, leaving out the emotion, collapsing hours of painstaking work into a few short sentences. No doubt he was looking forward to leaving The Home, getting some sleep at last. Until the next horror swallowed him whole.

Geoff closed his eyes. He let the facts swirl together, regroup, form into an orderly queue.

Bernard headed it. Faceless, unknown. And yet in a way responsible for all of this. Both crimes. What had really motivated him? Latimer seemed to say the man was proud of what The Home could offer, his part in it. He'd been so proud he'd enthused to these other men, made them want to see the excellence, learn from it. He'd told them about the rape too. And one of them had seized the chance for revenge which had almost destroyed Geoff personally. Was it his professional cynicism, or had Bernard really been flaunting his crime? Subtly, covertly maybe, but wanting them to be impressed – not by his sensitivity and caring but by his daring. Was he in reality one of those criminals who felt no remorse, no sense of responsibility for his crime? Had he gloried in Hassan's attempt to emulate him? Imitation, they said, was a form of flattery. Was his ego flattered?

Flattery. How easy it was to get caught up in its seduction. It was a temptation Geoff recognised. Was he even now feeling flattered that he had penetrated Simon Fenton/Hassan's disguise? Flattered by the glowing tributes to his success in court? Had he really been flattered by Marilyn's attentions? Flattered by his own ability to resist temptation? Was he even now flattering himself that he had so far resisted Angela's temptation?

He dragged his thoughts away.

His eyes focused back on Bill. He looked broken and old. Like the time Inspector Wexford's own wife was kidnapped and he felt his powerlessness personally. There was the same raw pain. Only here it was no clever acting. This was real. The shadow of what had happened to his beloved daughter would never leave Bill. No matter the evidence, he would always blame himself.

Beside his example Geoff's own reflection shattered into a thousand pieces.

Other books in the Living Literature Series

PATERNITY

When Judy agrees to marry Declan his happiness is complete. But from the first night of their marriage cracks appear in their relationship until eventually Judy reveals the demons which haunt her. When a child dies, the questions that follow unravel a past which rocks their security to its foundations.

What have they inherited? What are they passing on to future generations? This story of love and deception challenges the morality of what is done in the name of infertility treatment today and exposes the dilemmas and conflicts which society must address.

ISBN 1 85775 652 5   Paperback, £11.99

DOUBLE TROUBLE (a sequel to *Paternity*)

The Halleys are a close, successful, loving family. But relationships become increasingly complex following the marriages of identical twins Nicholas and Michael. Darker secrets and hidden emotions are revealed when an unplanned pregnancy and a surrogacy arrangement lead to discoveries which challenge their moral values and jeopardise their happiness.

This story probes beneath society's superficial acceptance of fertility treatment, revealing the potential for pain, distorted relationships, and far-reaching consequences, both medical and moral.

ISBN 1 85775 669 X   Paperback, £11.99